CHACE SCENE

A Grace Texas Murder Mystery

Cherry Northcutt

Copyright © 2020 Cherry Northcutt

All rights reserved

The characters and events portrayed in this book are fictitious. Any similarity to real persons, living or dead, is coincidental and not intended by the author.

No part of this book may be reproduced, or stored in a retrieval system, or transmitted in any form or by any means, electronic, mechanical, photocopying, recording, or otherwise, without express written permission of the publisher.

ISBN 13: 979-8-6831-5491-2

This book is dedicated to my family

CONTENTS

Title Page	1
Copyright	2
Dedication	3
Grace Texas Murder Mysteries	9
Chapter 1 – Monday, January 15	11
Chapter 2 – Monday, January 15	18
Chapter 3 – Tuesday, January 16	28
Grace Gazette - January 17	37
Jess Sayin' Blog Post – January 29	38
Chapter 4 – Thursday, February 8	40
Chapter 5 – Thursday, February 8	48
Chapter 6 – Thursday, February 8	57
Jess Sayin' Blog Post – February 8	68
Chapter 7 – Friday, February 9	71
Chapter 8 – Friday, February 9	80
Chapter 9 – Friday, February 9	91
Chapter 10 – Friday, February 9	101

Chapter 11 – Friday, February 9	110
Chapter 12 – Friday, February 9	117
Chapter 13 – Friday, February 9	124
Chapter 14 – Friday, February 9	133
Chapter 15 – Friday, February 9	141
Chapter 16 – Friday, February 9	155
Chapter 17 – Saturday, February 10	163
Grace Gazette – February 10	171
Chapter 18 – Saturday, February 10	173
Chapter 19 – Saturday, February 10	182
Chapter 20 – Saturday, February 10	193
Chapter 21 – Saturday, February 10	204
Chapter 22 – Sunday, February 11	213
Chapter 23 – Sunday, February 11	223
Chapter 24 – Sunday, February 11	234
Chapter 25 – Sunday, February 11	248
Chapter 26 – Monday, February 12	263
Chapter 27 – Monday, February 12	273
Chapter 28 – Monday, February 12	283
Chapter 29 – Monday, February 12	292
Chapter 30 – Monday, February 12	301
Chapter 31 – Monday, February 12	315
Chapter 32 – Monday, February 12	321
My Day with Donna - by Jessica Hart	326

Chapter 33 – Tuesday, February 13	328
Grace Gazette - February 13	338
Chapter 34 – Tuesday, February 13	339
Chapter 35 – Tuesday, February 13	347
Chapter 36 – Tuesday, February 13	356
Chapter 37 – Tuesday, February 13	360
Chapter 38 – Wednesday, February 14	369
Chapter 39 – Wednesday, February 14	379
Grace Gazette – February 15	391
Grace Gazette – February 16	393
Jess Sayin' Blog Post – February 16	394
Pie Hole Basic Pie Crust	396
Chocolate Pie	398
Miss America Pie	400
Chicken Fried Steak from the Grace Grill	402
Donna Vance's Vegan Protein Smoothie	403
Acknowledgements	405
About The Author	407

GRACE TEXAS MURDER MYSTERIES

Cherry Northcutt is the author of
the Grace Texas Murder Mystery series.
Visit amazon.com/author/cherry.northcutt
for information on other books in the series.

For more information about the author
visit www.cherrynorthcutt.com

CHAPTER 1 – MONDAY, JANUARY 15

3:20 p.m.

Alpaca Sweater. That's what the sign said. Jess squinted and looked out the window again. Yep, a man and woman were hanging up a sign above the door to what used to be the Happy Trails Travel Agency. The sign said *Alpaca Sweater.*

"Ms. Melody?" Jess called out toward the back of the cavernous Antique Emporium where she worked part-time. The rest of the time she was a free-lancer for the Grace Gazette, the one and only newspaper in the small town of Grace, Texas. That office was on the opposite side of the town square.

There was no answer. Ms. Melody must still be in the stockroom. Jess wondered if the Gazette might want a news story about the new shop. Or, she could always write about it on her blog, *Jess Sayin'.* The shop was in a prime location on the corner, facing the courthouse and across the street from Casa Maria Mexican Restaurant.

Jess watched out the window as the couple hung up a *Grand Opening* banner across the front window. It was a slow day. Maybe Ms. Melody wouldn't mind if she took a little break and went over to check it out. Jess began formulating a headline in her mind: *Couple Opens Sweater Shop.* She sighed, remembering her days as a features writer for the newspaper in Houston just a few years ago. *This is what passes for news in a small town,* she thought.

Just then the bells on the front door chimed. Jess looked over and was mortified to see Chace Perez and her mother, Tanya. Chace was engaged to Jack Ketchum, who just happened to be Jess's ex-husband. She was determined that she and Jess would be friends, no matter what. Jess plastered on her best fake smile.

Chace and Tanya breezed in, both wearing thick turtleneck sweaters and Ugg boots. "Jessica," Chace chirped in that fine Texas lady sing-song voice, befitting her status as a former Miss Texas. "Come here Sugar, and give me a hug." Chace rushed over with arms outstretched. Jess reluctantly stepped out from behind the counter to let herself be hugged. Chace was a hugger. Jess was not, at least not when it came to Chace.

Ever since she had met Chace, Jess had disliked her. Partly because she was going to marry Jack, but mostly because she was just too perfect. Chace was slim and tall with silky dark hair in a medium length bob. Jess, by contrast, was forever battling her untamed dark blonde waves. Chace had the personality of a game show host, always smiling and talking non-stop. Jess tried to avoid her as much as possible, which was like trying to avoid a tornado coming straight for your house.

Tanya Perez, on the other hand, was not so friendly with Jess. She was of the opinion that one should not embrace the ex-wife of your intended, not figuratively and never literally. "Hello Jessica," she drawled with a smile that said, *I'm tolerating you* and a stiff demeanor that said, *don't get too close*. Tanya was shorter than her daughter and had big, blonde hair. Jess could smell the Aqua Net from across the room.

"I was hoping you would be here," Chace said, glancing around the empty shop, "are you busy right now?"

"We're slow at the moment," Jess admitted, "but I've got some dusting to do."

Chace continued. "We wanted to ask you about your Aunt Patsy's property. I wondered if you might be free sometime so we could all go take a look at it."

"What are you talking about?" Jess asked. "Why would you want to look at my Great Aunt Patsy's old farm?" There was an awkward pause. "How do you even know about the property?"

Chace sucked some air in through her teeth. "Jack told me that your Aunt Patsy has a lovely old farmhouse down Turner Road," she explained. "You know I've been looking for a wedding location, since the original place fell through."

"That wedding barn place isn't available?"

"No, we tried them. We've tried everywhere. You know we want to have an outdoor wedding. The theme is kind of country chic. You know, sort of rustic and vintage. So I thought maybe the farmhouse would be good." Chace looked at Jess with a hopeful smile.

Jess was at a loss for words. "No... I don't think..." she stammered, "It wouldn't be right for a wedding."

"I just thought we could take a look," Chace pleaded. "I haven't been able to find anything nice."

Jess pictured her Aunt Patsy's old farmhouse, now boarded up. It was a huge, two-story, Victorian house with a wrap-around porch. Back in its heyday, it would have been a charming setting for a country wedding. Now though, it had been unoccupied for several years. Aunt Patsy was happily spending her days at the Heritage House, an assisted living home for the elderly.

"I don't think it would work," Jess said. "The windows are boarded up and there are probably spiders everywhere. Maybe even snakes or raccoons."

"See, it's not a good idea. I told you so," Tanya said to her daughter as she turned to leave.

"Oh, go on, it can't hurt to take a look," came a voice from across the store. Everyone looked up startled to see Ms. Melody, standing near a display of Fiestaware dishes. How long had she been there?

"In fact, you might as well go now," Ms. Melody added. "I can mind the store myself and you've still got a couple hours of daylight left."

Reluctantly, Jess agreed to show Chace the old farmhouse. The ladies decided to take Tanya's car for the twenty-minute trip out of town.

"Hold on," Chace said, tapping the face of her iPhone. "I want Jack to come too."

Jess was in no mood to see Jack. This whole excursion was bordering on ridiculous already. After a quick phone call, Chace informed her mother that they were to pick Jack up at his law office only two blocks away. Jess climbed into the back seat and off they went.

Chace leaned her head into the back seat. "Thank you for letting us take a look. I just know we're going to love it."

"We'll have to see," Jess said smiling back at her. *I hope you get bit by a field mouse while we're out there*, Jess thought.

When they reached the office of Woodley and Associates, Jack was waiting outside. He wore a gray suit and tie. His dark hair curled above his ears. He took the backseat next to Jess and flashed a nervous smile. Jess looked away.

"Do you want to switch with me and sit next

to Jack?" she asked Chace.

"No, you're already back there," Chace said. She leaned back and blew Jack a kiss.

On the drive out to the farmhouse, Jess tried not to look at Jack. She felt awkward about the whole situation. She couldn't help a few surreptitious glances. *Why did he have to be so good looking?*

At one point they made eye contact and Jack shrugged his shoulders, holding his hands out palm up as if to say *I don't like this any more than you do, but what can I do about it?*

Jack and Jess had eloped at the age of twenty-one, right after college. They weren't necessarily too young for marriage, but immaturity can have a long shelf life. Jack attended law school while Jess worked as a journalist. Jess had loved her life in the big city. Shortly after Jack's graduation, Jess's mother died in a car wreck. A few months later the newspaper laid off half the staff, Jess included. She was bereft and despondent. Their three-year marriage dissolved a few months later.

There was one other thing in the backseat between Jack and Jess. A big secret they were keeping from Chace and everybody else. A couple of weeks earlier, when Jack had taken a job in Grace, he and Jess had gone out for dinner to catch up. They talked about old times and had a few laughs. Then they spent the night together in Jack's motel room. So there was that.

That one night of passion happened before Jess knew there was a Chace. In the days after, in rapid succession, Jess discovered that Jack was engaged, the happy couple was moving to Grace, and Chace was pregnant. So Jess had plenty of reasons to be angry at Jack.

"Turn right here," Jess said abruptly. "It's going to be about another mile at the white mailbox."

They rounded a corner past a line of trees and saw the house in the distance. The farmhouse was badly in need of a paint job and some new boards here and there. The grass was overgrown and the steps up to the porch would have to be replaced. To Jess it looked like a haunted house, haunted with the memories of her childhood.

To Chace it looked like a dream come true. "It's beautiful," she gushed, "Oh Jack, just look at that porch!"

CHAPTER 2 – MONDAY, JANUARY 15

4:30 p.m.

Tanya parked in the gravel clearing several yards from the house.

"This is gorgeous," Chace said as she tramped through the overgrown brush. "We could set bales of hay out here for people to sit on," Chace was gesturing in semi-circles, "and we could stand on the porch with the pastor, right in front of the door. It's going to be beautiful!"

"But sweetie, this place is falling apart," Jack reasoned. "No offense Jess."

"None taken." Jess was hanging back, checking her phone. She could feel the heat rising in her neck. *This was not happening! There was no way she was going to let the love of her life marry this... this... spoiled brat right here at her own Aunt Patsy's house. No way in hell!*

"What about the inside?" Chace asked. "It might be just the place for the reception."

"Um, I don't think I brought the key with me," Jess called out, fingering the key in her handbag.

"Honey, an outdoor wedding is not such a good idea," Tanya said. "We won't be able to predict the weather. It could be cold or raining."

"You don't have the key? Really?" Chace whined, still looking around and making plans.

Jack walked over to Jess who was leaning against the SUV. He looked her in the eyes. "I know you have that key," he said softly.

She stared back up at him defiantly. "No, I don't."

"What's that in your hand?" he asked, pulling her hand from the handbag. "She found the key," he shouted out to Chace.

"I hate you Jack!" Jess whispered through gritted teeth as she trudged up to the front door.

It was the staircase that did it. The wood bannister curved at the foot of the stairs as the steps got wider. Jess had never considered it to be particularly grand, but Chace thought it was *to die for*. The house itself was not in bad condition. They explored the ground floor with their cell phone flashlights. The furniture was covered in drop-cloths and the rugs were rolled up.

"How long has it been unoccupied?" asked Tanya.

"About two years. A little longer maybe," Jess said. "Jack actually helped close it up when we moved Aunt Patsy to the retirement home." Maybe this subtle reminder of her previous marriage to Jack would nudge Chace away from the farmhouse as a wedding venue.

"I think all it needs is a good cleaning," Chace said, "we could have the reception in these two front rooms, take pictures on the stairs and out on the porch."

"We've turned the power off," Jess stated, "and the house needs some repairs. Aunt Patsy can't afford that." She hoped that settled the matter. Everybody was heading back out to the porch for what remained of the sunlight.

Chace was not giving up. "What if we pay for the repairs and the cleaning?"

"No Honey," Tanya said, "it's too much work, there are much better places out there."

"Mom, we have looked everywhere," she pleaded. "Every place is either booked or else it's terrible. I haven't seen anything I like as much as this farmhouse. It's perfect."

Nobody spoke.

"It won't cost that much, we can fix this place up with the money we would have spent renting a wedding hall," Chace continued.

"Couldn't you just get married in a church?" Tanya sighed.

Chace pouted.

Jack turned to her. "Is this what you really want, Chacie girl?"

Jess couldn't believe he had called her that. Her heart ached, remembering when he used to call her Jessie girl.

"It's what I really want," Chace said, looking up at him piteously.

"So, what do you say, Jess?" Jack asked.

NO!!! Jess wanted to shout. She wanted to run away from all of them down to the creek that ran along the northern side of the property. That had been the spot she retreated to anytime she got mad at her cousins, or her parents, or even sweet old Aunt Patsy. *NO!!!* She wanted to scream in Chace's face. More than that she wanted to push Jack off the porch.

Instead she said, "Well, it's not up to me. I'll have to ask Aunt Patsy."

"Thank you so much," Chace gushed, clasping her hands together and jumping up and down.

On the drive back to town, Jess stared out the window, trying not to listen to Chace natter on with her plans for the wedding. She heard snippets, something about Mason jars and a harpist and things she saw in *Texas Bride Magazine*. Jess thought it sounded kitschy and tacky, but also possibly kind of cool.

Back in town Jess said her goodbyes and got into her own car. Finally, she was alone. *How could this be happening?* Jess wanted nothing more than to pop open a beer and indulge in a solitary movie night in her apartment. She checked the time. Dinner would be in full swing at the Heritage Home. *Let's get this over with,* Jess thought as she started the car.

Jess parked in the lot at the Heritage House Assisted Living Home and practiced what she was going to say as she walked up to the building. She found Aunt Patsy in the dining hall, holding court with her passel of old biddies. Aunt Patsy was the Queen Bee in her gang of four, which included Myrtle, Pearl, and Ruth.

"Good evening ladies," Jess spoke in a slightly louder than usual voice. Aunt Patsy stubbornly refused to wear a hearing aid. Jess leaned down to give her great aunt a kiss. Aunt Patsy backed up a few inches on her mobility scooter to get a better look at Jess.

"Well, Jessica, darlin' – to what do I owe the pleasure?" Aunt Patsy asked.

"I have something I wanted to talk to you about," Jess said, "but it can wait until you're done with dinner."

"We're about done anyway," Patsy said, looking down at what was left of her meatloaf, new potatoes, and asparagus, "but I would like to have a dish of ice cream."

Jess greeted Myrtle and Ruth. "Where is Pearl tonight?" Jess asked.

Myrtle sighed and looked down at her plate sadly. "Pearl is no longer with us."

Ruth shook her head. "She went to be with the Lord."

Jess was taken aback. She held her hand to her chest, "Oh no, I'm so sorry. When did she pass away?"

"She's not dead. She just went on a retreat with the Baptist church," Aunt Patsy said, matter of factly. All three ladies burst into a fit of giggles.

Jess shook her head. "Why do y'all do me this way?"

After everyone had finished their vanilla soft-serve, Aunt Patsy shooed away her friends, "Now y'all let us have some privacy, Jess has something to say." She didn't care about ruffling anybody's feathers.

"What is it, darlin'? Do you need some money?" Aunt Patsy asked in a loud whisper.

"No, actually… here's the thing," Jess began. She relayed the story of how Chace had come to believe that the farmhouse was an ideal spot for her wedding. She tried to make it sound like a ridiculous idea, laughable, and foolish. She explained that the repairs would be extensive, it was probably not safe, not big enough, and the weather would be unpredictable.

Jess laughed nervously. "Why does anyone have outdoor weddings in Texas anyway?"

When Jess was all talked out, she could tell that her attempt to quash the wedding idea had failed. Aunt Patsy's eyes were gleaming.

"A wedding out at my farm? Why that sounds absolutely wonderful," Aunt Patsy gushed. "And they say they'll get it all fixed up? I would love to see my house put to good use."

"But Aunt Patsy, come on," Jess tried to reason. "It's not a good idea."

"I know what's bothering you, child. You still have feelings for Jack." Aunt Patsy sighed. She wasn't one to beat around the bush. Usually, she beat right through it. "You're just going to have to swallow your pride and move on. He's got someone else now, honey."

Jess fumed and pursed her lips. "That's not it at all. I am over him."

"I know it's hard, but this will be a good thing, you'll see," Aunt Patsy said, patting Jess's hand.

Jess said her goodbyes to Aunt Patsy and her friends and went home to her apartment, glad to finally be completely alone. She was looking forward to putting her feet up and bingeing on Netflix. She wanted nothing more than to forget about the ordeal her day had become. She reached into the fridge. The better part of a Corona Light six pack was hiding in the back, behind some leftover Chinese takeout. *Let's get this party started*, Jess thought as she grabbed the beer and the leftovers.

Settling into her sofa she located the remote and turned on Netflix. She decided on *Kimmy Schmidt* and was halfway through her beer when she heard footsteps coming up the outside staircase to her front door. *Dang it*, Jess thought as she set down her takeout. Ms. Melody was a good boss and a nice landlady, but her frequent drop-in visits could be annoying.

Jess could also hear the rhythmic thump of Ms. Melody's orange cat, Sweet Tea. There was a knock and the door opened a crack as Ms. Melody peered in. Sweet Tea did not wait for an invitation. The cat trotted in and jumped onto the sofa next to Jess for some neck scritches. Jess obliged.

Ms. Melody was only a little less forward. "Jess, I fixed you a plate." She came into the room with a covered dish of baked chicken, dirty rice, and green beans. "But I see you've already eaten."

"Actually, I just got started," Jess said, "Thank you, this looks better than soggy cashew chicken any day." This was no lie. Ms. Melody was well known for bringing the best covered dishes to all the church potlucks. Jess dug in.

"So, I went over to that new sweater store. It's run by this cute hippy couple. Their names are Sonny and Skye. They seem nice." Ms. Melody said.

"They're new in town? What do they sell?" Jess stuffed a big bite of chicken into her mouth.

"They have sweaters and socks and bags and stuff, all made from Alpaca wool," Ms. Melody said. "I felt it. It's very soft."

Jess nodded, her mouth full.

After a pause, Ms. Melody could hold in her curiosity no longer. "So, what happened at the farmhouse?"

"Well," Jess swallowed and wiped her mouth on a paper napkin. "That whole thing went just *peachy.* Chace wants to have her wedding at my Aunt Patsy's farmhouse and whatever Chace wants, Chace gets!" She didn't bother hiding her aggravation.

"Did you talk to Patsy about it?"

"Oh, she thinks it's a splendid idea," Jess said with exaggeration. "Her eyes just lit up like it was Christmas."

There was a pause while Jess kept eating. Ms. Melody waited patiently for the rest of the tirade.

"I mean, why did you say, 'go right now –

there's still daylight'?" Jess said in a mimicking tone, gesturing with her hands. "That was a *brilliant* idea."

Ms. Melody interjected, "I didn't see any harm in it."

"You knew what would happen. Chace just loved the farmhouse, wants to fix it up and put Mason jars all over the place." Jess rolled her eyes. "This whole wedding is going to be a complete disaster. They've only got four weeks to put it all together."

Jess munched some more, deep in thought. "I can't let this happen, not at Aunt Patsy's house."

Ms. Melody made sympathetic noises and nodded.

"Who does Jack think he is anyway, barging in and taking over like he can do whatever he wants? I just can't believe..." Jess stopped herself.

"But Aunt Patsy likes the idea?" Ms. Melody asked.

"Yep," Jess answered with a sigh. "So I guess that's that. I don't have any say in the matter."

That night Jess lay awake. She kept replaying everything in her mind and coming back to thoughts of her mother. *If her mother were still around, none of this would be happening. She wouldn't stand for this. Not for one minute. Would she?*

CHAPTER 3 – TUESDAY, JANUARY 16

7:00 a.m.

Jess's alarm sounded for her opening shift at the Emporium. She hit snooze. Ten minutes later she got up, showered, brewed some coffee and unplugged her phone from the charger. Before the coffee was done brewing, her phone dinged with a new text.

Chace: Did you talk to Aunt Patsy about the house?

Jess groaned and ignored the text.

When she got to the store Shaun was already there sliding the till drawer into the register. Shaun was a retired history teacher who never let his pudgy, balding appearance dissuade him from flirting with all the ladies. He had a large booth space in the back of the shop with sports memorabilia, old record albums, movie posters, and other fun relics from the not too distant past.

"Good morning," Jess said as she came over to the counter.

"Good morning, fair lass," Shaun said with a bow. "You are looking gorgeous today."

"Thanks," Jess said bristling ever so slightly. Shaun's flirtatious manner never failed to annoy her. "What are we working on today," Jess asked.

"I have some new merch to set out," he said, indicating a couple of plastic bins on the floor.

"New?" Jess asked dubiously. "Don't you mean old?"

"Touché. They are older than you to be honest." Shaun opened a bin to show Jess his new treasures. "I scored a number of vintage Marvel comic books dating all the way back to the 1970s and '80s."

Jess was impressed. "Wow! Where did you get those?"

"One of my neighbors was cleaning out his garage and wanted to get rid of them. They're in excellent shape."

Jess pulled out a plastic wrapped copy of *The Amazing Spider-Man #21*, the special wedding issue. "I didn't know Spider Man got married," she said. She started to open the plastic, but Shaun swatted her hand away. Gently, he took it from her.

"No reading the comic books," he said sternly, pointing a finger at Jess. "In fact, I'm going to make a sign that says exactly that."

"Okay, fine. You go work on your booth. I'll hold down the fort up here," Jess said, taking up her position behind the counter.

Shaun carried a bin back to his space and returned for another one. He was just in time to see Chace and her mother walk into the store.

"Well, if it isn't our very own Miss Texas and her older sister, the lovely Tanya," he said as they entered the store. Shaun was very good with names, especially the names of pretty ladies.

"Former Miss Texas," Jess grumbled under her breath.

"Oh, hi there," Chace said to Shaun, trying to remember when she had met him.

Tanya hadn't forgotten. "Good morning, I remember you helped us with some centerpiece ideas for the wedding."

"Mason jars with fresh flowers, right?" Shaun said pointing. "If you need some jars, we've got about sixty in the back."

"We'll take about half that," Tanya said.

"As you wish," Shaun said with a bow. "I'll be right back."

"So, um, did you see the new sweater shop?" Jess asked.

"What?" Chace asked. She turned to look out the window across to the new Alpaca Sweater store. "Oh, no. We walked right by there and didn't even notice." Chace approached the counter with a nervous smile.

Jess steeled herself. She had decided this wedding would not be happening at Aunt Patsy's farmhouse. She had to draw the line somewhere.

"So, we just wanted to check back with you," Chace began, "about the farmhouse."

"Did you talk to your Aunt Patsy yet?" Tanya asked.

"Well, um," Jess looked at both of them and swallowed, "the thing is...." Jess was having a hard time. Chace was actually a nice person and she looked so eager. Jess began again. "I did talk to her and she's just not sure it would be um, safe for people to be out there... you know, with all the loose boards and... stuff." It was a lie, and not a very good one.

"Oh, but we'll fix everything," Chace said pleadingly.

"The thing is, if we're going to do this, we need to get started on repairs right away," Tanya said. "So we need an answer."

Jess shook her head and looked down. "I'm afraid the answer is no, then."

Chace was crestfallen. "No?" she repeated. She actually teared up. "Then what am I going to do? I only have four weeks to put this wedding together and I've got nothing."

"I'm so sorry, Chace," Jess said.

Shaun came back from the stockroom with

three packs of twelve Mason jars. "Here you go, three dozen. Will that work?" He noticed the forlorn look on Chace's face. "Oh Sweetheart, don't cry."

Chace began fanning her eyes and blinking away her tears. "It's okay; we'll just keep on keeping on." She managed to force a smile.

Tanya leaned over and slapped a credit card down on the counter. "Here," she said. "For the jars."

Jess began silently ringing up the Mason jars.

Around lunch time Ms. Melody came to the store and Shaun took a break. She and Jess began setting out some new Valentine merchandise on an endcap. There was a rack of cute cards, silk roses, and other gift items.

"Isn't it a little early for Valentines?" Jess asked.

"Candy's Candies has already started with the heart-shaped boxes of chocolates. I've got to stay ahead of the game." Candy's Candies was a sweet shop on the square on the North side of the courthouse. They specialized in custom made chocolates and candy gift baskets.

"You know these technically aren't antiques either," Jess teased.

Ms. Melody said, with mock indignation, "We sell antiques, collectibles, and gifts."

Jess laughed as she opened a box of little ceramic teddy bears holding hearts that said, *I Wuv You*. "Bleah," she said. "These are sickening."

Ms. Melody cleared her throat. "I saw Chace and her mother going into the Pie Hole earlier. Have you talked to them?"

"I did," Jess admitted. She opened a box of necklace and earring sets. She did not elaborate.

"And you told them no?" Ms. Melody asked.

"I told them no," Jess confirmed.

"Even though Aunt Patsy said it was okay?" Ms. Melody asked.

"Yep," Jess said, "I lied."

"Okay, good for you," Ms. Melody said. She stood up from her crouching position and dusted off her hands like the matter was settled. But, Jess felt far from settled.

The bells on the door jingled as Jack walked in. "Good afternoon," he called out as he came toward them.

"Good afternoon to you," Ms. Melody said.

Jess remained on the floor and continued setting the jewelry onto the rack. "Hey," she said without looking up.

"Jess, can we talk?" he asked.

"I'm working right now."

Ms. Melody interjected, "Why don't you go

into the office? Shaun should be back soon."

Jess scrunched her face at Ms. Melody. "Great idea. Thanks," she said sarcastically.

She and Jack went into the office. Jess took a seat at Ms. Melody's desk and reached into the mini fridge for a bottle of cold tea. She didn't offer one to Jack. Then she swiveled around to face him. "So, what's up?"

"Well, Chace is heartbroken about the farmhouse," he said.

"So what?" Jess said, her anger rising. "She ought to be upset because she's got a cheating fiancé."

"Well, thank you for not revealing that bit of information," he said with aggravation.

Jess glared at him. "I told you before that I wasn't going to say anything. Is that it? Or, have you come to beg me to change my mind about Aunt Patsy's house?" she asked.

He shook his head. "No... I came to say I'm sorry. I can see you're still angry," Jack said. "I'm sorry about that night. I let my feelings for you get the better of me."

Jess's eyes started to get teary. She blinked and took a breath.

"It wasn't fair to you. I wish things were different," he went on.

"You should have told me," Jess said. "Then nothing would have happened."

"I know I should have told you about Chace and the baby. It was just, seeing you again..." His voice trailed off. "I never meant to hurt you."

Jess took a deep breath. "Okay, thanks for the apology." She stood up. "We have to let go of the past and move on."

Jack stood. "Take care of yourself," he said. Then he walked out the door, out of her life, again.

Jess sunk back into the chair and allowed herself to cry. She took a big gulp of her tea. It did nothing to wash down the burning lump in her throat.

Jess left the store around 2:00 p.m. and drove out to Turner Road. At the farmhouse, she climbed up onto the porch. Finally alone, she let the memories wash over her. Her brother Tom peeking out from the side of the house to shoot her with a water gun, her Mom reading story books while they rocked in the porch swing, and Aunt Patsy baking cookies in the kitchen. It was a charming house. Jess understood why Aunt Patsy would love to see it again, all fixed up with people enjoying its beauty.

Jess looked out from the porch and envisioned rows of white wooden chairs full of nicely dressed people. She pictured garlands of flowers and kids running around in their Sunday best. She saw a bride in white lace, and Jack lifting the veil to reveal

Chace smiling up at him.

"Is this what closure feels like?" she asked herself. Jess picked up her phone and started a group text with Jack and Chace.

Jess: Good news. Aunt Patsy says you can have the wedding at the farmhouse!

Then she pressed send.

GRACE GAZETTE - JANUARY 17

New Shop Opens on the Town Square – by Jessica Hart

A new retail store has opened in Grace on the town square facing the World's Largest Hanging Flower Basket. The store, Alpaca Sweater, will be holding their Grand Opening Event throughout this week. All merchandise will be 10% off during the Grand Opening Sale. Alpaca Sweater offers sweaters, scarves, socks, hats, blankets, and bags made from authentic Alpaca wool imported from Peru.

The owners of Alpaca Sweater are Sonny and Skye Bleu. The couple is new to Grace having recently moved from El Paso where they ran their own dog grooming business.

Alpaca fleece is reported to be hypoallergenic and softer than sheep's wool.

JESS SAYIN' BLOG POST – JANUARY 29

Renovations at the Farmhouse

Preparations for the big wedding are underway at Aunt Patsy's old farmhouse and I have to admit, it is breathing new life into the place. Boards are being replaced and the whole house is being repainted. The interior is getting some much-needed TLC as well, for the official wedding portrait on the grand staircase. My Great Aunt Patsy is thrilled to see her home getting all spruced up and, if she's happy, I'm happy.

Who's getting married? Why none other than former Miss Texas Chace Perez to local attorney Jack Ketchum. Yes... that Jack Ketchum... my ex-husband. But, we're all great friends now, so no worries.

The nuptials are taking place on February 14. How sweet is that? It will be an outdoor wedding in front of the farmhouse, weather permitting. If it rains, everyone will just crowd into the front parlor, I guess. Unfortunately I will have to miss the festivities as I will be holding down the fort at the Antique Emporium. But, if you happen to see Chace out and about, maybe you can finagle an invitation.

Stop by the Antique Emporium this week and, if you mention my blog, save 20% on all Valentine's Day merchandise.

Jess clicked submit. "I don't think I've ever written anything so full of bull," she admitted.

Sweet Tea meowed from the sofa in agreement.

"Oh well," Jess said, as she grabbed her shoulder bag. "No time for regrets, Jack and I are over. This wedding is happening, and I have accepted it."

Sweet Tea gave her a dubious look. She wasn't buying it.

"I have," Jess insisted. "Anyway, I've got to get going so, see ya." On the way down the outside steps of her garage apartment, Jess shook her head. *I can't believe I'm having a conversation with a cat*, she thought, *I'm officially a crazy cat-lady.*

CHAPTER 4 – THURSDAY, FEBRUARY 8

9:00 p.m.

More than three weeks had passed since Jess's decision to let the wedding proceed at the farmhouse. Except for a couple of trips out with Aunt Patsy to check progress, she and the happy couple had been keeping out of each other's way. Now, the wedding would be happening in less than a week.

At the Gazette office, the small staff of the local newspaper was busy at work. Jess was in the middle of the bullpen at what had become known as the freelance table. It consisted of two craft tables pushed together. There were a handful of desks dotted around the big open room with a copier against the back wall and a small coffee bar.

Jess was on her laptop, writing up her interview with Reverend Fincastle about the restoration of the First Church of Grace after a recent fire. The sanctuary was being rebuilt and he expected it to be completed by Fall.

Near Jess sat staff reporter, Clarence Irvin, a wiry older gentleman with white hair. He was speaking in hushed tones into his desk phone.

Brittney Barnes, the Associate Editor, strode purposefully out of her office with a large box and approached the table. "Sorry, Jess. You gotta scoot." She tilted her head and gave Jess a fake smile that was all too familiar from their high school days. Brittney and her group of mean girls had tormented Jess and her group of misfits every chance they got. Now, Brittney no longer had the cheerleader body or the army of skanks to back her up. Adulthood had a way of leveling the playing field, sometimes.

Jess flashed her own fake smile, "What's up Brit?"

Brittney set the box down and gleefully announced, "Donna Vance is coming to our office tomorrow!"

Clarence put his hand over the mouthpiece of his phone. "Donna who now?" he asked.

"Donna Vance," Brittney gushed. "She's the Queen of Texas Chic. She has her own show, *Lone Star Living*." She pulled a copy of *Texas Bride Magazine* out of the box. "She's coming here with her entourage to do a story for Texas Bride. So, I'm giving them the freelance table as their workspace."

"Texas Bride, you say?" Clarence pretended to be impressed. "I forgot they were part of Lone Star Publications." He whispered something into the phone and ended his call.

"Lone Star is our parent company, right?" Jess asked.

"Right, they also publish *Texas Bride Maga-*

zine. It has all the details of the top weddings in the state," Brittney explained. "So, shoo." She motioned for Jess to move away. "I've got to fix up the table for her. You will just have to work from home this week." In the box Brittney had a gold colored tablecloth and various decorations and supplies including a gold toned stapler, pencil cup, and post-it dispenser.

"I take it she likes gold?" Jess said as she gathered up her laptop and handbag.

Wanda, the receptionist, came over from the front desk, her crisp, blue cotton dress swishing from side to side. Wanda was a large woman of that indeterminate, over forty age bracket. She had wavy blonde hair, bright blue eyes, hot pink lipstick and a smile as big as Texas. Jess couldn't help but like Wanda.

"I'm so excited. I love Donna Vance. I've got all her cookbooks," Wanda gushed. "Let me help you with that." She began shaking out the table cloth.

"You can share my desk, Jess," Clarence said as he cleared a space for her. "You know, my wife enjoys that Donna Vance program with all the southern cooking and decorating."

Brittney placed a vase of yellow roses in the middle of the table.

Jess finished shifting her things over to Clarence's desk. "Why is Donna Vance coming here though? What's the story she's doing?"

"She's only covering the wedding of the century," Brittney beamed. "Some of you may not know this, but Chace Perez has relocated to Grace and she's having her wedding here."

"And who would that be?" Clarence asked.

"She was Miss Texas three years ago," Jess answered. "I never realized Chace was such a celebrity though." Jess couldn't believe it. *The wedding of the century? That was a bit much.*

Brittney looked affronted. "She's going to be on the cover of the magazine!"

Everyone looked up as the editor, Bob Barnes, came out of his office and joined the group. "I see that Brittney has told everyone the big news."

Brittney placed a number of sharpened pencils into the gold pencil cup. "I'm trying to explain it Daddy."

Clarence piped up, "I understand we'll have a celebrity in our midst."

Bob chuckled. "Right, so while Donna Vance is here with her crew to cover the wedding, I want everyone to make her feel welcome."

"You got it, boss," Wanda said with a wink before she made her way back to the front counter.

"Anyway, I just got off the phone with Mandy Lynn. She won't be in today. One of her kids is sick," Bob said.

"What else is new," Clarence grumbled.

Bob ignored the remark. "So, Jess. I've got another assignment for you. I want you to interview Katy Hockley about the flower basket." Bob handed Jess a page with all the details. She was to interview the president of the Grace Garden Club about the new spring flowers they were planting in the hanging basket on the courthouse lawn.

Brittney smiled as if this were a plum assignment. "Oh, that's right. It's time for the new spring flowers."

"The garden club members are busy planting flowers as we speak. You'll need to get some pictures," Bob explained. "Katy Hockley will be here around ten for the interview."

"You know Katy, right?" Brittney asked.

"Oh, I know Katy," Jess said. "She's a neighbor of mine."

"Great," Brittney cooed. "You'll need to borrow the camera from Wanda. We want good photos. Not cell phone pictures this time, okay Jess?"

Jess rolled her eyes. She had taken a few cell phone pictures for her article on the church restoration and Brittney had rejected them. "Okay. What do you want me to say, though? I mean, it's just flowers," Jess said.

"Just give us five hundred words on the new varieties they're planting and how important the flower basket is to the community," Bob said.

"And to the look of the courthouse lawn," Brittney said. "After all, it is the *World's Largest Hanging Flower Basket.*"

Jess wasn't likely to forget that fact. The flower basket hung from a large pergola on the northwest corner of the courthouse lawn, just across the street from the Antique Emporium.

"But, if you don't think you can do it ..." Brittney began.

"I'll do it," Jess cut in. "No problem."

Jess checked the wall clock. She had half an hour, just enough time to get some questions together. Everyone got back to work and Jess pulled a chair over to the side of Clarence's desk.

He smiled warmly. "You've been here going on a month now and I still haven't given you a tour of the print room."

"Well, I need to prep for my interview with Katy," Jess said. "Anyway, I've seen it already."

"Oh, you need the grand tour. Come on. This won't take a second," Clarence said, waving away her protests. "Besides, how much prep do you need for a story about a flower basket? You could write that in your sleep."

Jess laughed at this as Clarence led the way to the room with the printing press in the back.

"Welcome to the world of journalism," he said as he swept his hand across the machinery before him.

Jess spoke up, "I used to work at the newspaper in Houston. I do have some experience."

"Oh, well you're an old pro then," Clarence said.

The printing room ran the width of the bullpen and offices. It housed the digital laser printer. Jess was impressed with the long row of connected machines including a huge roll of newsprint that fed into the laser printer, a cutting machine, a collator, and a folding machine.

"Very cool, I have to admit. When I started here I wasn't expecting such modern methods," Jess said as she got a closer look.

Clarence smiled. "We're high tech. We switched to digital printing a couple of years ago."

"Nice going. I guess that's more efficient for a print run of only five hundred?"

Clarence continued. "We've got this operation down to a science. Everything's done on computers now. Wanda does the typesetting and Brittney handles the layout. I remember back in the old days…"

Clarence was interrupted when Brittney opened the door and stuck her head in. "There you are," she said with annoyance. "Katy is here for her interview."

"Already?" Jess had expected to have time to prepare questions. "She's early isn't she?"

"I don't know. She's here now," Brittney replied as she gestured toward the front. "Chop chop." With that she moved away and let the door swing shut.

Jess looked at Clarence who shook his head. "Chop chop," he said, mimicking Brittney's tone.

Jess smirked. "Now you stop that."

"Are you ready to face the garden club president?" Clarence asked jokingly.

"I'm just gonna have to wing it," Jess said with a shrug.

"It's easy," Clarence said reassuringly. "Just let her talk."

Brittney opened the door again. "One more thing Jess, don't forget the camera." Brittney tilted her head slightly, flashed her fake smile, and again let the door swing shut with a loud thunk.

"We really need to hire a staff photographer," Jess said.

CHAPTER 5 – THURSDAY, FEBRUARY 8

9:45 a.m.

Jess met Katy at the front of the office where she was chatting with Wanda. Katy Hockley was the mother of three boys, all in elementary school. She was slightly overweight and had short auburn hair. She sang soprano in the church choir, won awards for having the best yard in the neighborhood, and had a husband who was frequently away on business.

"Hi Katy. I'm doing your interview today," Jess said in greeting.

"Oh, I thought I was meeting with Mandy Lynn," Katy said.

"She couldn't make it," Wanda said. "Her little girl has strep."

"Oh, poor thing. Tell her I'll be praying for her."

"So," Jess said, pretending she was prepared, "Why don't we start with some pictures of the basket and then we can sit down for an interview."

"Oh, let me get the camera for you," Wanda said. She grabbed the camera bag out of her bottom drawer and passed it over.

Jess slung the bag over her shoulder. "All right, let's go."

It was a bright sunny day with just a little nip in the air. They crossed the street and began the walk around the courthouse lawn. Katy began chattering away. "The club members are there at the basket now, putting in the new spring plants."

"Great," Jess said, "I can take some pictures of that, while they're planting."

"That would be good," Katy agreed. "Then, take a few more pictures after it's all done. It's going to be beautiful."

They made their way around the side of the courthouse and Jess saw several ladies industriously replanting. They had lowered the basket and propped it onto the ground with four sawhorses. The members were busily laying in compost and fertilizer. A large assortment of flowers in pink, orange, yellow, and red were spread out in rows on little plastic trays nearby.

Jess took several pictures of the activity around her. Katy beamed with pride as she directed the group. "We've been planning this day for months," she said. "We only replant twice a year."

"Let's sit down so I can take some notes," Jess suggested. They took a seat on one of the park benches which had been moved away from the pergola for the replanting.

"So, what is the actual size of the hanging basket?" Jess asked, pulling a steno pad out of her bag.

"The basket is ten feet wide," Katy recited. "It's the largest hanging basket in the world and we are very proud of that fact."

Jess found that her pen was out of ink so she began recording on her phone. "So, what flowers are you putting in today?"

"Today we're planting petunias, begonias, impatiens, geraniums, and some lantana."

Clarence had been right. All Jess had to do was let Katy talk. The basket had been erected twenty-nine years ago. It was a collaborative effort of the Grace Garden Club and the city government. They held a fundraiser and Easter egg hunt on the courthouse lawn every spring.

"This is going on the front page, right?" Katy asked.

"I believe so," Jess said. "I'm not really in charge of that. What time do you think you'll be finished with the planting?" she asked.

Katy didn't even have to think about it, "We'll be packing it up around two thirty."

"I'll come by and take some more pictures then," Jess said as she got up to leave. She glanced behind them and noticed the Alpaca Sweater shop. "Say, Katy, have you ever been in that new sweater store?"

Katy looked over at the shop and scrunched up her nose. "Sweaters made from Alpaca skin?"

"Alpaca wool," Jess corrected her.

"I don't know. It sounds scratchy. I'll talk to you later," Katy said. She then joined her club members, instructing them on the placement of the flowers.

Jess packed up the camera and went home for lunch. Sweet Tea greeted her at the foot of the stairs to her apartment, rubbing up against her legs.

"Stop it," Jess admonished. "You're going to make me trip." Once inside, Jess poured some kibble into a bowl for the cat and made herself a sandwich. "Sweet Tea, my career is in the garbage. I'm writing a puff piece about a flower basket," she lamented.

Sweet Tea gave Jess a look of total indifference. "Mew," she said.

"I guess you're right," Jess said, setting her phone out on the table. "Stay positive. Thanks, Sweet Tea. That's good advice."

Sweet Tea continued to eat without looking up.

After transcribing the interview and researching each type of flower, Jess was ready for a break. She saved her notes on her laptop and stretched.

Just then her phone dinged with a text message. It was her best friend, Avery, who was going to culinary school in Austin.

Avery: Skype tonight?

Jess: Sure, what time?

Avery: 9 p.m. okay?

Jess: Okay. See you then.

Jess rinsed her dishes and began repacking her laptop bag when her landline rang. It was her father.

"Hi Dad," Jess said into the phone.

"Jess, darling. I'm glad I could catch you at home. How are you doing?"

"Really great. How are you?"

"Just fine. Eleanor says hello."

"Tell her hello from me. How are Chad and Jeremy?" Jess said. She still wasn't used to her father being remarried. Eleanor was her stepmother. Chad and Jeremy were Eleanor's boys, aged twelve and ten.

"Oh, they're okay I guess. Listen Jess, I wanted to see how the job search is going for you?"

"Well, I've been pretty busy writing freelance for the Gazette here in town. And I'm doing the monthly newsletter for the church. So, I'm keeping busy."

"Jessica, I'm talking about a real job, something with security."

Jess cringed at the disappointment in her father's voice. "Well, I've sent out applications. There just aren't a lot of openings in journalism."

"Have you thought about medical billing? Eleanor knows some people …."

Jess interrupted, "I've got to get back to the office Dad. I'm working on a story right now."

"All right Darling, I just worry about you," he said.

"I know you do. I love you Dad," Jess said.

"Love you too."

Back at the office, Jess was at Clarence's desk finishing up her story. She had taken photos of the finished basket and sent them to Brittney for the layout. She checked her notes transcribed from the recording but couldn't find the dimensions of the basket.

Hmmm, she thought, *maybe the garden club website has the info.* She keyed *World's Largest Hanging Flower Basket* into the search engine. A video popped up from a garden center in Georgia. She scribbled down those dimensions, twelve feet wide weighing two tons. Jess also scribbled down the phone number. *This can't be the biggest*, she thought.

Jess keyed in *Grace Texas Garden Club*. The website home page featured a picture of the flower basket with a group photo of the garden club members. She clicked on the tab for the hanging basket. The dimensions were listed as having a ten foot width with no weight given. But ten feet was considerably smaller than twelve feet.

Jess watched the video from Georgia again. The post was from four years ago. Jess glanced around. Brittney had gone into her father's office so the room was deserted, except for Wanda on the phone at the front desk. Jess picked up Clarence's phone and dialed the number.

"Atlanta Garden Center," a man's voice answered.

"Hi, I just saw a video about your *World's Largest Hanging Basket* on YouTube, but it was from a few years ago. Do you still have that basket?"

"Yes we do," the man said with pride, "it features over two hundred plants."

"Okay and what are the dimensions?"

The man confirmed what Jess had seen in the video. "You really should come out and see it for yourself."

"Okay," Jess said, "and is it really the largest in the world?"

"Nobody has challenged us on that yet," the man said, "have you heard of a bigger one?"

"No, I haven't," Jess said. "Thank you." She ended the call and took a deep breath. *How can this be*? The Grace Garden Club had been claiming their basket was the biggest in the world for years. Jess wasn't sure what to do. *Maybe the website is wrong*, she thought. She called Katy, who picked up on the second ring.

"Hello, Jess?"

"Hi Katy," Jess said, "I'm just double checking my notes for the article. What did you say the dimensions of the hanging basket are?"

"It's ten feet wide," Katy answered.

"Okay," Jess said, "and do you know how much it weighs?"

"I really don't know. I'm not sure how we would weigh it," Katy said laughing.

"How many different plants did you put in?"

"We put in a hundred and fifty plants today," Katy said proudly.

Jess took a deep breath. "Well, the reason I asked is... there's a larger hanging basket in Atlanta."

Silence.

"No way." Katy was clearly not having it.

"I googled 'world's largest hanging basket' and saw a video about a hanging basket at the Atlanta Garden Center. It's twelve feet wide and has two hundred individual plants."

"You have got to be kidding me," Katy said. "Hold on, let me go to the computer."

Jess waited while Katy looked up the info. She heard the video playing on Katy's computer. "No, no, no, this cannot be," Katy moaned. "How did this happen?"

"I don't know. It's a surprise to me."

"Well, you can't print that," Katy said tersely.

"I can't say ours is the largest when I know that's not the truth."

"Listen, don't print anything about this Atlanta basket," Katy demanded. "What people don't know won't hurt them."

"Is it really that big a deal?" Jess asked.

"Yes, of course it's a big deal," Katy spat out. "Having the world's largest hanging basket is Grace's claim to fame. Without it we're just a tiny little back-water with nothing special."

"We still have the biggest hanging flower basket in Texas," Jess offered.

Katy was emphatic. "Do not change the story."

"I have to check with Bob."

"I want to see the article before it goes to print," Katy demanded.

"I can't do that," Jess said.

Katy fumed. "Well, we will just see about that!" Then Jess heard the unmistakable clunk of the phone hanging up.

CHAPTER 6 – THURSDAY, FEBRUARY 8

3:45 p.m.

Jess walked across the room to Bob's door. She could see through the glass window that Brittney was in the office having a discussion with him. Jess knocked on the glass and gave a little wave when the two looked up. Bob gestured for her to come in.

"What is it?" Brittney asked with aggravation.

"Hi, sorry to disturb you," Jess said as she entered the office. "I have a little problem with Katy Hockley."

"Okay, what exactly?" Bob asked.

"It turns out there's actually a larger hanging flower basket in Atlanta."

"Really?" Brittney asked, her eyes wide.

"Yeah, I called the place and it's two feet wider."

Bob ran his hand through his hair and shook his head. "I really don't think it's that big a deal. Just change the story."

"So, should I put in the info about the basket in Atlanta, or just say ours is the second largest, or...."

Brittney interrupted, "Jess, we are in the middle of something. Just change the story." She waved her hands dismissively, motioning for Jess to leave the office.

"Okay," Jess said as she backed out of the door and closed it gently. She went back to Clarence's desk and made a few tweaks to the story with a brief mention of the Atlanta Garden Center's flower basket at the end. She referred to the hometown basket as the largest in Texas. She gave her story the title: *Grace Garden Club Replants Hanging Basket for Spring* and clicked submit.

After work, Jess pulled out of the parking lot behind the Gazette and into the town square. As she drove by the T-shirt shop, Corporation T-Shirt, she saw Clarence on the side of the building. He looked both ways as if he might cross the street but instead ducked into an unmarked door along the side.

Where is he going? Jess wondered. She circled around the block and came up along the side of Corporation T-Shirt. She had never noticed the door before and figured it probably went into the stockroom of the T-shirt shop.

She debated whether or not to go in. Her curiosity got the better of her and she parked the car in front of the shop. She casually walked around the side of the building and tried the door. It opened onto a small landing with a staircase going down. She could hear voices below and began tiptoeing down the steps. *What is this?* Jess wondered.

As she got to the foot of the stairs she saw a long dark mahogany bar with barstools and a few booths along the opposite wall. The walls were exposed red brick and it was dimly lit with Edison bulbs hanging down the length of the room. Clarence was seated on a barstool with a mug of dark beer.

Norman, the owner of Corporation T-Shirt, was behind the bar mixing a drink. He looked up. "Well, hello there. Welcome to the Side Bar."

"Jess, you found me," Clarence said beaming. "Come here and take a load off." He dusted off the barstool next to him.

Jess was dumbfounded. "What is this?"

"You have just stumbled upon Grace's best kept secret," Clarence said with a grin.

Norman wiped off the counter in front of Jess. "This used to be a speakeasy back in the days of prohibition. When I opened Corporation T-Shirt, this basement was being used as storage. I cleared it out and decided to get a liquor license and open my own bar."

"Wow. How long have you been here?" Jess took a seat.

"Oh, the Side Bar's been around nigh on

twenty-five years or so," Clarence said.

"That's basically my whole life. How did I not know about this?"

The two men chuckled. "I'll be right back," Norman said. He took the drink to a gentleman seated at the end of the bar and then returned. "Now, what can I get for you?"

"Um, how about a Corona Light?"

"Coming right up."

Jess still had questions. "Why don't you have a sign outside or advertise or anything? How come nobody knows about this place?"

"I think it's kind of fun if not a lot of people know about it," Norman said as he popped the cap on an ice-cold bottle of Corona and added a wedge of lime. "I'm not in it for the money. I just enjoy shooting the breeze with old-timers like Clarence here."

"Who are you calling old?" Clarence asked in mock offense.

Jess was still incredulous. "My whole life there's been a secret bar here and I never knew." She sipped her Corona. "I like the name Side Bar."

"That works for the newspaper and the courthouse," Norman said.

"How so?"

Clarence asked. "Well, you know what a sidebar is in the paper biz?"

"A little box on the side of the article with call-out information," Jess said, gesturing with her hands. "It's usually in the form of a list."

Clarence chuckled. "Journalism 101," he joked.

Norman leaned in. "And in the courtroom, a side bar is when the judge calls the lawyers over to the bench for a private talk."

"Oh, I see." Jess said, very pleased to be in on a secret.

"There's one very important thing to remember about the Side Bar," Clarence said, looking serious.

"What's that?"

"Do not... under any circumstances... tell Brittney."

Jess crossed her heart and smiled conspiratorially.

That evening, Jess opened Skype and called Avery, her best friend since junior high. Avery's parents owned the Pie Hole. She looked a lot like her mother, tall, trim, and African American.

Jess: Hey, how's it going? I miss you so much.

Avery: Miss you too. What's up?

Jess: Not much. I've been working at the paper all day.

Avery: How is it?

Jess: Not too shabby. Brittney is annoying but that's nothing new.

Avery: I could not stand her in high school. Remember in P.E. when she took my clothes out of my gym locker and threw them into the shower stall?

Jess: Yes, that was horrible. You had to go the rest of the day dripping wet.

Avery: I will never forgive her for that.

Jess: She was the worst. She's not so bad now though, just kind of a jerk. Listen, I want to ask you something. Did you know about a secret bar underneath Corporation T-Shirt?

Avery: No. What kind of bar?

Jess: It used to be a speakeasy. Norman runs it. I followed Clarence in this door on the side of the building. There are no signs or anything. It's been there for twenty-five years.

Avery: What? How come I didn't know about it?

Jess: That's what I said.

Avery: You'll have to show me next time I'm in town.

Jess: Hey, how are your culinary classes

going?

Avery: It's going okay. I have this one instructor though, Chef Pierre. He is really tough.

Jess: I'm sure you can handle it.

Avery: He wants us to cater an event.

Jess: What kind of event?

Avery: Anything really, a party, a meeting. The thing is, we have to find our own clients. How am I supposed to do that with no references? Who would be willing to take a chance on a student?

Jess: I'll let you know if I hear of anything.

Avery: What did you do today?

Jess: I spent the whole day writing about the flower basket. The garden club replanted for spring and that's what passes for hard-hitting news in this one-horse town.

Avery: Come on, you love Grace and all its little quirks.

Jess: Yeah, I do. It's unique. But the highlight of my day was finding out there's a bigger flower basket in Atlanta.

Avery: Oh wow! Really?

Jess: Yeah, Katy was not happy.

Avery: I'll bet.

Jess: Oh, I almost forgot. Guess who's coming to town?

Avery: Umm ... I give up. Who?

Jess: Donna Vance.

Avery: Donna Vance? You mean, *the Donna Vance*? TV star, lifestyle maven, the Queen of Texas Chic?

Jess: No, the other Donna Vance. (laughing)

Avery: Ha ha. What brings her to Grace? Is she covering the flower basket too?

Jess: No, she's doing a story on the wedding of the century, of course.

Avery: Oh no, how awful.

Jess: Well ... it's for *Texas Bride Magazine*, which I just found out is owned by the same parent company as the Gazette.

Avery: Great, so she's coming to your office? It's like you can't get away from this wedding.

Jess: It's okay. I'm fine, really.

Avery: Sure, you are. It's only your ex marrying a former Miss Texas, at your Aunt's house.

Jess: (sigh) I know, but, I'm over him and I'm just going to try to steer clear of this whole wedding brouhaha. I told Ms. Melody I would work at the Emporium so she could go to the wedding.

Avery: You need to get away. You're still coming to Austin for South by Southwest, right?

Jess: I think I'm a little old for Spring Break.

Avery: You're never too old for good music.

Jess: Maybe so, if I can afford to take time off from my various part time jobs.

Avery: I'm sure you can find a way. You know, I'm really surprised that Chace would want Donna Vance to cover her wedding.

Jess: Why? Chace loves being the center of attention.

Avery: I don't think she wants that kind of attention.

Jess: What do you mean?

Avery: Donna Vance makes fun of brides and critiques weddings. She's merciless. You should check out her website.

Jess: How do you criticize a wedding?

Avery: She comments on everything like it's a bad movie review. She rips into the decor, the dress, the bridesmaids, just everything. She even has a blooper reel of wedding mishaps.

Jess: You mean like wedding guests falling into the cake?

Avery: Yeah, stuff like that. Some people think it's funny, but I think it's downright mean.

Jess: Hmm, well, I'll have to check it out.

Avery: So, what else is going on? Did you get together with that hot detective?

Jess: Chris Connor? No, that didn't go anywhere.

Avery: What do you mean? I thought you two were going out.

Jess: He said we should catch a movie or something, but then he never called me.

Avery: So, call him! Don't man the phone, phone the man!

Jess: If you think he's so hot, why don't you call him?

Avery: First, I am in Austin. Second, he said he wants to go out with you, not me. Third, I am so busy with this culinary program that I have no life.

Jess: Okay, maybe I'll call him.

Avery: Good. I better get going. I've got an early class tomorrow.

Jess: Later Gator.

After ending her skype session, Jess felt curious. She opened Google and keyed in Donna Vance. There were several options, news, images, and books to buy. Donna had been a lifestyle maven for over twenty years. There were books on decorating, entertaining, weddings, marriage, and several cookbooks.

Jess clicked on the official website and found the *Weddings* tab. She found wedding advice, trends, and a blooper reel dubbed *Epic Wedding Fails*. Jess clicked on it. A montage of wedding videos was played with mishaps including a father of the bride whose pants fell to his ankles as he was dancing with his daughter, a bouquet being tossed into a ceiling fan pelting the crowd with chopped up bits of flowers, and an outdoor wedding with a bride who slipped along a muddy center aisle and fell on her behind. She spent the entire wedding with a muddy stain on the back of her dress as the couple said their vows. The voice of Donna provided snarky, running commentary throughout the entire clip reel. She referred to the bride who fell as "Soggy Bottom" and said, "Look at the size of that derriere!"

There were also several clips from a cowboy themed wedding in which Donna criticized everything from the decorations and dresses to the food and music. Donna said, "Why do you have to act like a bunch of ignorant rednecks? This is why people in other states think Texas is full of hicks. Your wedding is a formal occasion. Take off the stupid cowboy hat!"

Oh no. Chace is toast, Jess thought.

The identities of the people in the videos were protected by a black bar covering the eyes. Even so, it had to be humiliating to be included in the *Epic Wedding Fails*. Jess felt an instant dislike for Donna. *One more reason to stay as far away from this wedding as possible,* Jess thought.

JESS SAYIN' BLOG POST – FEBRUARY 8

Wedding Movie Marathon

Valentine's Day is coming soon and romance is in the air, and what's more romantic than a wedding? Well, to be honest a lot of things, but that's not the point. The point is, weddings are full of pomp and pageantry, romance, stress, family drama, and there's cake! So, bonus.

Weddings are also the perfect setting for a good old fashioned rom com. Luckily for me, I have inherited my mother's extensive collection of DVDs and Blu-rays so I can binge watch these modern-day classics anytime. So, without further ado, I give you my:

All Time Best Wedding Movie Binge List:
1. Four Weddings and a Funeral - By far, the best wedding movie ever. Back in the day, Hugh Grant was a hottie! This movie has everything: wardrobe malfunctions, embarrassing speeches, awkward flirting ... just everything you could want. This movie even transcends Andie MacDowell's famously bad acting. Put on your best turquoise underpants and enjoy.
2. My Best Friend's Wedding - Julia Roberts tries every dirty trick in the book to break up the happy couple. Also, back in the day, Dermot Mul-

roney was a hottie!

3. My Big Fat Greek Wedding - Very good family comedy. Best line from Maria, mother of the bride: "The man is the head, (of the household) but the woman is the neck, and she can turn the head any way she wants."

4. Bridesmaids - A lot of folks can't get past the scene with all the vomiting. Get over it. The movie is very funny, and full of the kind of inappropriate humor that male characters get away with on a regular basis. Best line from Megan, played by Melissa McCarthy: "I took nine (puppies). I did slightly over commit to the whole dog thing. Turns out I'm probably more comfortable with six."

5. Father of the Bride - Welcome back to the 90s, Mr. Banks! This movie is so cute and sentimental. The sweet father/daughter relationship gets me every time.

6. 27 Dresses - A fun romance with unrequited love, sisters at odds, and that thing where the wrong guy turns out to be the right guy. Also, a publicly humiliating revenge melt-down. And, once again, back in the day, James Marsden was a cutie.

7. Bride Wars - Pranks, hijinks, and another publicly humiliating revenge melt-down. Also best friends at odds and that thing where the right guy turns out to be the wrong guy. That wrong guy is Chris Pratt looking oddly un-hot. (Note - anytime a male character says, "People will think I've lost control of you, already," you know he's the wrong guy.)

Honorable Mention - It's not a wedding movie but **About Time** has one of the best movie weddings I've ever seen. There's a huge storm with heavy winds and pouring rain which absolutely destroys the outside reception. It blows the tent over, pouring cold water on the guests. They laugh it off and make the best of it. It's perfectly imperfect.

CHAPTER 7 – FRIDAY, FEBRUARY 9

8:30 a.m.

In the morning, Jess went downstairs and picked up her copy of the Grace Gazette on the lawn. She always got a thrill seeing her name in the byline.

Jess got into her blue Ford Fusion and started the car to warm it up a bit. Then she opened the newspaper. Her story was front page news, featuring several of her pictures and the headline: *World's Second Largest Hanging Flower Basket.*

Shoot, Brittney changed the headline, Jess thought. That wasn't unusual. The headline had to fit on the page right so sometimes it was shortened. But this gave her a feeling of dread. Katy would not be pleased.

Jess drove to the Gazette office and saw a number of garden club members through the windows at the front desk. *I think I'll go in the back way,* Jess decided as she turned the corner to use the parking area behind the building.

Jess slipped in the back door but she could hear the cacophony of complaints coming from the front. Over the din, she heard Katy Hockley's distinctive shrill voice, "This is an outrage! I demand you print a retraction! I want to see Bob Barnes right this instant!"

Jess tried to be unobtrusive as she made her way over to Clarence's desk. Clarence looked like he was hiding behind a copy of the paper, ignoring the group of ladies at the front. Wanda was holding her own at the front desk, not letting anyone behind the counter.

"If you will just take a seat please," Wanda said in her calming voice, "I will see if Mr. Barnes is available."

Then, Katy spotted Jess. "There she is!" Katy shrieked, pointing directly at Jess. "That's the one who wrote this piece of trash." Katy raised her copy of the paper and slammed it down on the counter.

Brittney came out into the bullpen and went up to the counter. Jess couldn't hear what she said but it seemed to appease them. There was some general mumbling.

Clarence gave Jess a sly smile. "Looks like you ruffled some feathers."

Brittney came across the room. "Jess, I'd like a word with you please."

Jess followed Brittney into her office. They took seats, Brittney behind her desk. "You're in a heap of trouble," Brittney said, "this situation is out of hand."

"Trouble?" Jess was confused. "You were

there when I told Bob about the larger basket in Atlanta."

"Be that as it may," Brittney said, "I think you could have handled it better. Ms. Hockley said you had promised to call her before running the story. Is that right?"

"No, I didn't say that…"

At that moment, Bob came into Brittney's office. "I see we have quite a crowd here this morning."

"Hi Dad," Brittney said. "I was just talking to Jess about her hanging basket story." She cleared her throat. "Under the circumstances, I don't think we can use Jess as a freelancer anymore."

"No," Jess protested. "That's ridiculous."

"Katy told me you promised her final approval on the article," Brittney said.

"Nonsense," Bob said. "We don't give outsiders approval on our stories. We're journalists, we print the truth."

"But this story has a lot of people upset."

"Brittney, it's called journalistic integrity. Jess did a fine job on the piece and we've sold more copies than we have in weeks."

"Thank you," Jess beamed.

Clearly peeved, Brittney pursed her lips. "Did you forget that we have Donna Vance and her people arriving today?

"I did not," Bob said. "I'll go smooth things over with the garden club." He started to leave and then turned back to Jess, "Jess, I may have another assignment for you today, do you mind hanging out for a little while?"

"Not at all," Jess said, glad that she was not being let go after all. Bob held the door for her and they left Brittney alone in her office.

Bob went to the front desk and talked with the club members. Jess had no idea what he said to assuage them but they quieted down.

"What are you working on, Clarence?" Jess asked as she pulled a chair up to the side of his desk.

"Oh, I've got a few irons in the fire. Good piece about the flower basket, by the way."

"Thanks," Jess said. "I wonder who picked that headline."

"That would be Bob," Clarence answered with a twinkle in his eye.

Jess heard a gasp from several of the garden club ladies. She and Clarence looked up to see Donna Vance and two other people coming into the lobby.

"Oh my goodness, it's Donna Vance!" Katy squealed.

"Well, hello. Is this my welcoming committee?" Donna joked as she basked in the adoration of her fans. She swept into the room like she owned the place, looking much the same as she did in her videos. She tossed her short, ash blonde hair. She was wearing a cream colored designer coat over tan slacks.

Bob lifted up the pass-through counter for Donna and her people. "Good morning. I'm Bob Barnes. Welcome to the Grace Gazette."

Brittney walked briskly up to the front while Jess looked on. Bob and Brittney introduced themselves and shook hands with everyone.

"This is my husband Garrett. He's the photographer on this project," Donna said.

Garrett nodded and shook hands. Jess thought he looked odd with his gelled brown hair, parted on the side, and an equally gelled handlebar mustache. He was shorter than Donna and carried a large, black, camera bag.

"And this is my personal assistant, Crystal Clearwater. Isn't that name just a hoot?" Donna said as she indicated the very plain woman next to her.

Crystal smiled weakly, peering out through her mousy brown hair, which hung down in her face. "Pleased to meet you," she said.

Jess and Clarence stood as Brittney led the group over to the freelance table in the middle of the room. Bob introduced Clarence and Jess. Everyone shook hands.

Now that the initial excitement was over, the garden club began trickling out. Donna gestured toward them. "So, who are they?"

"Oh, that would be the Grace Garden Club," Jess said.

"They're upset about a story Jess wrote in today's paper," Brittney said, showing a copy of the Gazette.

"Is that so?" Donna mused. She turned to Jess, "Let me give you a word of advice, honey. You've got to develop a thick skin. Don't worry about stepping on some toes if you want to be a good writer."

Jess nodded.

Then Brittney proudly offered Donna what had been the freelance table. "So, I put together a little workspace for you. I think there's room here for everybody and ...."

Donna interrupted, "Oh, this won't do at all." She looked around at the bullpen. "I need my own office. There are too many distractions out here." She looked at Crystal, "Didn't you make that clear when you made these arrangements?"

"Well, I, uh..." Crystal stammered.

Brittney was at a loss for what to do. "Nobody mentioned anything about a private office," she said.

Donna looked across at the two offices along the side of the bullpen. "What about this one right here?" she asked, pointing at Brittney's office. Without waiting for an answer, Donna brushed past her assistant and made her way over. Everyone followed her inside.

"Well, this is my office," Brittney said.

"Very nice," Donna said, assessing the space. "Charming little rug."

"Thank you," Brittney beamed.

"This will do nicely. How soon can you move your things out?" Donna said. Brittney was clearly taken aback, but Donna failed to notice.

"It's fine, Brit. You can have the freelance table," Jess said cheerily.

Brittney gave her an angry look.

"You can share my office, Brittney," Bob said, "It's only for one week. Come on, let's clear the desk."

Donna walked over to Brittney's small seating area with a loveseat and coffee table. "You two can set up over here," she said to her two-person team.

Everyone began bustling about, moving Brittney's things into Bob's office and setting up her computer on the conference table. Jess brought in Brittney's briefcase and purse and set them in a chair near the computer.

Donna and her assistant followed Jess into

Bob's office. "Let's have a little pow-wow about this magazine story," she said.

"Absolutely," Bob said, taking a seat behind his desk. "What can we do for you?"

Jess, in an effort to be helpful, began looking for a power strip under the conference table while Brittney adjusted her speakers.

"I'm new to Grace," Donna said, "I'd like to have someone to show me around, someone who knows the town. Sort of a liaison, if you will."

"I can do that," Brittney piped up.

"I want someone who could help me organize my notes, keep up with the wedding itinerary, someone with writing experience."

"I am at your service," Brittney said as she came over and stood next to her father.

"This would be in addition to your assistant?" Bob asked.

"Crystal is my personal assistant, not a writer," Donna explained. "And she doesn't know this town."

Crystal nodded in agreement.

Jess emerged from under the conference table, covered in dust. "I found the power strip," she said.

"How about her?" Donna said, gesturing toward Jess. "You're a writer. You know the town."

Jess stood up and dusted herself off. "You want me to help you write the story?"

Brittney said, "Oh, I don't think Jess wants to work on this story."

"Well, why ever not?" Donna asked.

"Jack Ketchum, the groom, is her ex-husband," Brittney said.

Jess scrunched up her face in aggravation. "Brittney," she started. "That's not ...."

"What? It's true," Brittney said defensively.

Donna looked intrigued. "Well then, you've got the inside track. That settles it."

CHAPTER 8 – FRIDAY, FEBRUARY 9

9:45 a.m.

Despite her misgivings, Jess knew that working with Donna on a cover story for *Texas Bride Magazine* would be a good career move. "Sure, I'll be your liaison," she said, dusting off to shake hands with Donna.

Brittney flashed her fake smile. "Fantastic. I guess y'all better get on over to your office then."

"We don't have time for a pow-wow at the moment," Donna announced. "We're meeting the happy couple in a few minutes." Donna got up and snapped her fingers. "Jess, you and Garrett are with me."

"Oh," Jess said, realizing that she would now be thrust into the wedding activities.

Out in the bullpen Donna began issuing orders. "Garrett we have to get to the hotel and set up for pictures. Crystal, I need a mini fridge in that office for my smoothies."

Jess gathered up her notebook and her bag. Clarence was not at his desk, so she slipped her laptop into his bottom desk drawer and grabbed her coat.

The Bluebonnet Hotel was only two blocks from the town square but Donna insisted on driving her red Cadillac Escalade. On the way, Jess texted Jack.

Jess: I am helping Donna with the magazine article. On our way to the hotel now.

Jack: Great! I want a word with you before we begin the interview.

Jess wondered what that was about.

As they entered the hotel, Jess gestured to the grand entrance. "This is Grace's oldest hotel, built in 1890. It's rumored to be haunted."

The hotel had a meeting room reserved for the interview. Garrett began setting up lights for photos.

Jack came out to greet everyone. "Chace will be down in a moment," he said.

Donna held out her hand. "Pleased to meet you. I'm Donna Vance."

Everyone shook hands. Then Jack asked, "Could I just have a quick word with Jess?"

"Oh, certainly," Donna said with a curious look.

Jack led Jess to the other side of the lobby and ducked into a hallway, in an effort to get out of earshot of Donna.

"What is this all about, Jack?"

"It's Chace," Jack whispered. "She doesn't want word getting out that she's pregnant."

"Okay, that's fine by me," Jess said. "But it is the twenty-first century, you know. People get pregnant before getting married all the time now."

"Her grandmother, her abuela from Mexico, is very old fashioned so we don't want her to find out," Jack explained. "We don't want anything in the article about the baby, okay?"

"Got it." Jess nodded. "It should be easy since she's not even showing yet."

"And just, keep it a secret from the bridesmaids, if you can."

Jess mimed zipping her lips and locking them shut. "Oh, there is one thing," Jess said.

"What?" Jack asked worriedly.

"Whose idea was this magazine story? Have you seen Donna's website where she slams weddings and has a blooper reel?"

"I don't know who contacted the magazine. Anyway, what are you talking about?"

"Donna makes fun of brides and their weddings. It's vicious, like she's reviewing a bad movie."

Jack looked confused.

Jess continued. "Chace must have known this when she agreed to it."

"That doesn't sound good. I don't want anything to upset her."

Just then Chace peeked around the corner. "There you two are," she cooed. "I met Donna and she told me you're helping her with the story, Jess. That is just great!"

Jess motioned for Chace to come closer. "Donna is not nice to brides. Have you seen her website?" Jess asked.

"Oh," Chace laughed. "I have seen those *Epic Wedding Fails*. That is just too funny. But don't worry, *Texas Bride Magazine* is different. It's all about wedding cakes and dresses and fun stuff." Chace gave Jess a pouty look, "You are just so sweet to be worried about me."

At that moment Donna poked her head around the corner. "Are we having a three-way over here?" she joked.

Chace laughed hysterically while Jack and Jess looked uncomfortable.

"Come on," Donna said, "let's get on with this interview."

They went back across the lobby to the room set up for the interview. Jack and Chace sat together on a loveseat for a portrait. Jack looked dapper in a navy jacket and red tie with khaki trousers. Chace wore a striking emerald green long sleeve dress with a draped neckline and a side tie that gathered loosely above her left hip. *Excellent job hiding the tummy*, Jess thought. A long string of freshwater pearls completed the look. Jess peered at her, wondering just how far along Chace was in her pregnancy. From what Jess could tell, she wasn't showing yet.

Garrett moved lights around and took several shots. "Now, I'd like to get some with the two of you standing. Jack, let's put you behind Chace with your arms around her shoulders." The couple stood and let Garrett direct them through several poses before he was done and the couple returned to the loveseat.

Donna and Jess took seats in the chairs across from them.

Chace reached into her bag and handed Donna a couple of pages. "This is our pre-wedding itinerary," she said. "I emailed this to your assistant."

Donna handed the itinerary to Jess. "Here, you can take this one. I already have a copy."

Jess glanced over the list and couldn't believe the number of activities leading up to the wedding. "You have a dress fitting in an hour," she said, "and the bachelorette party tonight?"

"Yeah, it's quite a whirlwind," Jack said.

"Jess, you're invited," Chace said. "In fact, you're invited to everything."

Jess shifted uncomfortably in her seat. This

meant she would have to go to the wedding after all, as a journalist covering the event. She had specifically told Ms. Melody that she would work at the Antique Emporium on Valentine's Day. Now she would have to take the day off. "Thanks," she said.

"She'll be with me," Donna interjected. "Now, tell me how you two lovebirds met?"

"That's kind of a funny story," Jack said, "It was at a baseball game."

"It's like right out of Harry and Sally," Chace said.

"*When Harry Met Sally*," Jess muttered under her breath. She got out a small notebook and began taking notes.

"I had been going out with Guy," Chace said.

"Who was this guy?" Donna asked.

Chace giggled, "His name is Guy."

Jack continued, "We worked together in Houston."

"The Astros game was only my third date with Guy," Chace clarified. "Anyway, he asked me if I had a friend I could fix up with his friend, Jack."

"Right, because he had four tickets," Jack said.

"So, I immediately thought of my friend Taylor. She was always complaining about not having a boyfriend," Chace said with a laugh.

"We all four went to the Astros game. It was

Astros vs. Rangers. And the Astros won," Jack said.

"Nobody cares about the game, Honey. They just want to know how we met."

"Just to clarify, you were both on dates with other people?" Jess asked.

"Yes," Jack said. "I was on a blind date."

"When was this?" Donna asked.

"Last August," Jack said, "I'm not sure exactly when."

"It was August 31, I'll never forget it," Chace said. "Anyway, at some point Taylor had to get up and go to the bathroom."

"Then Guy said he was going to go get beer," Jack said, "so it was just Chace and me."

"And then they turned the kiss cam on us!" Chace laughed. "Everyone was looking at us!"

"We tried to wave it away," Jack said. "But everyone started chanting - Kiss! Kiss! Kiss!"

"So, we just had to kiss! Then everybody cheered, it was so funny," Chace giggled.

"After that, I was hooked," Jack said.

"Wow, that must have been some kiss!" Donna said. "What did your dates think of that?"

"Well, Taylor saw it on the big screen as she was walking back to our seats. She wasn't too happy, but she got over it." Chace explained. "In fact, she's one of my bridesmaids so it all worked out."

"I talked to Guy later that night and said I wanted to ask Chace out," Jack said.

Jess spoke up, "So, you've only known each other six months?"

"Less actually," Donna said, making a note on an index card.

"Yeah, about six months," Jack agreed.

"Okay so now, tell me about the proposal. I'm sure that's a romantic story," Donna said.

Jack and Chace exchanged a look for a moment. "It's not that romantic," Jack said.

"Of course it is," Chace said, reaching over and touching his arm. "It was on a Sunday," Chace began slowly.

Jess got the distinct feeling that Chace was making this up on the spot.

"So, Jack came over to take me out to Sunday brunch."

Jack nodded in agreement.

"And he brought a box of Cracker Jacks. You know, because we like baseball," Chace continued. "So, I just said, I'll save those for later, we're about to go have brunch."

Donna looked at them both curiously.

"But, Jack insisted that I have some Cracker

Jacks right then and there."

"Right," Jack interjected, "I said, there's a surprise inside." Jess figured that he had finally caught on to where this story was going.

"So, I didn't know what he was getting at and I was a little agitated, but he kept insisting."

Jack picked up the story, "She didn't know that I had put the engagement ring in a little pouch inside the box of Cracker Jacks."

"Oh my goodness," Donna said with a big smile.

"No, I had no idea. So, I was getting pretty aggravated so I just ripped the box open."

"And then, some of the Cracker Jacks spilled out and went flying across the room, and so did the little pouch with the ring in it. Chace ate some of the Cracker Jacks from the box."

"And I said, I had some. Are you happy now? But he was searching around on the floor."

Jack was really getting animated now. "She said, what the heck are you doing? I said, I'm looking for the prize."

"And then he found it and he was on his knees and he held it up to me."

"Chace was still annoyed with me so she grabbed the pouch and ripped it open. Then she saw the ring."

"And I started crying and then he said ...."

"I said, will you marry me?"

"And I said, yes."

"Isn't that sweet," Donna said. "When was this?"

"October," Chace said.

While at the same time Jack said, "December."

Chace laughed like something was hilarious. "Jack, no Honey. It was in October. How could you forget that?"

Jess smiled at them dubiously. *What a load of rubbish*, she thought. Probably the proposal had happened in the bathroom while looking at a positive pregnancy test.

"Now, I'd like to ask you about the Miss America Pageant," Donna said.

Jack interrupted, "I'd better get going, I'm meeting Guy for a round of golf and I've got to get changed."

"Your friend Guy who was dating Chace?" Donna asked.

Jack got up, "Yeah, he's my best man." He got up and kissed Chace on the cheek. "I'll see you this evening."

"I didn't know you played golf," Jess mused.

"I'm going to have to go soon too," Chace said, "I'm meeting all my bridesmaids in front of that dress shop downtown."

"Buttercup Dresses and Formals? That's our next stop. I can drive you there," Donna said, "We need to cover it for the magazine. But first, one quick question about the Miss America Pageant."

"Oh, that," Chace said dismissively. "I never even made it past the semi-finalist stage."

"That's just it. You were a semi-finalist and you were one of the favorites to win," Donna said.

"Oh, I don't think so," Chace said.

Donna continued, "But then you tripped on the hem of your dress during the talent competition. That stumble took you out of the running and cost you the Miss America crown."

Chace laughed, "Oh no, I wouldn't have won anyway." She stood up, "but we really do have to go meet everybody now, I don't want to be late."

"What was your talent?" Jess asked.

"Singing," Chace answered. "I grew up singing in the church choir."

"Chace has a lovely singing voice," Donna said. "You should take a look at the pageant video on YouTube."

CHAPTER 9 – FRIDAY, FEBRUARY 9

11:10 a.m.

Buttercup Dresses and Formals was on the town square, directly across the courthouse from the Pie Hole. Donna pulled up and parked in front. There were three young women milling around and looking at their phones.

"Oh shoot, we're late," Chace remarked as she got out of the Escalade.

"Chace, oh my goodness! There you are," one of them said as she gave Chace a big hug.

Jess and Donna emerged from the vehicle and introductions were made. Garrett began unpacking his tripod from the back of the vehicle.

"Donna, Jess, these are my bridesmaids; Madison, Taylor, and Kennedy," Chace said. Everyone shook hands. Madison was a round faced young woman with long chestnut hair. Taylor was shorter with loose blonde curls. Kennedy was a real looker. She had long curly red hair and a tall slender figure.

"And we all know who this is," Taylor gushed, pumping Donna's hand excitedly, "I am just so glad to meet you."

"So, you're all three named after Presidents,"

Jess pointed out.

"Wow, I never thought about that," Chace said. "Let's get inside and try on our dresses. Then we'll have our photo shoot. Is my sister here?"

"Conlie? I haven't seen her," Madison said.

"I'm sure she's just running late," Chace said as they entered the dress shop.

Fiona, the proprietor of the store greeted everyone at the front. She was a trim little woman in her mid-forties with her graying hair pulled into a tight bun. She shook hands with Donna. "I am just honored to have you in my shop. I'm a big fan."

Donna smiled, "Thank you. It is a charming little store."

Everyone crowded into the small shop. A young assistant was waiting near the dressing rooms at the back pointing to a rack of pink taffeta dresses with full billowy skirts.

At that moment the bells on the door jingled, and Crystal came in holding a plastic bottle filled with an ugly green liquid.

"There you are!" Donna hissed at her assistant. "I am starving to death here!"

Crystal silently held the bottle out to her, but Donna pushed her hands forward, palms up. Flustered, Crystal rummaged in her bag and came out with a little bottle of hand sanitizer. She poured a small amount into Donna's hands. After Donna had rubbed them together, she snatched up the foul green concoction.

"I just can't live without my protein smoothies," she said to the group.

"So, I've got your dressing rooms all set up," Fiona said, "We have the bride in here." She indicated the largest dressing room in the back. Chace went in and Kennedy followed.

"I'll help you do up your buttons," Kennedy said.

"I'm the maid of honor," Madison informed the assistant. The girl handed her one of the frothy pink dresses with an extra bow on the back and pointed her into a dressing room.

Taylor got her dress off the rack and went into the third dressing room.

Donna sat on a bench outside the dressing rooms to wait. Crystal stood nearby with a napkin in hand while Donna sipped her smoothie.

"I can't wait to see those dresses," she called out to everyone.

"Do I really need to be here for this?" Jess said, feeling out of place.

Donna patted the bench next to her, "take a seat."

The bells jingled again and Garrett came in. "Honey Bunches, how long is this going to take?" He made his way to the fitting room area.

"Sir, you're not supposed to be back here," Fiona informed him.

Donna gave her a tight lipped smile. "He's with me," she explained, as if that made it all right.

Fiona threw up her hands and walked away, shaking her head.

Donna looked annoyed with Garrett. "It takes however long it takes, maybe half an hour. I don't know. Are you all set up for the photo shoot outside?"

He stroked his mustache. "Not yet. I need to get the heart-shaped boxes from that candy store next door. You know, for the girls to hold up since the wedding is Valentine themed."

"Sure, you go do that," she said dismissively. "Don't eat too much candy though." She patted him on the behind as he left the store.

Madison called out from her dressing room, "this Maid of Honor dress is way too small for me. Didn't you get my measurements?"

Fiona hustled in with her tape measure and pins. "We got everybody's measurements, let me see about that."

Chace emerged from her dressing room with her gown undone in the back. Even so, the dress was stunning. The white chiffon dress sparkled with beads and pearls sewn into the lace sleeves and bodice. It had an empire waist and cascading ruffles down the front and back of the full skirt.

"There must be some kind of mistake," Chace began.

Her voice was drowned out by the loud noise of a motorcycle approaching. It stopped just outside the dress shop and parked next to Donna's SUV. A petite woman in a leather jacket stepped off the bike and removed her helmet. She shook out her thick mop of platinum blonde hair with two inch black roots.

"Who is that?" Donna asked.

"That's my sister, Conlie," Chace answered with an embarrassed smile.

Conlie entered the shop and looked around. "What's up, bitches?"

"Conlie," Chace laughed nervously, "you made it."

"Hell, I wouldn't miss this shotgun wedding for five dollars," Conlie quipped as she sauntered back to the dressing room area.

"Girls, you know my sister Conlie," Chace said. Each bridesmaid stuck her head out of the dressing rooms and greeted the newcomer with a wave and a smile.

Jess and Donna stood up to shake hands. Conlie was in such stark contrast to her sister. She removed her jacket and Jess saw a snake tattoo on one arm and a skull on her neck, just below her ear.

Conlie gave her sister a hug and then stepped back. "Will you look at my big sister? Doesn't she make a pretty picture?"

"It is a beautiful dress," Donna said, "go ahead and do up the back."

"That's just it," Kennedy said emerging from the dressing room, "it's too tight. Chace, have you put on weight?"

"Nothing is fitting right," Madison complained as she came out of her dressing room holding the pink dress on a hanger. "This maid of honor dress is so small a child could wear it."

"That's because it's not your dress," Conlie said sharply. "I'm the maid of honor."

"What? No, that's ridiculous," Madison said. She looked toward Chace, who had an expression of surprise.

Jess saw Donna tap Crystal on the arm. Crystal reached into her bag and very inconspicuously pulled out a small mini cassette recorder. Nobody else noticed.

"Why is it ridiculous? I am her sister," Conlie insisted, stepping right up to Madison.

Chace went over to the two of them, as if to break up a fight. "Maddie, I'm sorry. I did tell Conlie she could be the maid of honor."

"I don't believe it," Madison said looking around for support. "I'm your oldest childhood friend. I should be the maid of honor."

Taylor came to her side. "She even planned the bachelorette party. She put a lot of work into that."

"Well there's nothing we can do about it now," Chace said nervously.

"I can't believe they're just now working this out," Donna whispered to Jess. "The wedding is less than a week away."

"Can I have my dress now?" Conlie asked, holding out her hand for the hanger.

"Fine," Madison said in that way that meant nothing was fine. She dropped the hanger into Conlie's outstretched hand.

After everyone's dress was tried on Fiona determined that only the wedding gown would need alterations. Then everyone put on floral print sundresses with pink, springy cardigans for the photo shoot on the courthouse lawn.

"It's too cold out for these sleeveless dresses," Taylor complained, "Why did you pick these? It's not Spring yet."

"It will be when the magazine comes out," Donna said, "Besides, the dressmaker is a sponsor."

"Is that right?" Conlie asked, putting her jacket on over the dress.

"I'm sorry, I know it's kind of chilly out today, but we'll just take a quick picture and then change back," Chace said. "And then y'all can wear these to the couple's shower on Sunday."

What in the world is a couple's shower? Jess wondered.

Out on the lawn Garrett had set up a tripod to take a group photo in front of the hanging flower basket.

"It's literally freezing out here," Kennedy said through gritted teeth.

"Conlie, you can't wear your jacket. Put on the sweater," Chace pleaded.

"Okay, okay, don't get your knickers in a twist," she said as she complied. At least the sweater covered one of her tattoos.

Garrett gave each bridesmaid a large heart-shaped box to hold as a prop for the photo. Chace's box was the biggest.

"How hokey is that?" Jess muttered as she stood with Donna and Crystal.

"The chocolate shop, Candy's Candies is also a sponsor for the article," Crystal said. "Valentine's Day will have passed, but they're doing a half page ad for their Easter candy."

"Sounds like this wedding is one big sponsorship deal," Jess commented.

"Pretty much," Crystal agreed.

While they looked on, Jess noticed Katy Hockley standing off to the side holding a large wooden plaque. *What is she doing?* Jess wondered.

"Are we done yet? I am getting frostbite out here!" Madison complained as a gust of wind blew her skirt up.

Jess checked the temperature on her phone. It was fifty-five degrees. She pulled her coat tighter around her.

"I've got everything I need," Garrett said, "We're done here."

The girls raced back to the dress shop, leaving their candy boxes with Garrett. He began packing up his equipment.

"You take Garrett over to the hotel," Donna said to Crystal, "get us all checked in and meet me back at the office." She gave her the keys to the Escalade.

As soon as the wedding party had left the area, Katy marched over to the flower basket with her new sign. Jess peered over as Katy removed the sign in front of the basket which had said, "The World's Largest Hanging Flower Basket presented by the Grace Garden Club and the City of Grace." The new sign read, "The World's 2nd Largest Hanging Flower Basket presented by the Grace Garden Club and the City of Grace."

Jess sighed and shook her head.

CHAPTER 10 – FRIDAY, FEBRUARY 9

12:30 p.m.

The wedding party dispersed, leaving Jess with Donna and her entourage.

"Why don't you show me around a little bit, Jess. You've got a lovely town square here."

"Sure. Can we stop for lunch along the way?"

"Of course."

Jess led Donna around the square pointing out the interesting shops along the way. The dress shop was wedged between the hair salon on the corner and Candy's Candies. Corporation T-Shirt was on the end. They sold custom embroidered shirts and offered a variety of t-shirts with band logos and humorous sayings. Norman, the owner, waved at Jess from behind the counter.

They passed by the Gazette office and a woman who looked to be in her thirties rushed out. She had auburn hair in a spiky wedge cut and wore a black trench coat over black slacks.

"Mother, there you are!" she said in exasperation as she approached. "I have been waiting for more than an hour."

Donna's face turned ashen as if she were looking at a ghost. "Virginia, what a surprise. How long has it been? Two years?" Donna said in a monotone voice. "Jess, this is my daughter Virginia."

Virginia gave her mother an awkward hug while Donna stood stiffly. "The woman at the counter wouldn't tell me where you were," Virginia complained. "I need to talk to you."

"No doubt, it's about money," Donna said. "I'm busy at the moment. Jess and I are working on a magazine story."

Jess was surprised by Donna's demeanor. "We can do this another time," she said.

"Nonsense," Donna said impatiently. "Getting to know the town is part of my research."

Virginia looked annoyed. "Seriously, mother. Can we go somewhere? Maybe get some coffee?"

"Jess, is there any place around here for a decent cup of coffee?" Donna asked doubtfully.

Jess's stomach growled. *So much for getting any lunch.* "The best place for coffee is right around the corner at the Pie Hole," she said.

"Fine," Donna replied to her daughter. "But I can only spare a minute. We have a tight schedule."

The trio rounded the corner and made their way to the Pie Hole. "They also have great pies," Jess said proudly. "It's a genuine Mom and Pop shop. My friend Avery's parents own it."

"How quaint," Donna replied.

Avery's father, Todd Perkins, stepped out to greet them. "Good afternoon ladies. Lots of excitement out by the flower basket today." Mr. Perkins was a tall, slender, African American gentleman who was graying at the temples. He had sparkling eyes and a wide grin.

"Good afternoon Mr. Perkins. This is Donna Vance and her daughter Virginia."

"Pleased to make your acquaintance, ladies," he said, tipping an imaginary hat. "Come on in. You have got to try one of our pies."

Donna smiled, "It sounds tempting, but just coffee this time."

Virginia brushed past Todd and began perusing the menu board.

Once inside the aroma of fresh baked pie crust filled the air. "I think I'll get myself a mini chocolate pie," Jess said.

"So charming," Donna said as she took in the small café.

There were booths along one side and a self-serve coffee bar next to the bakery case. Avery's mother, Ms. Erika was at the counter. Like her husband, Erika was tall, thin, and African American. She and her husband both wore crisp white shirts and khaki pants.

"Jess, you will never guess what's happened,"

Ms. Erika exclaimed. "We're expanding into the space next door! I'm opening my own tea room."

"That is wonderful news!" Jess said. "I want to write a story about it."

"A tea room sounds charming," Donna said. "It's so nice to see a couple working together as a team. Just like me and my husband Garrett. We are so devoted to each other."

"Thank you," Erika said, beaming.

"I'm Donna Vance, by the way."

"Oh, we know who you are," Todd declared. "It's not every day we get a celebrity in here."

"What can I get for you ladies today?" Erika asked.

The three ordered coffee and Jess got her mini chocolate pie. "I haven't had lunch," she said by way of explanation. They took a seat at a small round table near the counter.

"Cut the crap, Mom," Virginia said, rolling her eyes. She mimicked her mother, "We are so devoted to each other."

"What do you want, Virginia? I haven't seen you in years and now you waltz in like nothing has happened."

Jess was surprised that they were going at each other already, right in front of her. She opened her coffee cup and blew on it to cool it down.

Virginia shot daggers at her mother. "Can we talk without your new assistant hanging around?"

Jess looked up from her coffee. "I'm not Donna's assistant."

Donna cut in, "Jess is my liaison with the local newspaper. Crystal is still my assistant."

Virginia looked surprised. "Wow, that's a new world record. Your assistants don't usually stick it out that long. How long have you had her now? Three years?"

Donna took a sip of her coffee. "About that long. Now let's cut to the chase. Why are you here?"

"My podcast got cancelled. Do you happen to know anything about that?"

"But Darling, your podcast was hysterical. How do podcasts even get cancelled?" Donna asked with mock concern.

"All my sponsors pulled out and then I Heart Radio dropped us," Virginia explained, "as if you didn't pull the strings on that."

"Sweetheart, I had nothing to do with it," Donna said. "Couldn't you just run your little podcast on your website?" Donna took a sip of her coffee.

"Not if I want to make any money from it," Virginia complained.

"Aw, you poor thing. I had a hunch it was

about money."

Jess couldn't tell if Donna was sincere or poking fun at her daughter. She realized she hadn't touched her pie yet and cut herself a bite.

Virginia took a sip of her coffee. "Damn, that's hot!" she said, spitting the hot coffee into a napkin.

"Do you want me to give you a job, Virginia? Is that it?" Donna asked.

Jess didn't know if Virginia would get angry and storm out, or if this was the olive branch she had been looking for.

"Do you have a job for me?" Virginia asked hopefully.

"I'm sure we could find you something to do," Donna said.

At that moment the door opened and Chace rushed in.

"Oh, hello," she said, surprised to see Jess and Donna there.

Donna greeted her, "Chace come meet my daughter, Virginia."

Introductions were made but Chace looked distracted. "I need to talk to Ms. Erika about the pies for the shower," she said.

"Chace, darlin' what can I help you with," Ms. Erika called out. "I'm premiering a special fruit pie at the shower, just for you."

"Oh, thank you," Chace gushed, "So, the thing is...." Chace went up to the counter.

Donna sat back down and put a finger to her lips. She cocked an ear in Chace's direction. Virginia got out her phone and began texting.

Jess didn't think eavesdropping was fair, or necessary, but she remained silent.

"The thing is," Chace began in hushed tones, "our caterer for the reception fell through and I wanted so see if y'all could do a wedding cake and a light lunch?" She had a huge, hopeful smile on her face with desperation in her eyes.

"Oh, Honey, I just don't see how we can pull that together on such short notice," Erika began.

Jess stood up. She had an idea. "How about Avery?" she blurted out. "Avery needs to do a project for her culinary class. I'll bet she would love to cater the reception."

Chace looked over at Jess with her mouth open. "Oh my gosh! That's a wonderful idea," Chace sang out. She rushed over and hugged Jess. Never mind that it was obvious everyone had been eavesdropping.

Jess let herself be hugged as Donna watched with a dubious look on her face.

"You will have to call her and ask," Jess said.

"It's a brilliant idea. I just know she'll say yes," Chace said.

"We need to get moving," Donna said, tapping her watch.

"Thank you so much," Chace said. "I'll see you all at the bachelorette party tonight."

"We wouldn't miss it," Donna said as they stepped back out onto the sidewalk.

"So, where is Garrett and your little sycophant?" Virginia asked.

"Crystal and Garrett should be back from the hotel soon," Donna answered. "Now we'll have to get you a room too."

Jess pulled out her itinerary to see what time the party was. She glanced at the other activities. That's when she noticed the location of the upcoming couple's shower. "This shower is at my Aunt Patsy's house," she exclaimed.

"The old farmhouse?" Donna asked. "Your aunt owns it?"

"Well yes, she's my great aunt."

"How did you not know about that until now?" Donna asked. "Secondly, are you telling me your ex-husband is getting married at your aunt's house?"

Jess smiled sheepishly and shrugged, "it's a small town."

"This whole thing is just thrown together last minute," Donna mused.

Virginia pretended to sneeze. "Hicksville" she said into her cupped hand.

Jess ignored the sneeze. "Let me show you the Antique Emporium," she said. "It's where I work part time." She pointed to it across the intersection.

"Okay, fine," Donna said with forced patience, "but then we have to get back to the office. I've had about all the small town charm I can take for one day."

Jess felt a bit peeved at the disparaging remark.

CHAPTER 11 – FRIDAY, FEBRUARY 9

1:15 p.m.

Jess was with Donna and Virginia outside of Alpaca Sweater. "I'm going to skip the antique store and go into this sweater shop," Virginia said. "I'll text Crystal to get me a room and meet you back at the newspaper office."

"It was nice meeting you," Jess called out to Virginia.

"So, you work at the antique shop?" Donna asked as they crossed the intersection. "I thought you were a full time journalist."

"I'd like to be," Jess said. "I used to write newspaper stories in Houston."

Donna laughed derisively. "Newspapers are a thing of the past," Donna said.

"I also write a blog, called Jess Sayin'."

"Blogs are on the way out too, Honey. People don't read anymore. You should do a podcast."

That didn't work out so well for your daughter, Jess thought, feeling a bit perturbed. She held the door open for Donna and they walked into Nesbitt's Antique Emporium. Ms. Melody called out a cheery hello from behind the counter.

"Hi there," Jess said as they approached the counter. "This is Donna Vance. I'm showing her around town."

Shaun popped out from behind an old roll top desk that he had been dusting. "Pleased to make your acquaintance," he said, as he bowed before her.

"It's lovely to meet you," Ms. Melody said. "What brings you to Grace?"

"I'm doing a magazine piece on the big wedding," Donna said. "Jess has agreed to be my liaison while I'm here. I must say, your charming little village is like a Norman Rockwell painting."

"Liaison? How exciting," Ms. Melody said.

"That reminds me. I wanted to ask you if I can have the week off." Jess said hopefully. "I will have to go to the wedding after all."

"I don't think that will be a problem," Ms. Melody said. She turned to Donna. "Does that mean we'll see you at the couple's shower on Sunday?"

"Definitely. Jess just found out it's being held at her Aunt's farmhouse. I can't wait to see it," Donna said.

"Then you'll be needing shower gifts," Shaun said. "Are we thinking about dishes or maybe something more personal?"

"Oh, I hadn't even thought of that," Jess said. "What would be good?"

"I have an idea," Shaun said, "follow me."

Donna noticed a display of handmade jewelry. "You go ahead. I want to look at these necklaces. They're exquisite."

Shaun led Jess toward the back of the store, to his large booth of memorabilia. "So, you're working with Donna Vance. I'm impressed," he said.

"Yes," Jess said, "and she has quite an entourage. Her husband, an assistant, and her daughter Virginia just showed up."

"Virginia Vance? I love her podcast," Shaun exclaimed.

"Well, that's too bad. Apparently it just got cancelled."

Shaun looked crestfallen. "Cancelled, but it was such a riot."

"What was it about?"

"Mostly it was her complaining about her mother and what an awful childhood she had. It's called *Yeah Right*."

"You can make a whole podcast about that?" Jess asked.

Shaun shrugged. "It was funny. Now, about that shower gift." He held out his hands like a car show hostess, indicating his racks of old movie posters. "What's better for the couple just starting out than some classic wall art?"

"You think a movie poster would make a good gift?" Jess tried to imagine Chace having a big poster on her living room wall.

"Sure, everybody loves movies," Shaun said, "and I can have it framed and gift wrapped for you."

"I don't know," Jess said dubiously, as she began looking through the posters. She had no idea what movie would be appropriate. She flipped through *Star Wars*, *The Maltese Falcon*, and *Dirty Dancing*. Nothing seemed right.

"I have some Monty Python posters," Shaun volunteered, "*Holy Grail, The Meaning of Life*."

"I don't think the former Miss Texas would be a Monty Python fan," Jess said. She kept flipping.

Then she saw the poster for *When Harry Met Sally*. She remembered the first time she and Jack had seen it in her dorm room when they were in college. Jess's mother was a big movie buff and had recommended it. Even though Chace had made reference to the movie, Jess didn't think it was a good idea.

Shaun had been searching through a second rack. "I've got the perfect thing," Shaun said. He pulled out the movie poster for *Bridesmaids*, with Kristen Wiig and Melissa McCarthy.

"That is a terrible idea," Jess said, "I'll take it." She and Jack had seen that movie in her dorm room too. He had not enjoyed it.

"I'll just pop this into a frame right now," Shaun said.

They were both startled by Donna's loud voice from the front of the store. "What the hell do you mean, we don't have reservations?"

Jess and Shaun came to the front to see what was going on. Crystal, Garrett, and Virginia were there and Donna was none too happy.

"The hotel is all booked up," Crystal said meekly. "We don't have rooms."

"Can't you do anything right?" Donna groused.

"I can't believe there's only one hotel in this stinkin' town," Virginia griped, throwing her hands in the air.

"There's a motel nearby. It's called the Oasis," Garrett said.

Donna shrieked, "I am not staying at a cheap motel, you fool! I'm Donna Vance, for crying out loud!"

He winced in the wake of her tirade.

Jess took Ms. Melody aside. Shaun followed. "Remember how you were talking about turning your house into a B&B?" she asked.

"What are you getting at?" Ms. Melody said. "You want me to invite this lot into my home?"

"It could be worse. I'm sure they would pay

well," Jess said.

Ms. Melody contemplated this. "I guess it would work. I do have three extra bedrooms upstairs."

Shaun had been listening too. "Great idea," he said. Before Ms. Melody could change her mind, he went back to the group near the front door. "Problem solved," he sang out. "There happens to be a vacancy at a lovely bed and breakfast just a few blocks away from here."

"Bed and breakfast? Seriously?" Donna asked.

Shaun continued, "Ms. Melody, the proprietress of this fine establishment, also happens to run a charming B&B."

"What's it called?" Donna asked.

"Pecan ... Tree ... Inn," Ms. Melody answered, slowly.

"We need two rooms for the next week," Crystal said.

"Make that three rooms," Virginia interjected. "Don't forget about me."

"You must be Virginia," Shaun said. He reached out to take Virginia's hand and gave it a kiss. "Enchante."

Virginia drew her hand back and eyed Shaun with trepidation. "And you are?"

"I'm Shaun Johnson at your service. I'm a big

fan of your podcast."

Virginia smiled, "Thank you."

"It's been cancelled," Donna barked. "Back to this bed and breakfast. Let's go take a look at the place." She sighed. "This is going to throw my whole schedule off. Jess, I will meet you back at the newspaper."

Ms. Melody gave them directions to her house and left to go let them in. On her way out she pointed at Jess and muttered, "What have you gotten me into?"

CHAPTER 12 – FRIDAY, FEBRUARY 9

1:50 p.m.

While Shaun wrapped her gift, Jess popped over to the Grace Grill for a quick sandwich at the counter. Brooke happened to be waiting tables. Her long blonde ponytail swished from side to side as she walked the length of the counter, wiping up crumbs.

"Brooke, have you ever heard of a couple's shower?" Jess asked between bites.

Brooke paused from wiping down the counter. "I think that's where it's not just a shower for the bride, but for the groom too," she said. "Unless this is a baby shower."

"Ix-nay on the aby-bay," Jess said, "Chace doesn't want anyone to know she's pregnant, especially not Donna Vance."

"Oh, is she pregnant? Brooke asked with a wink. She leaned in and said, "I heard Donna Vance is in town writing a story about the wedding."

"You got that right, and I am her liaison."

"Sounds fancy," Brooke went back to cleaning the counter and another customer came in. Brooke almost gushed. "Well good afternoon, Detective

Connor. It's always a pleasure."

Jess turned to see Chris Connor walking up to the counter. She couldn't help noticing how his sandy blonde hair curled around his ears and his mischievous green eyes seemed to sparkle.

"Hey Brooke," he said nodding. "Jess, how's it going?"

Jess had her mouth full at that moment. "Fine," she mumbled, chewing rapidly.

"I've got your to-go order ready," Brooke said as she set a couple of bags on the counter. "It all comes to $27.96."

"Al-righty," Chris said as he pulled out his wallet.

Jess swallowed. "So, it's been awhile," she said.

"Yes, I've been meaning to call you," he said. He gave Brooke a couple of bills.

"I'll be right back with your change," she said as she made her way to the cash register.

Jess remembered her conversation with Avery and decided to go for it. "I'm going to a wedding shower thing Sunday night, out at my Aunt Patsy's farmhouse."

"Oh, that sounds nice," he said.

Brooke came back with the change. "Here you go," she said, handing him a few bills and counting out his pennies.

"Thanks so much, and this is for you," he said, handing her a five dollar bill.

"Thank you kindly, sir," Brooke said with a big smile.

Chris turned to leave with his order. *It's now or never*, Jess thought. "Do you want to go with me?" she blurted out. "You know, to the shower?"

Chris turned to look at her. Brooke stood staring.

"You mean as your date?" he asked.

"Well, yeah. I'm allowed to bring a date," Jess said, "I'm invited." She was holding her sandwich up and a dollop of mustard squished out and plopped onto her shirt.

Brooke handed her a napkin.

Chris cleared his throat, "Is this the wedding shower for Jack and Chace?"

"Yes," Jess said as she dabbed at the mustard stain.

"Sure, I would be happy to accompany you to the shower. What time should I pick you up?"

"About three thirty."

"Well isn't that sweet," Brooke said, having been privy to the whole thing. She trotted off to wait on some other customers.

"Do I need to bring a gift?" Chris asked.

"Oh, no. that's not necessary."

"Okay then, I'll see you at three-thirty on Sunday." Chris smiled before he turned and walked out.

Brooke came back to refill Jess's drink. "Well aren't you the luckiest girl in town?"

"You think so?" Jess asked, still working on her mustard stain.

"He's a fine looking man," Brooke said with a sigh. She offered Jess a wet wipe. "For a while there last month I thought you and your ex might rekindle the old flame."

Jess laughed nervously, "No, of course not. He's getting married."

"Yes he is," Brooke said as she continued wiping down the spotless counter. "But I did hear a rumor that he had some woman in his motel room one night."

Jess looked up and Brooke met her gaze. Brooke continued, "You know, back before his fiancé got into town."

Jess swallowed hard. "Well, that is just a vicious lie," she lied. She dug a twenty out of her bag and slapped it on the counter. "You shouldn't go around spreading rumors like that."

Brooke picked up the money. "Thanks for the

tip."

Jess stalked across to the Emporium to pick up her wrapped poster from Shaun. She then carried it across the courthouse lawn to the Gazette office, still fuming about what Brooke had said. Obviously, Brooke knew about the night with Jack. The last thing she wanted was for Chace to find out. Sure Chace was an annoying airhead, but this news would crush her. Jess stashed the poster into the backseat of her car and went in the back door.

Wanda was coming across the room holding a big pink heart-shaped box of chocolates and a vase of yellow roses.

"What do you have there?" Jess asked.

Wanda shifted the candy under her arm to reach for the doorknob to Brittney's office. "These were left on the front counter for Donna Vance. There's a card. It's from somebody called Dean Cartwright."

Through the glass Jess could see Donna, her assistant Crystal, Garrett, and Virginia gathered in Brittney's office. Bob and Brittney were nowhere to be seen. "So you read the card?"

Wanda stuck her nose in the air and joked, "I'm just doing my job." She started to open the door. "Oh, I forgot. Donna wants to see you right away." Wanda slipped in quietly and set the gifts down on the desk.

"Where did these come from?" Donna asked. She tore open the card and read, *"Happy Valentine's Day to my best gal.* It's from Dean." A note fell out of the card and flitted onto the desk.

"From Dean? How nice," Garrett said.

"Nice?" Donna barked. "What the hell is he thinking? He knows I can't eat sugar. Blech." Donna tossed the candy into the trash.

Jess sidled over to Crystal. "Who's Dean Cartwright?" she whispered.

"He's her business manager, up in Dallas," Crystal whispered back.

"Don't throw away good chocolates," Garrett said, fishing the box out of the trash.

"Garrett, you are getting on my last nerve!" Donna shouted. She pointed at her husband, "Get that frickin' box of candy out of my face before I slap you!"

He dropped the candy back into the trash, threw up his hands and silently walked over to the seating area across the room.

Still angry, Donna turned to her assistant. "Crystal, I need a smoothie!"

Crystal stopped arranging note cards and rushed over to the new mini fridge in the corner of the office. She repeated the hand sanitizing ritual before handing over the foul concoction.

Jess couldn't believe how harsh Donna was with everyone. Virginia did not look up from her phone the whole time.

Donna took a long sip of her smoothie, which calmed her down a bit. "Jess, we just got back from your friend's house. It's not really a bed and breakfast, is it?"

"Technically, you are her first guests," Jess admitted.

Donna laughed and looked over to Virginia. "See, I told you so."

"I'll be glad when we can blow this one horse town," Virginia said, still not looking up. "What else did Dean say?"

Donna picked up the note. "He says good luck on the magazine story," she said. She kept reading, "What the hell?" She tossed the handwritten note onto the desk and stood up. Donna turned toward Crystal and almost threw her cell phone at her. "Get me that son of a bitch on the phone now!"

CHAPTER 13 – FRIDAY, FEBRUARY 9

3:35 p.m.

Donna began pacing back and forth.

"What is it Mom?" Virginia asked, suddenly concerned.

"My book deal, my next cookbook," she said. "He's gone and screwed up the whole thing! He says the publisher has backed out!" Donna balled up her fists like she wanted to punch someone.

Jess looked longingly at the door.

Crystal rushed over and handed Donna the phone, "I have Mr. Cartwright on the phone."

Donna put her hand over the phone and looked at the group. "A little privacy please?" Everyone started toward the door, "Oh, and Crystal, please give those notecards to Jess. You don't know what you're doing. Jess, if you could sort those out, I'd appreciate it."

As they left the room Jess heard Donna shout into the phone, "Damn it, Dean! I'm gone for one day and you manage to screw up everything!"

Outside of Brittney's office, Wanda and Clarence were looking dumbfounded. The glass walls didn't provide much in the way of soundproofing.

In fact, everyone could still hear Donna yelling into the phone.

"Would you and your dad like a cup of coffee?" Wanda asked Virginia.

Annoyed, Virginia answered, "He's my stepdad."

"That would be very nice. Thank you," Garrett said as he smoothed his mustache. He followed Wanda to the coffee bar.

Virginia sauntered over to the freelance table and took a seat, once again disappearing into her phone.

Crystal took a deep breath and tossed her dark hair out of her face. It fell right back into place, covering one eye. She held up the note cards to Jess. "So, um, here are Donna's notes about the wedding story," she said meekly.

"Thanks," Jess said, "I'll just take a look." *Poor girl*, Jess thought, *if that's how Donna treats her, why does she stay?*

"Crystal, do you think you can find me a diet coke in this god-forsaken town?" Virginia asked.

"Um, well, I don't know," Crystal stammered.

"Um I dunno," Virginia said mimicking her.

"There are some canned sodas at the T-shirt shop," Jess said, pointing out the front window toward Corporation T-Shirt. "They have a fridge case by the register."

"Thanks," Crystal said. "I'll be right back." She scooted out to procure the beverage.

Jess sat across from Virginia at the table. She thought about it and decided to say something. "You could be nicer to her, you know."

"Whatever," Virginia said. "She knows I'm joking around." She leaned back and put her feet on the table.

Jess shook her head and began reading the note cards.

Virginia regarded Jess for a moment. "Mom told me you used to write for the newspaper in Houston, and that you have a blog." She said 'blog' laughingly, as if the idea were preposterous.

"Yeah, I did write features in Houston," Jess said.

"I hope you're as good as Mom thinks you are. She's got high standards."

"I'll do my best."

Virginia went back to her phone and Jess went back to the note cards. There were notes on the interview with Jack and Chace. There was a card that said *Cracker Jack Proposal* and under that Donna had written *Fake?* The next card read: *Dress fitting very last minute. Sister Conlie - wild card. "Shotgun wedding" - is bride pregnant? Couple together only 5 months, why the rush?* The next card read: *Wed-*

ding details, catering, bridesmaids, thrown together slap dash. Like a barn dance. The next card read: *Hick town full of country bumpkins.* On the next card Donna had scribbled: *Ex-wife helping out with wedding? What's up with that?*

Jess couldn't believe her eyes. Was this the story Donna wanted to write?

The noise from Brittney's office had died down. Donna opened the door and walked over to the table in the middle at the same time Garrett came back with his coffee. She had a smug look on her face.

"Well, I finally did it. I fired Dean. Virginia, how would you like to be my new manager?"

Virginia jumped up, her eyes wide. "You fired Dean?"

"He's an incompetent fool," Donna said. "A monkey could do a better job."

Virginia looked around. Jess couldn't tell if she was excited or overwhelmed. "Great! I will take over, effective immediately." She turned toward Jess. "We'll start with this wedding story."

"We have that handled," Donna said. "As my new manager you can start with getting those publishers on the phone and undoing the damage Dean has done."

Virginia smiled and held up a finger, "Right, I need to make some phone calls and I need my own office."

"You can always have the freelance table," Jess said, patting the table with a smile. She wished Brittney was around.

Donna cut in, "Jess, let's compare notes from this morning."

Jess gathered up the note cards and her own notebook.

Crystal came back in, empty handed. "They were out of diet coke," she explained, nervously.

"Oh, for goodness sake, Crystal! Can't you do anything right?"

Crystal cowered. "Sorry."

Virginia began barking orders at her. "I need you to get the book publishers on the phone for me, stat. And I'll need a laptop to use."

Crystal looked confused.

"Don't just stand there," Virginia yelled. "You're looking at the new manager for Donna Vance Enterprises."

Crystal began bustling about.

"Garrett, I need to look at those pictures," Donna called out. She snapped her fingers. Garrett flinched and spilled some of his coffee onto his shirt. He rushed into the office behind Jess.

Virginia followed as well. "I need to be part of this meeting," she announced.

Garrett held the camera up for Donna to see and began scrolling through the pictures. "Here are the shots I took at the interview," he said.

Donna grabbed it and began swiping through the photos herself. "The happy couple, isn't that just sickeningly cute," Donna said.

Jess looked over her shoulder and saw pictures of the bridesmaids out on the courthouse lawn. There were the posed photos and several candid shots that looked like the bridesmaids were arguing. Jess saw a photo of Conlie near her motorcycle in her leather jacket and floral print dress. It actually looked kind of cool. There was also a photo of Katy Hockley hammering in her new sign next to the flower basket. Jess wondered how that was relevant to the article.

"Excellent pics," Donna said, "I definitely want to use this one." She pointed to the photo of Madison glaring at Conlie.

"Is that really the focus of this story though?" Jess asked. "Isn't this really just a puff piece to make the bride look good and sell wedding dresses?"

Virginia gasped.

Donna shook her head. "Nothing I do is ever a puff piece. I mean, of course we want to make the sponsors look good, but we also want to cover the story from all angles. This story has a lot of angles. Believe me, boring puff pieces don't sell magazines."

"I know," Jess held out the notecards, "but some of these notes are harsh."

Virginia cut in, "don't play goody-two-shoes with me, Jess. I've been reading your blog. It's full of biting sarcasm. It reminds me of me actually."

"And your podcast?" Donna asked with a sly smile.

Virginia ignored her mother's comment and kept going, "Jess, I know you used to be married to Jack, so what gives?"

"Exactly, Jess. You don't seem too keen on these nuptials. Don't you think a scathing article would be the ultimate revenge?" Donna asked with a wicked grin.

Jess couldn't believe these two. She looked from one to the other, expecting them to cackle like witches at any moment.

Virginia held her hands out, "this is your chance."

"I don't want any part of a revenge story," Jess said, tossing the notecards onto the desk. "That's not what I'm here for."

Virginia pursed her lips, "Okay, Pollyanna, just what are you here for?"

Donna held up her hand like a traffic cop, "Let's back it up a bit." She turned to Crystal and pointed, "Could we get some coffees here?" She turned to the others, "would you like some coffee?"

Jess nodded.

"Yeah, whatever," Virginia said, throwing up her hands.

"Why don't you go down to that pie shop around the corner? We don't want to drink the stale crap that passes for coffee here." she waved her hand in the general direction of Wanda's coffee bar.

"Can I go?" Garrett asked from his perch on the loveseat.

"Good idea, honey bunny," Donna said in a baby-talk voice, "you've been a good boy and you deserve a treat."

"What's good there?" Garrett asked.

"You should try the chocolate pie. It's amazing. And, can you make my drink a caramel macchiato?" Jess asked.

"Virginia, what would you like?" Crystal asked timidly.

"I like my coffee the way I like my men," she said, "strong and hot."

Donna let out a peal of laughter. She was the only one who did.

Once Garrett and Crystal had left the office, Donna looked at Jess. "I understand, you don't want to hurt anybody's feelings. I get it."

"I have no ill will toward my ex," Jess said, her arms folded, "or Chace."

"We just want to have a little fun with the story," Donna said, "but I'll tone it down. Don't quit on me now."

Jess looked dubiously at Donna and Virginia.

Virginia turned to her mother, "You know Mom, Jess really is a good writer. I think you should read some of her blogs."

"Is that right?" Donna looked thoughtful. She turned to Jess. "How would you like to have a co-writer credit for this piece?"

"It's going to be a cover story for the magazine," Virginia said.

"It would look really good on your resume," Donna said.

Jess smiled in spite of herself. "That would be great." They shook hands on it. Jess was excited, but a small part of her felt like she had just made a deal with the devil.

CHAPTER 14 – FRIDAY, FEBRUARY 9

7:05 p.m.

Jess had never expected to be invited to the bachelorette party, but here she was getting dressed for the event.

She called Avery. "What do you wear to a bachelorette party?" Jess asked.

"I don't know. Where is it going to be?"

"Franklin Hall. I'm going with Donna Vance and her entourage."

"Are you part of the entourage now?" Avery asked.

"I guess so. I'm her cowriter on the story!"

"Wow, co-writing with Donna Vance! I'm impressed."

"I know! It's weird though."

"You think it's weird to write an article about your ex-husband's wedding?" Avery asked teasingly.

"Nah, that's not weird at all," Jess said.

"Well, would it be weird if your best friend was catering the wedding?"

"That's great news," Jess said excitedly.

"Thank you. Chace called and said you recommended me."

"I'm glad. It looks like we're all getting roped into this wedding one way or another," Jess said. "Will this work for your project?"

"Oh yes, big time. I'll be in town tomorrow to meet with the bride and my other professors will let me make up the classes I miss. I'm so excited!"

"Me too. I wish you were here now so you could go to this bachelorette thing with me."

"It might be fun," Avery said.

"Oh wait, I forgot to tell you," Jess said, "I asked Chris Connor out on a date."

"Oh my gosh! You should have led with that. Did he say yes?"

"Of course he said yes. We're going to the couple's wedding shower," Jess said.

"That's not a real date," Avery said.

"It is so," Jess said defensively. "Anyway, I'd better get dressed. Later Gator."

Jess decided to wear some dark skinny jeans and a shimmery blue top with spaghetti straps. She wondered if it was too fancy for Franklin Hall, a western style bar with weathered picnic tables around the wooden dance floor.

She squeezed her feet into her dark leather cowgirl boots and put on a brown suede jacket. *Not bad*, Jess thought, checking herself out in her full length mirror before she headed downstairs.

Sweet Tea slipped into the house along with Jess. Everyone was gathered in the kitchen where Crystal was mixing up another batch of the foul smelling green protein smoothies for Donna.

"Ew, what is that?" Jess said, waving her hand in front of her nose.

"Mom's vegan protein smoothies," Virginia said with a laugh. "They taste worse than they smell. Here try it." Virginia poured a little bit into a juice glass and held it out to Jess.

Why do people do that? Jess thought. *If it tastes bad, why give me a taste?* Jess held her nose and took a sip. "Oh, that is awful," she said.

Donna gave Jess a withering glare. "We can't all just eat whatever we want," she said. "You'll see when you get older and all those caramel coffees catch up with you."

Jess back-pedaled. "I'm sure it's very healthy," she said. "It must be working. You two are very trim and fit." She indicated Donna and Crystal.

"That's because Crystal is bulimic," Virginia teased.

"I am not," Crystal said, flipping her hair out of her eyes. The other side of her long bangs fell into her face obscuring one eye.

Donna bent down to pet Sweet Tea. "What a

darling little kitty cat," she said. Sweet Tea eyed her dubiously, then arched her back and hissed.

Jess admonished the cat. "Sweet Tea, no!" The cat ran off into the den.

"Time to get going," Donna said, clapping her hands loudly.

Crystal packed up the smoothies into a cooler bag and slung it over her shoulders. As they all left the kitchen, Ms. Melody came in from the back yard and noticed the dirty blender, cups and utensils all over the counter. "No, don't worry about it, I'll clean up," she groused. Nobody heard but Jess.

"Technically, that is your job as owner of a B&B," Jess said jokingly.

Ms. Melody threw a spinach leaf at Jess's retreating figure.

Donna said she would be the designated driver for the night. Jess piled into the back seat of the Escalade along with Garrett and Crystal. Donna and Virginia were in front.

They stopped at the Gazette so Crystal could refill the mini fridge with smoothies. When she tried the door, it was locked.

"Oh my gosh, Crystal. Figure out your life!" Donna yelled with annoyance as she fished her key out of her purse. "They gave me a key. Here." She thrust the key at her assistant.

Crystal dashed inside with the smoothies for the next day while everyone waited in the SUV.

Jess bristled at this but didn't say anything. She looked over at Garrett. *He doesn't say much*, she thought. "What are you going to do, Garrett?" Jess asked, "This party is girls only."

Garrett started to speak but Donna interrupted. "He's coming with us, I have to get pictures."

The group stopped at the hotel bar where the pre-game drinking was already in progress. Taylor, Kennedy, and Madison were in matching pink T-shirts, provided by Corporation T-Shirt, that said *Bride Squad!*

Donna and her entourage descended on the wedding party and introductions were made. Jack's best man, Guy, was busily shaking hands and smiling like a used car salesman.

"So, what are the guys doing this evening, Guy?" Virginia asked. "Strippers? Drugs? Debauchery?"

Jack laughed, "No, nothing like that." He pulled a paper out of his pocket. "We're doing a pub crawl, I've made a map."

"That would be good if there were any pubs in Grace," Jess said. She looked at the map.

"We're starting here at the hotel bar, obviously," Jack said pointing at the map. "Then we're walking the two blocks to Casa Maria for dinner and tequila shots. Then we'll hit the Grace Grill for a beer," he said.

"That's only two places," Donna said. "Garrett, get a picture of this map."

"After that we'll walk three blocks in the other direction and hit the Burger Barn," Jack said.

"For another beer?" Jess asked.

"Yeah, or a milkshake maybe," Jack said.

"Lame!" Virginia said, pretending to sneeze. "Good thing I'm hanging with the chicas tonight."

Jess took Jack's map and drew a star on the side street next to Corporation T-Shirt. "There's a door right here, it's not marked but it's a speakeasy. Take the guys here," Jess whispered to Jack.

"Thanks," he whispered back and folded up his map. "By the way, I have a favor to ask." He took Jess aside, away from the group. Donna and her entourage were busy talking with the bridesmaids.

"Do you have another big secret?" Jess asked.

"Same secret," Jack replied. "So far the bridesmaids don't know about the baby. Chace and I were hoping you could help her pretend to get drunk tonight?"

"How does one pretend to get drunk?"

"Well, just work something out with the bartender that she gets virgin drinks and you know, don't let her friends buy her shots or anything."

"Wow, that is a tall order," Jess said, shaking her head. "I'll do my best."

Just then Chace and Conlie joined the group at the hotel bar. "Hey party people! Are we having fun?" Conlie called out. They were also in pink T-shirts. Conlie's said *Maid of Dis-Honor* and Chace's simply said *Bride*.

Jack and Jess joined the pre-game partiers.

Chace looked at Jess and mimed drinking. Jess gave her a wink and a thumbs-up. Chace put her hands together to make a heart. *I guess we speak each other's unspoken language*, Jess thought.

"Bottoms up," Kennedy said, handing Chace a gin and tonic. "Let's get this party started!"

"I'll take that," Jess said, grabbing the drink out of Chace's hand and taking a swig. *And so it begins*, Jess thought.

"Let's get going," Chace called out.

"Pictures first," Donna said. She helped pose Jack and his groomsmen for a group photo. Then Chace and the bridesmaids. While no one was looking, Jess poured the drink into a potted fern. Then she realized it was plastic.

The ladies walked to Franklin Hall which was next door to the hotel. "No stretch limos for this bunch," Virginia remarked.

"That's the great thing about such a small town," Chace said cheerily. "You can walk everywhere."

"Redneck," Virginia said under the guise of a sneeze.

"Bless you," Chace sang out with a clueless smile.

CHAPTER 15 – FRIDAY, FEBRUARY 9

8:30 p.m.

The group entered Franklin Hall and headed to the back room. The entire area had been decked out in pink and gold with a balloon banner spelling out *Last Fling Before the Ring*. There were balloons in the shape of diamond rings and bottles of champagne. Jess was relieved to see that there was nothing lewd or improper. She didn't think that would go over well with the magazine.

As soon as she walked in the door, Madison put a tiara on Chace's head and a pink feather boa around her neck. Already at the party were Brittney and police officer Beverly Frick, off-duty. Both were wearing feather boas.

"Everybody gets one," Madison said, passing out boas.

The girls settled in for a night of drinking and party games. Jess pushed past Madison and took a seat next to Chace.

"Let's start the night with shots!" Taylor roared.

"Actually, I'm kind of hungry," Chace said, "I didn't have any dinner. Can we get some appetizers?" The group ordered loaded potato skins, boneless chicken wings, and nachos.

"I made badges for everybody," Madison said as she began handing out pink glittery buttons with ribbons attached. "Conlie, this is yours and I made one for you too Jess." Jess's button said *Hot Mess!* Conlie's said *Bad Influence.*

"You got me pegged," Conlie said as she fastened the button to her shirt.

Jess looped her button around the strap on her top, not wanting to stick it through her suede jacket.

"*Trophy Wife,*" Chace squealed as she put her button on. "That is so funny."

Madison passed out the rest of the buttons. Kennedy's said *Lush*, Taylor's said *Call me Maybe.*

"This is what you think of me?" Kennedy asked, giving Madison a hurt look, which everyone ignored.

Madison passed the box around to the others. "Y'all can just pick what you want," she said. Donna chose one that said *Diva*, Virginia chose *Wild Child*, Beverly Frick chose *Kiss Me,* Crystal chose *Hot Stuff*, and Brittney chose *Sassy.* Madison then attached her own button. It said *Girl Boss.*

The waiter brought over a tray of tequila shots and everybody took one, except Donna. As the designated driver, she asked for a glass of water.

"To the bride," Taylor said. While everyone

else was downing their shots, Jess bumped Chace's hand, causing her tequila to spill out onto the table. Chace then lifted it to her lips, pretending she had downed the shot.

"Let me get you another gin and tonic," Jess said. "I owe you one since I stole yours at the hotel." She got up to go to the bar.

"Thanks," Chace said, flashing her stunning smile.

At the bar, Jess asked, "Could you possibly serve the bride only non-alcoholic drinks that look like the real thing? She doesn't want her friends to know she's not drinking."

The bartender eyed her quizzically. "Okay, any particular reason for this?"

"Nope, she just wants to keep her wits tonight," Jess said. As an afterthought she slid a twenty dollar bill across the bar. "Okay?"

"You got it," he said, pocketing the money.

Jess came back to the table with two virgin gin and tonics.

Chace took a big sip. She gave Jess a wide eyed look. "Woah, that is so strong! Is this a double?" she asked.

"Um, yeah. Why the hell not?" Jess answered.

Chace drank deeply and her friends began chanting, "Drink... Drink...Drink!"

She drained the glass and banged it down on the table. She held her fingers to her temples. "Oh, no, that really went to my head." Chace was putting on a good act.

"Here," Jess pushed her own drink over. "Have mine."

The appetizers arrived and everybody dug in. Jess noticed that Garrett was in the corner taking pictures.

"Okay, let's play a party game," Madison said, clapping her hands. She got out two boxes from under the table. "For this we need to break into two teams."

"How about the bride and Donna Vance as team captains," Kennedy suggested.

Chace went first and picked Conlie. Donna picked Jess and so on until the group was divided into two teams. Virginia was the last to be chosen for her mother's team.

Madison placed two brightly colored buckets on the floor about ten feet apart. "Chace, your team is shooting for the pink bucket. Donna, y'all get the blue bucket." Then Madison handed the boxes to each team captain. Each box was full of lacy thong underpants. Chace's box had pink thongs and Donna's had blue. "So, the game is called *Thong Shot*. You each take a thong and shoot it, like a rubber band, and try to get it into your team's bucket," Madison explained.

"I don't think these are my size," Virginia joked.

"Do we get to take these home?" asked Beverly.

"So, everybody on the team has to shoot a thong one by one, until the box is empty," Madison began, "whichever team gets the most in, wins, and. ..."

Madison got hit in the face with a pink thong.

"Conlie, don't," Chace admonished her sister.

"Oops, my bad. I was just practicing," Conlie said.

Madison tried to laugh it off. "Oh, you are so silly. Anyway, the winning team gets prizes." She held up a bag of ring pops.

"Oh, it is on," Conlie said.

They began the game with lacy thongs flying through the air, most of them missing the buckets. Garrett moved quietly around the room taking pictures. Everyone was laughing and shooting thongs at each other. In the end, Donna's team claimed the victory and received their prize.

"Gee thanks," Virginia said, taking her ring pop and displaying it proudly on her finger.

Donna declined her ring pop and looked at her daughter with disdain. "I guess that's the only engagement ring you'll ever get."

Virginia's mouth fell open in shock. Donna ignored her daughter's hurt expression.

More tequila shots were passed around and more appetizers were ordered. Jess drank her shot and surreptitiously switched glasses with Chace so she could pretend to drink it. Chace ordered another fake gin and tonic. Almost everyone was starting to feel tipsy. Jess noticed that even shy, quiet Crystal was enjoying the music and having a conversation with Officer Frick. Brittney had managed to move closer to Donna and was chatting away, while Donna sat sipping her iced water with lemon.

Then suddenly the music stopped. A police officer strolled into the room. "We've had a complaint about some rowdy behavior in here," he said, peering at the group through aviator sunglasses and brandishing a large flashlight as if it were a weapon.

"What are you talking about?" Madison asked, confused.

"Are you new to the force?" Frick asked.

Jess noticed a smirk on Conlie's face.

"I'm Officer Goodbody. I hear you ladies have been bad," he said, "bad to the bone." The George Thorogood song *Bad to the Bone* began playing as the officer ripped open his shirt and began moving to the music. Everyone shrieked as he tore away his pants, and wearing only black leather shorts and his police hat; he danced over to the bride.

Chace's face turned bright red as the dancer wiggled and twerked right in front of her. Then several of the ladies got up to dance with the young man and slipped dollar bills into the waistband of his shorts.

Officer Frick, by now three sheets to the wind, was very energetic as she popped and locked her way over. She was wearing an orange sweater dress, from Alpaca Sweater, that was about two sizes too small for her plus size frame. She seemed enamored with the young man. "You know, I really am in law enforcement," she said to him. "I could have you arrested for impersonating an officer."

"Are you a good cop, or a bad cop?" he asked suggestively as he gyrated to the music.

"I may have to take you into custody," she said, looping her feather boa around his neck and pulling him closer to her.

Jess noticed that Garrett was now taking video of the dancing. She swayed over in his direction and began twirling around wildly, bumping him and knocking the camera from his hands.

"Damn it," he yelled and bent down to rescue his camera.

"Whoopsy daisy," Jess said. "Sorry about that."

After a few songs, the stripper bid them farewell, but not before Officer Frick had slipped her phone number into the front of his waistband.

Jess was starting to feel tipsy. She excused herself to go to the restroom. *No more drinks*, she said to herself in the mirror. She went into a stall and a moment later heard a couple of the others come into the ladies room.

Jess overheard, "I mean, she's acting like they're best friends. It's pathetic." Jess wondered if they were talking about Conlie.

"Don't you think it's sad that she's working on an article about her ex-husband? I mean, who does that?"

"Yeah, she still has feelings for him. It's obvious. Did you see them talking in the corner at the hotel?"

"What a loser."

Jess heard them laughing and couldn't believe her ears. She tried to peer around the side of the stall door to find out who was talking.

Just then, she heard a stall door open a few spaces away and the unmistakable voice of Chace. "You two need to stop it this instant! Jessica and Jack have been divorced for a long time and we are all good friends now. She's a top notch journalist and I'm glad she's working on this story."

Jess heard mumbled apologies and the sounds of the sink. *Wow.* Chace had come to her defense. That was a surprise. She waited until the three of them left before coming out.

Back in the party room, Jess looked around for Garrett, hoping she hadn't broken his expensive camera. He was not around. "Where did Garrett go?" she asked Donna.

"He's had enough of this hen party," Donna said. "He said he would walk back."

"I don't think I can take any more shots," Chace said, pretending to stumble back to her seat.

"I'm ready to call it a night ladies," Donna said to the group.

"Aw, the party's just getting started," Virginia whined.

"You've had enough to drink, Virginia. It's time to go," Donna said.

"Boo, party pooper!" Virginia slurred. "You're just no fun anymore."

Donna turned to Virginia and said, "Watching you get drunk is not my idea of fun." She stood and gathered her coat and bag.

Jess began looking around for her purse.

Donna waved to the group. "Goodnight, everyone. We'll see you in the morning for the expo." She turned to go. "Virginia, come on, we're leaving."

Virginia stood up and chugged her screwdriver. Then she pointed a finger in her mother's face. "You used to know how to party!" She stumbled a bit as she turned toward the group. "Back when I was growing up, my Mom and Dad were swingers! They used to have pool parties where everybody was naked. I wasn't allowed because I was only a kid." She laughed drunkenly. "And look at you now, the Queen of hearth and home. What a joke!"

Donna looked at her daughter, her eyes burning with fury. Through clenched teeth she hissed, "Virginia, that's enough! You are embarrassing yourself."

"Don't treat me like a child."

"Stop acting like one."

Virginia got right into her mother's face. "Screw you, you old bitch!"

Donna laughed and stepped back, shaking her head. "I should have known better. I can't believe I made you manager of Donna Vance Enterprises. You are nothing but a worthless, ungrateful brat!"

"Oh, look out. The great and powerful Donna Vance has spoken!" Virginia said, waving her arms around in a sweeping gesture. Jess thought she might topple over.

Everyone else looked on in shock. No one said a word until Donna spoke again.

"We are through, Virginia. Don't come asking

for any more help from me." Donna chuckled derisively. "You won't last a day out in the real world. Just like your stupid little podcast... you are going to crash and burn."

Virginia's face fell. "My podcast had a lot of listeners," she said defensively.

"Ha! One word from me, and all your advertisers dropped out, just... like... that." Donna snapped her fingers. She was on a roll now, "You've got no talent, no prospects, and nobody loves you."

For a moment, Virginia looked crestfallen. Then she pulled herself up and shouted, "You better watch yourself woman! You don't know what I'm capable of!" She stormed out of the room. If there had been a door, she would have slammed it.

Donna sat back down and picked up her water glass with a shaky hand. She took a gulp, looking around. "Where's Crystal?" she asked Jess.

Jess looked around for Crystal but didn't see her. "I don't know, did she leave with Garrett?"

"Meet me at the car," Donna said to Jess before she also walked out.

"Okay, I'll just grab my bag," Jess said. She checked her chair but didn't see her purse.

Everyone felt awkward at having witnessed the spectacle. "Damn, that is one messed up family," Conlie said, putting her arm around Chace. "Come on, maybe Maddie has some more party games."

Jess searched the table for her purse and then remembered she had left it in the restroom. She went back and found it in the stall where she had been.

On her way out she stopped to say her good-byes. Most of the group had left and the bridesmaids were with Chace, trying to cheer her up.

"Well, your big magazine friends ruined everything," Madison said as if the drama had been Jess's fault.

Jess bent down and gave Chace a side hug. "I'm really sorry they acted that way," she said.

"It's not your fault," Chace said, "I'll see you tomorrow."

"What do we have tomorrow?" Jess asked.

Chace sighed, "The Bridal Expo in Juniper."

This reminder was met with a chorus of groans from the wedding party.

"Can't we just sleep in?" Kennedy asked. "Or is this another one of your *Miss Texas* appearances?" Kennedy did air quotes around Miss Texas.

"We have to go," Chace said forlornly. "We have photo ops at all the sponsor booths."

Jess put her jacket on. "Hey, I gotta get going. Donna's my ride." Feeling drained by the night of drinking and all the tension, Jess walked across to the hotel parking lot where Donna had parked the

Escalade. It wasn't there. *I was sure she parked over here*, Jess thought. She walked up and down the lot, looking for the SUV, but it was nowhere to be found. *Did she leave without me?* Jess wondered. She walked back to where she had started. No SUV.

Jess sighed and resigned herself to walking home. It was about seven blocks, but it was the middle of the night and it was cold out. *It has to be forty degrees*, Jess thought. Pulling her suede jacket tighter, she wished she hadn't worn such a skimpy top.

With her hands in her pockets she began the walk back across the town square. Along the way she thought about how nice Chace had been to defend her. There was no way she would let Donna write anything disparaging about the wedding now.

As she neared the Gazette office she looked up. There was Donna's SUV, parked right in front. The door to the Gazette was left open. Jess noticed a light on in the back, in Brittney's office.

Angrily, Jess went inside. "Why didn't you wait for me?" Jess yelled out as she made her way back to Brittney's office. She looked around but didn't see anyone else. "Donna, are you here? You're supposed to be the designated driver."

There was no answer. It felt eerie being in the office at night. Brittney's desk lamp was on, but she didn't see Donna through the window. She got to the door and swung it open.

Donna was on the floor near the desk. Her back was arched, her eyes bulged, and she had vomited on the rug. In her hand, half spilled out on the floor, was a plastic bottle of vegan protein smoothie.

Jess gasped and ran over to her. She nudged Donna's shoulder. Her body was stiff. The bulging eyes stared upward, unblinking. Donna was dead.

CHAPTER 16 – FRIDAY, FEBRUARY 9

11:45 p.m.

Jess screamed and ran for the door. She got out onto the deserted sidewalk and looked around. What had happened? Where was Crystal, or Garrett? She glanced over to the opposite corner and ran to the door of the Sidebar.

Jess burst through the door and descended the steps. Jack, Guy, and the other groomsmen were gathered at the bar. Jess was breathing heavily.

"Help," she yelled. "It's Donna! I think she's dead!"

An hour later, Detective Connor and his team were on the scene. Jess was in the middle of the bullpen in a daze. Bob handed her a cup of coffee.

"Have you called her husband?" Bob asked.

"No, I only called you and Detective Connor," Jess said. "Am I the one who needs to tell her husband?" She took a deep breath and gulped her coffee. Her hand was shaking and a little spilled out, burning her hand. "Owww," she cried, setting the cup down.

"I'll notify the family," Chris said, coming up

behind them.

"What happened?" Jess asked.

"When you came into the office, did you see anybody or anything unusual?" Chris asked.

"No, the place was deserted," Jess said. "Did she have a heart attack?"

"It's too early to tell. The coroner will have to determine the cause of death. What was in that bottle she was holding?"

"One of her protein smoothies. She drank them all the time."

"We're going to need to test that too," Chris said.

"You don't think there was something bad in her smoothies do you?" Bob asked.

"We've got to cover all the bases," Chris said.

At that moment the forensics team came out with Donna's body on a gurney, covered with a sheet.

"I can't believe it," Jess said. "Donna Vance is dead?"

"Detective, are you treating this as a suspicious death?" Bob asked.

"No comment," Chris said.

Connor held his hand out to Jess. "Ms. Hart, may I take you home. I need to notify the next of kin and I understand they are guests of Ms. Nesbitt."

"Yes, okay," Jess said, tossing her cup in the trash.

Once in the patrol car, Jess asked. "Do you think Donna was poisoned?"

"How much have you had to drink?" he asked.

Jess tried to remember, "I don't know, I was drinking for two." When Chris didn't laugh at her joke she said, "I had some shots and ..." her voice trailed off, "maybe five."

"Tell me about the bachelorette party. You said Donna had an altercation with her daughter?"

"They basically had a shouting match, right in front of everybody. Officer Frick was there."

"I'll talk to her later." Chris pulled into the gravel driveway in front of the three car garage that Jess lived above. He took a deep breath, "I hate this part of my job."

"I'll come with you," Jess said.

"Are you feeling up to it?" he asked, looking in her eyes.

"The coffee helped," she said.

"You do look nice tonight," Chris said.

"Oh, please. My mascara is smeared and I'm sure I look like a mess."

Chris noticed her button peeking out from

her open jacket. "A hot mess," he said.

"Oh no, I'd better take that off," Jess said, blushing as she removed the button from her strap.

"Okay, let's get this over with." Chris said.

He strode to the front door and rang the bell.

It took a while, but Ms. Melody came to open the door in her bathrobe and slippers. "What are you doing here at this hour?" she asked as she let them inside. "Jess, did you get arrested again?"

"I never got arrested," Jess said defensively.

"I apologize for waking you," Connor said. "I actually need to speak to Mr. Vance and to Virginia Vance."

"It's not Mr. Vance," Jess said. "His name is Garrett Nielson. Donna kept her first husband's last name."

Ms. Melody looked worried. "Okay, I'll go up and get them. Is everything okay?"

Jess shook her head. "Go ahead and get Crystal too," she said.

Ms. Melody went upstairs. Jess and Chris took a seat in the living room.

When Ms. Melody came back down, Crystal and Garrett were with her. "Virginia wasn't there. Her room is empty," she said.

"What's this all about?" Garrett asked.

"Mr. Neilson, I have some bad news," Connor began. "You might want to sit down."

Garrett looked confused, "What's going on? Where's Donna?"

"Sir, I'm sorry to have to tell you this," Chris said somberly. "After she left Franklin Hall last night, Donna went to the Grace Gazette office. She died there."

"What?" Crystal shrieked. "She died? How?"

Garrett crumpled into sobs. "Nooo," he wailed with his head in his hands.

Crystal seemed to be in shock. "I don't understand. Was there some kind of accident?" Crystal asked.

"No, she collapsed on the floor. We haven't determined the cause of death yet," Chris said.

"Was she alone?" Garrett asked. "Did my darling die alone?"

"I'm afraid so," Chris said. "Is there any way to contact her daughter?"

"I'll text her," Crystal said.

"Don't text her that her mother has died," Ms. Melody interjected.

"I'll call her," Crystal said, getting out her phone.

"If you give me the number, I'll make the call," Chris said. "It's best to deliver the news in person."

"Shall I make some coffee?" Ms. Melody asked.

Jess nodded.

Chris tried calling Virginia but the call went to voicemail. He left a message with a number to call back.

"I have to be getting back to the station. I'll be in touch when we know more about what happened," Chris said.

Jess walked him out to his car. "What a night," she said.

"Are you going to be okay?" he asked.

"I'm okay. I don't know about Garrett though. He seems devastated."

"Well, it's quite a shock."

Jess hesitated by the car. "So, do you think somebody did something to hurt Donna?"

"Let's just say, we haven't ruled it out," Chris said. "I need to get back to the crime scene. Call me if you think of anything else."

Back in the house Jess and Ms. Melody sat with Crystal and Garrett around the kitchen table.

"I'm just stunned," Crystal said. "I thought she was perfectly healthy."

"I should have stayed at the party," Garrett wailed.

"How did you get back here?" Jess asked.

"We walked back together," Crystal said.

"Where did Virginia go?" Garrett asked.

"No idea," Jess said. She noticed Garrett tearing up and got up to find a box of tissues.

Ms. Melody poured coffee for everyone and brought over a plate of shortbread cookies. "It's decaf," she said. They sat in silence, everyone deep in their own thoughts.

"I just can't believe it," Ms. Melody said.

"Tell me how you found her," Garrett said with tears in his eyes.

Jess filled them in on everything that happened after he had left the bachelorette party, toning down the altercation with Virginia.

After a moment, Garrett went up to get his camera. "I want to look at my pictures," he said through tears. "I think I have some good shots of Donna."

When he came back down Jess said, "I'm sorry I bumped into you last night. I hope I didn't break the camera."

Garrett patted her hand. "You didn't break it dear girl." He began scrolling through the photos. Then he let out a wail. "I should have stayed with her. If I had stayed, none of this would have happened."

Crystal spoke up. "There's nothing you could have done." She sighed heavily and shook her head. Her long bangs flopped into her eyes again and she took a sip of the coffee.

For a fleeting moment, Jess wondered what would happen to the magazine story now. Then she felt guilty about being so callous.

CHAPTER 17 – SATURDAY, FEBRUARY 10

6:00 a.m.

Jess got a group text from Bob saying he wanted to see everyone at the office at eight for an emergency meeting. She had only had a couple of hours of sleep. She groaned and set her alarm for seven.

When the alarm sounded, Jess was drooling onto her pillow. After a quick shower she pulled on a fresh pair of jeans and a gray cable knit sweater.

As she was pouring coffee into a travel mug, she heard footsteps coming up the stairs to her apartment.

Jess looked at the time. She had to leave for the meeting at the Gazette.

Jess opened the door just as Virginia was nearing the top step. Her face was red from crying.

"What happened?" she demanded, pushing past Jess into the apartment.

"Virginia, I am so sorry about your mother," Jess said.

"They told me you found her," Virginia said, as if she were angry at Jess.

"Yes, she had gone back to the Gazette office,"

Jess said. "I'm not sure why."

Virginia sat on Jess's sofa and took some deep breaths. Then she burst into tears again, "I never should have shouted at her," she wailed.

Jess patted her on the back awkwardly. "I hate to say this, Virginia, but I've got to go. I have a meeting at the Gazette in about five minutes."

"How can you go in to work at a time like this?" Virginia asked.

"Bob called an emergency meeting."

"Well, I'm coming with you," Virginia insisted as she stood and headed for the door, "I have a thing or two to say."

Jess descended the steps with a sense of dread.

On the short drive over Jess asked, "When did you get back? I was up until four with Garrett and Crystal."

Virginia looked away. "I needed to let off some steam so I stayed away."

"But where did you go in the middle of the night?"

The question annoyed Virginia. "I just walked around. I don't know. There's a park. I sat on a swing and just hung out for a while."

"But it was so cold out," Jess said.

"What is this, twenty questions?"

"We're here," Jess said as she pulled into the back parking area.

They went in through the back door and made their way to Bob's office. Brittney and Clarence were already assembled there. Everyone expressed their condolences to Virginia.

Brittney looked like she had been crying herself. She handed Virginia a box of tissues. "Your mother was a great woman," she said. "She will be missed."

"Thank you," Virginia said, sniffing loudly into a tissue.

"Take a seat everyone," Bob said, "we have a lot to get through."

"We need to do a tribute to Donna," Brittney said.

"Definitely, but first, we need to issue a statement to announce Donna's passing," Bob said. "That needs to happen ASAP."

Clarence piped in, "I've been on the horn with the coroner's office, still no word yet as to the cause of death."

"I'll release a statement," Virginia said, "As her manager, it should come from me."

"Okay," Bob said.

Brittney blew her nose loudly.

"The second order of business is the *Texas*

Bride Magazine story."

"Are we still doing that?" Jess asked.

Bob continued, "I spoke with the editor of the magazine and the head of Lone Star Publications on a conference call earlier this morning. They do want to proceed with the story. They want us to use Donna's notes and go from there."

Virginia cut in, "Jess should write it. Mom asked Jess to be her cowriter, so she should finish the story."

"I don't think Jess has the experience for this," Brittney said. "It's going to be a cover story."

"I can do it," Jess said.

"All right Jess, do you need any help?" Bob asked.

"I'll help," Brittney said, throwing up her hands.

"I don't think I need any help," Jess said, "but thanks."

"So, the magazine wants us to continue with the scheduled pre-wedding events and photo ops," Bob said. "They faxed this over." He gave Jess another copy of the wedding itinerary.

"You really think going to a wedding expo today is the best idea?" Jess asked. "In light of everything that's happened?"

Virginia said, "The group still needs to be

photographed at the sponsor booths."

"The show must go on," Clarence interjected.

They were all startled by a banging on the window from the street. A man in a suit and tie under a tan overcoat, peered in at them. He had brown hair with blonde streaks and a blindingly white smile. He motioned toward the locked front door.

"Who is that?" Jess asked.

"That's Dean Cartwright," Virginia sighed. "Mom's former manager."

Brittney went to the front and led Dean into the room. "Our business office is closed on Saturday," she explained as she led him to Bob's office.

"Good morning, all. I'm Dean Cartwright, CEO of Donna Vance Enterprises."

"Former CEO," Virginia clarified. "Mom fired you yesterday, remember?"

"Technically, I am still under contract, and I need to be a part of anything involving Donna Vance, her work, or her image. We need to put out a press release about her death right away, and put together a fitting tribute. Now...."

Jess interrupted, "Who told you about Donna?"

"Her assistant, she called me last night," he said. "I drove down from Dallas as soon as I heard."

"You can't just barge in here and take over," Virginia said. "I have everything under control."

Bob stood up, "Mr. Cartwright, I'm Bob Barnes, Editor in Chief of the Grace Gazette. We answer to Lone Star Publications. Our main concern is the magazine story. Apart from that, we have no interest in who runs Donna Vance Enterprises."

"And your point?" Dean asked.

"My point is, this meeting is over."

Everyone filed out of Bob's office.

"Mom had some more notes for the story," Virginia said as they walked over to Brittney's office. There was crime scene tape across the door. "Should we go in anyway?" Virginia asked. She peered through the glass. "I see her notecards right there on the desk. I could probably just go in and reach over."

"You better not do that," Clarence called out from across the bullpen. "The police don't want anybody in there."

Brittney looked through the glass as well. "I can't believe Donna Vance died in my office," she said miserably. "My rug is ruined."

"Your rug?" Virginia asked in disbelief.

"It really did tie the room together," Jess said. Then she turned to Virginia. "I can get the notes later. I remember what we talked about yesterday."

Virginia nodded. "You need to get the gals and head over to Juniper for the Bridal Expo anyway. I guess Garrett will have to go and take pictures."

"That's not going to go over well," Jess said. "Donna just passed away last night. Shouldn't you be taking it easy?"

Virginia ignored her. "I'll text Crystal. Should she go too?"

"Virginia, we need to talk," Dean said pointedly.

She gave him a dismissive wave. "Not right now, Dean. I have to write out a statement to release to the media." Virginia said. She sauntered over to the freelance table in the middle of the room. "Why don't you go get yourself some breakfast? We'll talk later."

Dean looked at her with annoyance before he stalked toward the front door and found it locked.

"Oh, let me open that for you," Brittney said, rushing to the front.

"I just texted Crystal about the expo today. She said she's out running errands and you should go without her. What errands could she possibly have at a time like this?" Virginia asked.

Jess sighed. "I guess I better gather up the bridesmaids and get on over to Juniper," Jess said with a feeling of dread. She headed for the back door and her phone dinged. It was a text from Avery.

Avery: Chace is here at the Pie Hole and she is freaking out.

Jess: When did you get here?

Avery: I drove in late last night.

Jess: On my way.

No point going to my car, Jess thought. "Hey Brit, will you let me out?" she called across to where Brittney was seated near Virginia.

Brittney sighed and made a big show of trudging up to the front again. "I'm putting together a tribute story for the front page," she said, "unless you need me to go with you to the expo?"

Jess could see that Brittney really did want to go. "I'll let you know," she said.

GRACE GAZETTE – FEBRUARY 10

Queen of Texas Chic Donna Vance Dead at Age 52

– by Clarence Irvin

TV personality and lifestyle maven Donna Vance passed away on Friday, February 9, in Grace, Texas. The much loved author and founder of Donna Vance Enterprises was only three weeks shy of her fifty-third birthday. The cause of death is still unknown at this time.

"The world has lost a beautiful soul," Virginia Vance, daughter of Donna Vance, said in a statement on Saturday. Virginia was with her mother in Grace working on a story for *Texas Bride Magazine* at the time of her death.

Donna will be missed by the many viewers of her TV show, *Lone Star Living*, as well as fans of her cookbooks, lifestyle website, and her signature line of home décor merchandise.

Donna Vance was married to Garrett Neilson, her second husband. Their marriage was the subject of her recent bestseller, *The Second Time Around ~ A Second Chance at True Love*. Garrett worked as a photographer for many of her cookbooks and other projects. A memorial service will be held in Dallas pending the completion of the investigation into her death.

Donna Vance is survived by her husband, Garrett Neilson and her daughter, Virginia

Vance.

CHAPTER 18 – SATURDAY, FEBRUARY 10

9:05 a.m.

When Jess got to the Pie Hole she saw Avery seated at a table with a large group of women and several plates of cake.

"I just can't believe it," Chace wailed. "I have the worst luck."

Avery looked up. "Jess, you're here!" She rushed over to give her friend a hug.

"I have missed you so much," Jess said.

"Jess, come over here," Chace said, "I just don't know what to do."

"Good morning," Jess said to the group. She knew Chace's mother Tanya. Madison and Conlie were also there.

"I think you know everybody, except this is my Aunt Tammy," Chace said.

Jess shook hands with Tammy, who looked like a carbon copy of her sister Tanya. They both had big blonde hair and more make-up on their faces than Jess would wear in a year.

"We're tasting some options for wedding cakes," Tanya explained.

"Except I don't know if there's even going to be a wedding," Chace wailed, "seeing how Donna Vance has gone and died!" She began crying and Madison offered her a tissue.

Avery rolled her eyes and looked over at Jess.

"I mean, why am I even getting married?" Chace said through tears.

"Of course you're getting married," Tanya said, "We have our whole family coming."

Chace blew her nose loudly. "Tell them I've changed my mind," she wailed.

Jess pulled out a chair and it scraped loudly on the linoleum floor. She sat down across from Chace. "Could someone get her a glass of water?" Jess asked.

"I'm on it," Madison said, rushing to the counter.

Chace looked up at Jess through her tears. "Jack told me you found her, lying on the floor at the newspaper office. Is that what's true?"

"Yes I did," Jess said calmly.

"What'd she die of?" Tammy asked.

"We don't know yet. The police are working on it," Jess said. "In the meantime, the magazine still wants to do the cover story."

"That means you have to go through with the wedding," Conlie said, nodding her head matter of factly.

"Without Donna Vance, who's going to write the story?" Tammy asked.

Jess cleared her throat, "I am."

Madison gasped, "You, by yourself?" She handed Chace the water.

"I have Donna's notes," Jess said defensively, "and some help from the Gazette staff."

"Honey, you do want to get married, don't you?" Tanya asked her daughter.

Chace gulped her glass of water. "Yeah, well of course I do. It's just that, what with Donna dying and all... Well, it seems like bad luck or something." She took a deep breath. "First I couldn't get a venue, then my caterer fell through, and now this."

"Oh, honey," Aunt Tammy patted Chace's hand. "It's gonna be alright. Donna Vance was a great lady, but you've got to move on with your life."

"You and Jack are in love. Love is forever," Madison said. "No bad luck in the world can mess with that."

Jess rolled her eyes. *What a load of crap*, she thought.

Nobody knew what else to say. Chace was still looking forlorn.

"You don't want to leave Jack at the altar. Not after he proposed with a box of Cracker Jacks," Jess said jokingly.

Chace looked up with a confused expression. "What?" She thought for a moment, "Oh, the Cracker Jacks." She began giggling.

"What is she talking about?" Tanya asked.

Chace burst into uncontrollable laughter. "That Cracker Jack story. Oh my gosh, Jess." She couldn't stop herself.

"Are you okay, Sis?" Conlie asked, patting Chace on the back.

Chace took some deep breaths. "I'm okay. I'm fine. Sorry."

"So, you're okay then?" her Aunt Tammy asked to make sure.

"I'm just fine. I'm sorry I made such a fuss. Of course we're going through with the wedding. Let's taste some cake!"

Everyone breathed a sigh of relief. Crisis averted.

While Avery commenced with the cake tasting, Jess got herself a cup of coffee. She slid into a booth by the coffee bar and waited for the right moment to remind Chace about the expo. *One thing at a time*, she thought.

Soon enough the decision had been made. Chace chose a three tiered lemon cake with raspberry jam between each layer and vanilla buttercream frosting. The reception lunch would be beef tenderloin with green bean and tomato salad and dijon roasted potatoes.

Chace and her group got up to leave. "That is just absolutely delicious," she cooed. "Thank you Avery. I am so glad Jess recommended you."

"You're quite welcome," Avery said, gathering up her notes on the wedding menu.

Jess stood up. "One other thing, Chace," she said. "We have to get over to that wedding expo today."

Chace's shoulders sank, "No, I can't. I just can't."

"Why can't we do that tomorrow?" Madison asked. "The expo is going on all weekend."

"We have your couple's shower tomorrow," Tanya reminded her daughter.

"What if we do the expo in the morning? The shower is not until four," Jess said.

"I think that could work," Chace said.

"I'll tell Virginia that's what we're doing," Jess said. "You just take it easy today."

"Thank you so much," Chace said, rushing over to give Jess a quick side hug.

After the group of ladies left, Jess sunk into the seat by Avery. "I am emotionally drained after all that," she said.

Ms. Erika poked her head out from the kitchen. "Are they gone yet?"

"They're gone, Mama," Avery said.

"Whew, that is one loud bunch of women," Erika said. "You know I'm catering pies for the wedding shower tomorrow. I'm debuting a new fruit pie."

"Mmm, can I get a preview," Jess asked.

"I thought you'd never ask," Ms. Erika said, she brought out a combination blueberry, strawberry, and raspberry pie with different sized star shapes forming the crust on top. She cut slices for Jess and Avery. "I call it the Miss America Pie," she beamed.

Jess took a bite and let the warm fruity flavors wash over her tongue. "Oh, this is so good," she raved.

"It'll taste better this summer when I can get fresh berries," Ms. Erika said.

"Too bad they ate all the cake samples, or you could have tried that too," Avery said. She got herself a cup of coffee and sat back down opposite Jess.

A customer came in and went up to the counter so Erika excused herself.

"I can't believe you found Donna Vance lying dead on the floor," Avery whispered. "Was she sick?"

"Not that I could tell," Jess said. "It's weird;

she died with a smoothie in her hand."

"A smoothie?"

"Yeah, she drank these protein, veggie smoothies all the time. I had a taste and it was awful."

"Maybe that's what killed her," Avery speculated.

"Let's change the subject," Jess said. "What do you think of the wedding party?"

Avery thought about this. "I'm grateful to have a catering client, but...."

Jess smiled, waiting for the rest of what Avery had to say.

"It's like herding cats."

"Yeah," Jess agreed, "I'll be glad when this is all over."

"So, tell me about Detective Connor," Avery said, prodding.

"What's to tell?" Jess said coyly. "We're going to the shower together."

"I still say that's not a real date."

"You're probably right," Jess agreed. "Maybe after all this wedding hoopla is over, we can go out to dinner or a movie."

"That's better," Avery said. "You do like him, right?"

"Well, when I first met him, I hated him. He was the cop who hauled me down to the station for questioning, remember?"

"How could I forget?"

"But then, when he brought up going out, I kind of saw a softer side to him. He's nice," Jess said.

"And he's easy on the eyes," Avery said.

"Yeah, there is that." Jess sipped her coffee. "The good thing about taking him to the shower is everybody will see that he's with me and they'll know I'm over Jack."

"Who are you trying to convince?"

"Those bridesmaids. I heard them talking about me last night in the ladies room, they said 'She's so pathetic, she's still in love with her ex'," Jess said, mimicking what she had overheard.

"And are you still in love with Jack?" Avery asked.

"No!" Jess insisted. She threw a wadded up napkin at her friend. "You know what, though? Chace defended me. She told them that I'm over Jack and we're all good friends now, and she said I'm a good writer."

"Wow," Avery said, "that's high praise. You two do seem chummier than I remember."

"Oh, don't get me wrong. She's a spoiled brat," Jess said. "That reminds me, I need to touch base with Virginia about the expo."

"Later Gator."

Jess walked back to the Gazette office only to find that Virginia had left.

"That cute police detective came by," Brittney said. "He took Donna's things out of my office and my nice rug. Oh, and here." Brittney handed her Donna's notecards. "He said you could have these."

"Thanks," Jess said, "Did he say anything else?"

"He wants you to call him," Brittney said. "Are you skipping the expo?"

"Yeah, we're going to do that tomorrow."

Jess got into her car and got the heater going. Then she called Chris. "Thanks for the note cards," she said, "Brittney said I should call."

"I want you to know, we're on our way to Ms. Nesbitt's house. The coroner found traces of arsenic in Donna Vance's system."

CHAPTER 19 – SATURDAY, FEBRUARY 10

10:40 a.m.

Arsenic? Jess couldn't believe it. She pulled into Ms. Melody's gravel drive right next to the Grace PD Squad Car.

Inside the house, Detective Connor and Officer Frick were in the living room with Garrett and Virginia. Ms. Melody stood nearby.

"How did she get poisoned?" Virginia was shrieking. "She never ate anything."

"The smoothies!" Garrett gasped and held his hand to his mouth.

Virginia became enraged. "That mousy little assistant poisoned my mother!"

Detective Connor cleared his throat. "Let's not jump to any conclusions. We don't know how she ingested the arsenic or even if that was the cause of death."

"Did anybody else drink any of these smoothies?" Frick asked.

Everyone else shook their heads.

"Wait, Crystal drank some of them," Jess said.

Garrett sobbed, "Who would poison my

angel?"

"Where is Crystal?" Frick asked.

"I don't know, she still hasn't come back from running errands," Virginia said.

"Do you think she may have been poisoned too?" Jess asked.

"Oh no! We need to call her," Garrett said as he worriedly pulled on the ends of his mustache.

"I'll try calling her," Virginia said as she got out her phone.

"So, where did these smoothies come from?" Connor asked.

"Crystal would mix them up for Donna and herself," Garrett answered.

While her call to Crystal was ringing Virginia added, "They were vile tasting."

"There are still some smoothies in the fridge," Jess said.

"We'll need to take those in for testing," Connor said, "and all of the ingredients."

"No answer," Virginia announced angrily as she switched off the call. "I think you need to find her and question her."

"Let me get those smoothies for you," Jess said. She and Officer Frick went into the kitchen.

Jess got out a grocery bag and found five bottles of smoothies in the refrigerator. Then she began looking for the items that went into the foul concoction.

Frick cleared her throat. "Ms. Hart, I just want to say ..." She stopped for a long pause.

Jess looked at her blankly. "To say what?"

"The truth is, I'm embarrassed by my behavior last night. I was hoping you could keep that to yourself. I would hate for Detective Connor to get wind of it."

"I am the keeper of secrets," Jess assured her as she put the protein powder into the bag along with baggies of dried spinach, kale, frozen banana, pumpkin seeds, and hemp hearts.

"Thank you," Frick said. "Is that all of it?"

"Oh, wait, she used soy milk." Jess got that out of the refrigerator. She handed the bag to Officer Frick and washed her hands, just in case.

When they came back into the living room Virginia was yelling at Detective Connor. "What do you mean; you can't release her body yet? We need to make arrangements for her memorial service!"

"I understand your concern, but we need to complete the autopsy," Connor explained patiently.

"You just told us she died from poisoning," Virginia yelled.

Connor took a breath, "The coroner found arsenic in her bloodstream. He has not done a full autopsy yet."

"Is that necessary?" Garrett wailed, rocking back and forth on the sofa. "I don't want them to cut her all up!" He collapsed into sobs.

Jess wanted to put her arm around him but felt awkward about it, since she barely knew the man.

"Get ahold of yourself, Garrett!" Virginia snapped at him.

Everyone looked at her in shock.

"Why do we need an autopsy?" Virginia asked.

Connor spoke calmly and with great patience, "In order to be certain of the cause of death. Anytime there's a suspicious death an autopsy is performed."

"And how long does that take?" Virginia asked impatiently.

"We should be able to release the body in about twenty-four hours," Connor said. "But we can't be certain about that."

Virginia huffed and plopped down on the sofa next to Garrett. "So, what are we supposed to tell the press?" she asked. "My phone will not stop ringing."

"Do not mention anything about poisoning

at this time," Connor said. He turned to leave, "I'll be in touch."

Jess followed the officers out to their car.

"Do you think it was the arsenic that killed her?" she asked.

"We are not at liberty to discuss the particulars of this case," Frick said as she slid into the passenger seat.

Jess looked up at Chris.

"It's too early to tell. Everything you've heard here is strictly off the record," he said.

"Definitely, just between us. So, do you think she was poisoned?"

"Just between us?" Chris asked with a mischievous smile. He came closer and leaned down to whisper in her ear. "No comment." His warm breath on her neck was surprisingly nice. He opened his car door. "See you later," he said.

Jess took a deep breath before marching up to her apartment. Sweet Tea trotted up too.

Donna was poisoned, she thought, *that means everybody down in Ms. Melody's house is a potential murderer.*

Jess set her bag down on the kitchen table and took a diet coke out of her fridge. She opened her bag and took out Donna's notecards. She read through them again before she got up and dropped all the notecards into the trash. "We won't be needing those, will we Sweet Tea?"

The cat had rolled herself into the shape of a crescent roll on the sofa and did not reply.

Jess got out her laptop and began working on the wedding story. *It would help if I could look at Garrett's photos,* Jess thought. Even so, she wasn't about to go back down stairs and bother the poor man now. She wrote a little blurb about the dress fitting and the photo shoot on the courthouse lawn. *Now what do I say about the bachelorette party,* she wondered, *especially considering what happened afterward.*

Jess got up and tossed her soda can into the recycling bin under her sink. She went back to her desk and took out a yellow legal pad. She began making a list.

Suspects

1. Virginia Vance: Motive – Shouting match at bachelorette party. Possibly take over Donna Vance Enterprises.
2. Crystal Clearwater: Motive – Donna was mean to her.
3. Garrett Neilson: Motive – Donna bossed him around.
4. Dean Cartwright: Motive – Donna fired him over the phone.

Jess pondered each suspect for a moment. They all seemed like weak motives. She wondered, *does Virginia want to take over the company? What good is Donna Vance Enterprises without Donna Vance?*

Also, Crystal doesn't seem like the murdering type. Besides, she may have been poisoned as well.

The next name was Garrett. *I can't see him murdering anybody, especially considering that he's downstairs crying his eyes out.*

That left Dean Cartwright. *I don't really know enough about him,* she thought.

She turned to the cat, "What do you think, Sweet Tea?"

Sweet Tea sat up from her nap and opened her mouth in a wide yawn, showing off all of her teeth. She leapt from the sofa to the floor and trotted over to Jess's desk. Jess reached down to rub her neck.

"I don't have very much to go on," Jess said to the cat. "Maybe it was a deranged fan."

Sweet Tea jumped onto the desk and began walking back and forth on Jess's list, wrinkling the page.

"Okay, okay," Jess said, "I give up."

Her landline rang with a call from the Pie Hole. "Hello?" Jess said.

It was Avery. "Things are getting crazy here on the square," she said.

"What do you mean?"

"I mean we've got reporters from all over trying to get the story about Donna Vance. There are news vans everywhere."

"I should have known. I guess when Virginia put out a statement, it was only a matter of time."

"We're sold out of the mini-pies and I'm brewing coffee as fast as I can," Avery said. "I'm going to need a margarita after this. Maria's at seven?"

"I'll be there," Jess said.

"I gotta go, these reporter types don't like to be kept waiting."

"Hey, I'm one of those reporter types," Jess said.

"Later Gator," Avery said before clicking off.

Jess turned on her TV and flipped to a news channel. There was a story on the death of Donna Vance, with a news reporter on the scene in front of the Gazette office.

"Donna Vance was in the small town of Grace, working on an article for *Texas Bride Magazine*. It was here at the office of the local newspaper, where Donna collapsed late last night. The cause of death is undetermined," the reporter said. Jess could see behind him that flowers, banners, and tributes to

Donna Vance had been laid along the windows of the Gazette. "In a statement released earlier today...."

Jess switched to Channel 11, the local affiliate station in Juniper. "Law enforcement in Grace would not comment on the cause of death for beloved lifestyle maven Donna Vance who died late yesterday," the local news anchor said. She continued, "Let's go live now to Leigh Ballou, on the scene."

Leigh was positioned in front of the Flower Basket. "We are here on the town square in Grace with local resident Brooke Calvin."

The camera panned over to show Brooke with the Grace Grill behind her. "Ms. Calvin, what can you tell us about Donna's time here in Grace?"

This was Brooke's shining moment. She smiled and said, "Well, Donna was here with her people. They were taking pictures of the wedding group over by the hanging flower basket." Brooke was chewing gum as she spoke and twirling her hair on one finger. "It's the world's second largest hanging flower basket."

"I understand Donna was in Grace for the wedding of former Miss Texas Chace Perez, is that right?"

"Oh yes," Brooke said nodding, "Chace is just the nicest person and she is just bereft over the whole thing."

"As are we all," Leigh said.

"It's just a *trajesty*, and I'll tell you what. Donna Vance dying like that ..." Brooke shook her head sadly, "it wasn't no accident."

Jess sighed and turned off the TV. She decided to go downstairs and check on everybody. When she got there, Ms. Melody was in the kitchen making her famous chili and cornbread.

"Oh, that smells so good. Where is everybody?" Jess asked.

"Garrett is in the den watching TV," Ms. Melody said, "I don't know about Virginia. She took off after the police left. I'm so glad they took all that nasty smoothie stuff. That took up half my refrigerator."

"Come to think of it, I had a taste of those smoothies yesterday. It was awful, but I feel fine," Jess said. "Are you cooking lunch for him?"

"I know it's supposed to be bed and breakfast, but I thought I'd make some chili," Ms. Melody said, "Garrett is just beside himself, bless his heart."

Jess looked up at Ms. Melody with puppy dog eyes.

"Would you like to join us for lunch?" Ms. Melody asked.

"Well, since you asked," Jess shrugged. "Sure, why not?" She got out three bowls and small plates for the cornbread. "I'll go see how Garrett is doing."

Jess came down the front hall toward the den and heard Garrett talking.

"Where are you? I need you here. We need to talk."

She came into the hall and saw that he was speaking into the phone. She kept quiet.

He continued. "Call me when you get this message." He ended his call and looked up, surprised to see Jess. "How long have you been there?" he asked angrily.

"I just got here," she said, feeling defensive. "Lunch is almost ready."

He eyeballed Jess suspiciously as he stood. "I'm sorry I'm so jumpy. You and Ms. Melody have been so kind. Thank you. I'll go wash up for lunch."

"Were you leaving a message for Crystal?"

Garrett looked taken aback. "Well yes. I'm worried about her. After all, she drank those poison smoothies too."

CHAPTER 20 – SATURDAY, FEBRUARY 10

6:45 p.m.

When Jess got to Casa Maria, she was a little bit early. She put her name on the list and was told the wait would be thirty minutes. The place was packed with out-of-towners. She texted Avery.

Jess: At Maria's. Thirty minute wait. I'm in the bar.

She went into the bar and looked for a seat. Everything was taken. She was about to give up and stand in a corner when she noticed Jack at a little table in the bar area. Sitting opposite him was a woman with a long blonde ponytail protruding from the back of a baseball cap.

The first thing Jess thought was, *she shouldn't wear a baseball cap inside a restaurant*. The second thing she thought was, *it's probably one of Chace's relatives*. Then Jack leaned across the small table and kissed the blonde. The third thing Jess thought was, *Oh hell no*.

Jess maneuvered through the bar, trying not to get bumped by the crowd. When she got to Jack's table she started in on him. "What's going on?" she asked loudly.

"Hello," he said, "how are you doing? This has

turned into a real media circus, right?" Jack indicated the packed restaurant.

"Yes. It's crazy," Jess agreed. "Who's your friend?" She turned to introduce herself to the blonde, who peered at her through pink tinted John Lennon glasses.

"Jess, it's me," Chace giggled. "Can you tell? I'm incognito so the reporters don't bother me."

"We thought we'd go out to dinner, just the two of us," Jack said. "We weren't expecting all this."

"Take a seat," Chace said, "I just want to say thank you. This day off has been just what I needed. I spent most of the day in the bathtub."

"I'm glad you got some rest," Jess said.

"You know, I never should have agreed to this magazine story," Chace said. "A wedding is stressful enough without all these advertisers and photo ops."

"I never knew how much planning and preparation went into a wedding," Jack said.

Chace looked at him and made a brushing motion. "We should have just eloped like you and Jess did," she said.

Jess felt a little awkward hearing that.

Just then the hostess called out, "Ketchum party of two, your table is ready."

"That's us," Jack said.

"Hey, I'll pick everybody up tomorrow morning around eight-thirty for the expo," Jess said.

"See you then," Chace said, as she got up to leave.

At least I've got a place to sit now, Jess thought. She put her purse in the other chair to save it for Avery.

At the end of the bar, Jess saw Virginia Vance with a big frozen margarita in her hand. She was laughing and talking with someone. Jess couldn't see the man she was with.

"Who are you staring at," Avery said.

"Oh, Avery, there you are," Jess said. "I didn't see you come in." She moved her purse and Avery took a seat.

"This place is packed tonight," Avery said. "So, really, who are you looking at?"

Jess leaned in. "The woman at the bar, with the auburn hair, that's Virginia Vance."

"Virginia Vance? Donna's daughter?"

"That's the one."

"She doesn't seem very upset about her mother," Avery said.

"No, she does not," Jess agreed. "I'm trying to see who she's talking to."

They both watched as Virginia leaned back in her seat laughing. The man seated next to her was

Dean Cartwright.

The hostess called out, "Jessica Hart, your table is ready."

Virginia heard and turned to look.

Jess stopped behind the two on her way to the table. "Virginia, hi." She turned to Dean. "And you are Mr. Cartwright; we met this morning at the Gazette. It seems like you two have buried the hatchet."

The two of them were momentarily taken aback. Virginia's mouth dropped open. "We're having a meeting," Virginia stammered.

"At a time like this, we have to be proactive. There's no reason we can't work together," Dean said.

"We better go get our table," Jess said, waving goodbye. "Talk later."

Jess and Avery made their way to the table and ordered drinks. A margarita for Avery. Jess stuck to iced tea.

"It seems odd that she's not upset about her mother," Avery said.

"Very odd," Jess agreed. Their waiter set down some chips and salsa and Jess dug in.

"Was Donna a nice person?" Avery asked. "It's just, from everything you said it sounded like she had a mean streak."

"Did she ever. You remember the wedding blooper reel?" Jess asked.

The waiter brought the drinks and Avery took a big sip of her margarita. "Oh yeah, I remember."

"Well, that's who she was, mean sometimes, nice other times, very unpredictable." Jess took a sip of her tea. "I didn't tell you the big news."

"What big news?"

"You can't tell anybody."

Avery drew an imaginary X across her chest. "Cross my heart and hope to die."

Jess leaned in and whispered, "They found traces of arsenic in Donna's system."

Avery's eyes widened. "So she was murdered?"

"I think so," Jess answered. "Chris said they have to do an autopsy, and then they'll know more."

"Wow, this is huge. Nobody knows?"

"Only the family, and me, and Ms. Melody," Jess answered.

Their waiter came to take their orders. They decided on chicken fajitas for two.

Jess dipped another chip into the salsa. "So, the Pie Hole was busy today?"

"We were swamped with all these out-of-towners. It's been great for business."

They were interrupted when Virginia stopped by their table and took a seat.

"Hi, I'm Virginia Vance," she said to Avery. "You've probably heard of my podcast *Yeah Right*."

Avery looked surprised, "Nice to meet you."

Virginia continued, "Anyway, I just wanted to stop over real quick to explain my meeting with Dean."

"You don't owe me any explanation," Jess said.

Virginia laughed. "I know we disagreed about who was in charge of Mom's company," she went on. "So, I suggested we should meet on neutral ground and see if we could work things out."

"So did you?" Jess asked.

Virginia smiled, "I think so. Dean's going to be a managing partner and maybe I'll take over where Mom left off. Continue her legacy, so to speak."

Avery asked, "So now, you'll write the books, run the website, do the TV show?"

"Maybe. It's early days right now," Virginia said. Then she thought about it, "Except writing, that's not really my thing."

"Okay," Avery said. It was a bit off-putting how happy Virginia seemed.

"Maybe I'll need a ghostwriter," Virginia

mused. "That reminds me," she pointed to Jess. "You're writing Mom's last magazine story so it better be a good one. It's sort of her swan song."

"I'll do my best," Jess said through gritted teeth.

"Oh by the way, Crystal finally showed up back at the B&B. Did you know?" Virginia announced.

"No. I didn't know. Where has she been all day?" Jess asked.

"First she said she had errands to run. Then she said the police took her in for more questioning. Can you believe that? I mean, they've already questioned all of us."

Avery's mouth dropped open. "Wow! Do they think she had something to do with your mother's death?"

"Probably," Virginia said. "She's a cagey one. She went straight into her bedroom and slammed the door."

"Hot plate," the waiter showed up with a sizzling platter of fajitas. The aroma wafted over them.

"I better get back to my table," Virginia said as she stood up to go.

"Bye," Jess said with a wave.

"That was weird," Avery said, "it's like she's happy that her mother died."

"I know. It's unsettling. Donna's husband is the only one who seems really upset." She touched the edge of the fajita platter, "Owwww!"

Avery laughed at her friend, "he said it was hot."

After dinner Jess went straight up to her apartment. Sweet Tea was waiting for her on the upstairs deck.

"Come on in, I'll open a can of seafood variety for you."

Sweet Tea darted into the apartment and Jess opened a can, as promised.

"I don't know why you like this stuff," Jess said as she spooned out the cat food, "it stinks to high heaven." She dished out half the can and then covered the leftovers in foil and placed it in her fridge.

I need to get some groceries, Jess mused as she peered into the mostly empty refrigerator. She grabbed a cold water bottle and plopped down on her sofa. She flipped channels for a while. The station in Juniper re-ran the interview with Brooke. That woman was a problem. Jess wondered if she would tell anyone what she had said about Jack having 'some woman' in his motel room. Obviously Brooke knew that the woman in question was Jess. But now, maybe that juicy piece of gossip was overshadowed by Donna's death. And what did Brooke mean by telling the TV reporter it wasn't an accident?

Jess turned off the television and went to her desk. She saw her list of suspects and put a big question mark next to Crystal's name. *Where did she go all day?* Jess wondered. She pondered the list a little bit longer. *I've got nothing*, she thought.

She decided to pack her messenger bag for the expo. She made sure she had a fresh notebook and her wedding itinerary. She reviewed her notes from the interview with Jack and Chace.

Then she printed up maps of the convention floor, one for each bridesmaid and one for Chace. She drew stars by each booth they would have to visit and planned the easiest route. *Without Donna it's all up to me to herd these cats*, she realized. "No offense, Sweet Tea."

Sweet Tea had finished eating and perched herself on the arm of the sofa to get a good view. She looked like a loaf of bread with a head.

Not yet sleepy, Jess went to Donna Vance's website. She read some of the comments from fans, expressing sorrow over the loss of the beloved icon. She watched the retrospective video that Virginia had posted with clips from Donna's TV appearances over the years. She read the tribute that Virginia had written:

The world knows Donna Vance as the Queen

of Texas Chic, an icon of style and good taste. They see her as the powerhouse behind Donna Vance Enterprises. While I agree, she was a force to be reckoned with, she was more than that. Growing up, my mother was the best at everything. The best cook, the best at crafts and decorating, and the best mother a young girl could ask for.

Making a home is more than just preparing good food and creating a warm, welcoming place to come to. Making a home means family and genuinely caring for those you love. That's the true legacy of Donna Vance. That's what I will remember about my mother.

It's funny, Jess thought, Virginia said writing wasn't her thing but this is quite touching. She wondered how Virginia would change things if she took over or even if she could step into her mother's shoes.

Jess clicked around to various pages and re-watched the *Epic Wedding Fails*. She hoped this feature would go away soon now that Virginia was in charge. There was the unfortunate father of the bride whose pants fell down. There was the poor bride who slipped in the mud and became known as Soggy Bottom. Jess paused the video and ran it back. When she fell, the bride's veil fell off and the woman's bangs slid into her eyes. The eyes were covered and the bride was about thirty pounds heavier and blonde but the bangs flipping from one side to the other across her face was unmistakable. Soggy Bottom had a strong resemblance to Crystal Clearwater!

CHAPTER 21 – SATURDAY, FEBRUARY 10

10:45 p.m.

Jess watched the video a few more times just to be sure. She couldn't believe it, but it had to be Crystal. She looked at the time on her phone. It was late so she decided she would call Detective Connor first thing tomorrow morning.

Jess double checked the lock on her door and went to bed. At some point in the middle of the night, Sweet Tea began wailing loudly. Jess covered her head with her pillow but the caterwauling would not stop.

Jess got out of bed and tromped into the front room. "What do you want, you crazy animal?" Jess asked through clenched teeth.

Sweet Tea stood by the door, demanding to be let out.

Jess opened the door and a blast of cool air blew into the room. Sweet Tea darted out. "Okay, bye," Jess hollered before she slammed the door, re-locked it, and went back to bed.

Jess was awakened again when Ms. Melody knocked loudly on her door.

"I was not intending to get up quite this

early," Jess said as she opened the door, aggravated at another sleep interruption.

"There's been a break-in," Ms. Melody said urgently.

"What happened?" Jess asked, suddenly wide awake.

Ms. Melody was pacing and wringing her hands. "Somebody broke in. I don't know when it happened. I didn't hear a thing."

"Did they steal anything? Is everybody okay? Did you call the police?" Jess asked.

"The police are on their way," Ms. Melody said. "I don't think anything was taken. Can you come downstairs? I haven't told the others." She sat at the table.

"Tell me what happened exactly?"

Ms. Melody took a breath. "Well, I came to the kitchen to get a glass of water and that's when I saw broken glass and the back door was open."

"And nobody else knows yet?"

"I didn't wake them up, after everything they've been through," Ms. Melody said.

"Let me put some jeans on."

When they went downstairs, Jess saw that one small pane of glass from the kitchen door was broken near the doorknob. They carefully stepped around the broken glass and went up to the bedrooms.

Ms. Melody knocked on each door. "Wake up. There's been a break-in. Is everyone all right?"

Virginia was the first one out of her room. "What the hell is going on here?" she barked angrily.

Garrett was next into the hallway. He rubbed his eyes and yawned. "What happened?"

"It looks like someone broke in downstairs," Ms. Melody explained. "I want to make sure you're all okay."

"A break-in?" Virginia repeated shrilly.

Ms. Melody knocked again on Crystal's door. "Wake up," she called out louder this time. "Crystal, are you okay in there."

There was no answer.

"Crystal," she said loudly and knocked again. She opened the door a crack and called again. "Crystal, wake up." She let the door swing open. Crystal was not there.

Everyone peered into the empty bedroom. The desk lamp was turned over, a chair had been knocked down, and the blankets from the bed were strewn into the floor.

Ms. Melody righted the lamp.

"Don't touch anything," Jess said, "we have to leave it like this for the police."

"Oh, that's right," Ms. Melody said. She gently

laid the lamp back on its side.

Jess surveyed the room. There was an open suitcase on the desk chair and a glass of water on a coaster on the desk.

Garrett was visibly upset and pulled the hairs of his mustache. "How could this happen? I was in the next room."

"Why would anybody kidnap Crystal? She's a nobody," Virginia said.

"I don't understand how we didn't hear anything," Ms. Melody said.

"Let's go downstairs and wait for the police," Jess said.

When Detective Connor and Officer Frick arrived, everyone was seated around the kitchen table.

"Good morning, Ma'am. I understand there's been a break-in," Frick said.

Ms. Melody showed them the broken window in the back door.

"There's broken glass here on the kitchen floor. The door was unlocked and standing open," Ms. Melody answered.

"Were there signs of a struggle?"

"Up in Crystal's room. I'll show you," Ms. Melody said.

Everyone followed the officers upstairs.

"This used to be Andrew's room. I was thinking about turning it into a craft room or something, but then I decided to run a B&B," Ms. Melody rambled as the police looked at the bedroom.

Frick went around taking pictures. "It appears there was a struggle," she said.

"Did anyone hear anything?" Connor asked.

"Not a thing," Ms. Melody said.

Virginia poked her head into the room. "Do you think this is related to my mother's death?" she asked.

"Maybe, but it's too early to tell," Frick said. "Was there a ransom note?"

"Not that I could find," Ms. Melody said.

"What time did you discover the break-in?" Connor asked.

"A little after five. I wanted to get some water from the kitchen," she said. "I saw that the window was broken and the door unlocked. So, I called you."

"Are there signs of a struggle anywhere else in the house?" Connor asked.

"No, I don't think so," Ms. Melody answered.

Everyone went back downstairs and Ms. Melody started a pot of coffee.

Garrett asked fearfully, "Do you think she

was killed?"

"We don't know that sir," Frick answered. "Please remain calm."

Jess took Connor aside. "There's something I need to tell you about Crystal." She held her finger to her lips.

He nodded. "Later," he whispered.

Virginia sighed heavily as she flopped into a chair. "Well, since you're here, do you have any more information about my mother and what killed her?"

"We're still waiting on the toxicology report," Connor said.

"Why would it take so long?" Virginia asked, exasperated. "You told us she was poisoned!"

"We tested the smoothies. No poison there," Frick said. She pulled out her notebook. "The coroner did examine the contents of her stomach. Ms. Vance had ingested the protein smoothie and also a large amount of chocolate."

"Chocolate?" Garrett asked with surprise. "She never ate chocolate. She never ate anything." He collapsed into another fit of tears.

"You don't know Mom very well," Virginia said. "I knew that box of chocolates wouldn't stay in the trash."

"What are you saying?" Garrett asked.

"I'm saying Mom would secretly binge on sweets. I used to find candy wrappers hidden all over the house when I was a kid."

"We did not find any box of chocolates," Frick said.

"So did the chocolate have the poison? Or was it the smoothie she had?" Jess asked.

"It's impossible to tell," Connor said. "Do any of you know where she might have gotten the candy?"

"It was sent from Dean along with some flowers," Garrett said with a gasp. "Dean killed my angel!" He burst into another fit of sobs.

"Dean didn't poison her," Virginia snapped.

"Where is that box of candy now?" Connor asked.

"She threw it away at the Gazette. But if she took it out of the trash and ate them, then I don't know," Jess answered.

Connor looked at Frick. "We'll need to search for that box just to be sure."

"I'm on it," she said snapping her notebook shut with a flick of her wrist. "Time for a little dumpster diving."

"Jess, a word," Connor said. He pointed toward the door. "We'll keep you posted," he said to the others.

Outside by the squad car Jess pulled out her phone and brought up the Soggy Bottom video. "What am I looking at?" Connor asked.

"This bride," Jess pointed, "the one with the mud on her dress, that's Crystal."

"Are you sure?" Connor asked. "This woman looks different."

"I didn't recognize her at first either," Jess said. "But, they both do this hair flip thing where the bangs flip from one side to the other. Crystal does it all the time and so does this bride. See, right there." Jess paused the video at the right moment. "Donna put her in this video about four years ago and called her Soggy Bottom."

"What are you saying, that the bride changed her appearance and became Donna's assistant in order to murder her for revenge?"

"Maybe. Stranger things have happened," Jess said.

"I'll have to look into it," Connor said.

Frick leaned over and called out from the passenger side, "are we leaving or what?"

"Just one more thing," Jess said, "I don't think Crystal was kidnapped either. I think she just did a runner."

"Why do you say that?" Connor asked.

"I find it hard to believe that nobody heard

anything. I think the room was staged to make it look like a struggle and she just snuck out in the night," Jess said.

Frick overheard this theory. "Leave the investigating to the professionals, Miss Hart," she said. "C'mon Connor, we've got to motor."

"I'll see you tonight for the shower," he said as he slid into the driver's seat.

CHAPTER 22 – SUNDAY, FEBRUARY 11

6:45 a.m.

Jess went back into the house and sat at the kitchen table next to Garrett, who was sipping his coffee morosely. She could smell Ms. Melody's breakfast casserole baking in the oven. "Is there enough for me?" she asked.

"Of course," Ms. Melody said, "you're always welcome."

"Thank you," Jess said. She then turned to Garrett. "So," Jess began gently, "we still have to go to that wedding expo today. I want to leave right after breakfast."

He looked at her and stroked his mustache. His eyes again filled with tears.

"We just need you to take the pictures," Jess said with a pleading smile. She patted his shoulder thinking maybe that would help.

"I just can't," Garrett said, "not after everything that's happened."

"I understand, but…"

"You take the pictures." With that Garrett stood and walked toward the stairs. "I just can't," he added between sobs.

Jess sighed. "Okay, I'll take the pictures." *How about I just do everything*, she thought. Instantly she felt bad about it. Changing the subject she asked, "Where's Virginia?"

"I have no idea," Ms. Melody answered grouchily. "It's time for breakfast and everyone has scattered."

Jess's cell phone rang and she fished it out of her pocket. It was Aunt Patsy.

"Jess, you're not at home. I already tried your landline," Aunt Patsy said. "I'm surprised you're up at this hour. I was giving you your Sunday morning wake-up call."

"Just a moment Aunt Patsy," she said. She took her phone into the den. "I'm at Ms. Melody's," Jess explained. "There's been a break-in and Donna's assistant is missing."

"Oh my Lord," Aunt Patsy exclaimed. "It's not safe for you to associate with those people!"

"Well, the police came over and they're going to look into it."

"You stay out of it," Patsy said. "First Donna Vance up and dies… and now this!"

"I will stay out of it as much as I can," Jess said. "I am finishing up Donna's magazine story about the wedding though."

"You poor thing, having to watch Jack get married to somebody else. Bless your heart."

"So, what did you call about, Aunt Patsy?" Jess asked impatiently.

"Just making sure you're picking me up for church this morning."

"I can't this time Aunt Patsy. I have to go to the big wedding expo in Juniper."

"Well whoever heard of such a thing?" Aunt Patsy groused. "You're not getting married."

"It's for the magazine story so you're going to have to find another ride. I'm sorry."

"Well, I won't say anything about it, but you're not supposed to be working on a Sunday. I guess I'll just take the shuttle van with Myrtle," Aunt Patsy said with a sigh.

"Great idea," Jess said. *Why don't you just do that every Sunday?*

"I hope you'll be back from Juniper in time for the wedding shower. I can't wait for you to see the house."

"I can't wait either," Jess said. "In fact, I'm bringing a date."

"A date? Who's your date?"

"Detective Connor," Jess answered.

Aunt Patsy was delighted. "He is quite a catch."

"Do you have a ride for the shower?" Jess asked.

"I'll ask Ms. Melody to bring me. I don't want to impose on you and your date."

"Okay, sounds good. I better go."

"I can't talk anymore Jess. I have to get ready for church," Aunt Patsy said.

Jess heard the clunk of the phone hanging up. *Okay, Bye*, Jess thought.

Jess joined Ms. Melody and Virginia at the kitchen table. Ms. Melody was dishing out her breakfast casserole made with eggs, bacon, and sausage. It was one of Jess's favorites.

Jess asked, "So, how long has Crystal been working for Donna?"

"I think it must be about three years," Virginia answered.

"What do you know about her?" Jess asked.

"Nothing," Virginia said. "She probably came from an agency or something. Mom was very particular about who she hired."

Jess wondered how she could check Crystal's background.

"Oh, before I forget," Virginia said. "Garrett can't go with you to the expo this morning. He's too distraught. I brought you his camera so you can take all the pictures." She pointed to the big camera bag she had placed on the counter.

"I don't know how to use that big camera,"

Jess said.

"You'll figure it out. Here are the keys to Mom's SUV. You should be able to fit everyone in." Virginia handed over the keys to the Escalade.

Jess took a deep breath. *Can I drive such a huge vehicle?*

At 8:30 Jess pulled into the hotel parking lot. She texted Chace.

Jess: I'm parked under the awning. Come on down.

Chace: I have to get everybody. It will be a minute.

While she waited, Jess began looking through the pictures Garrett had taken. Many from the bachelorette party were too embarrassing. Jess deleted them without hesitation. Likewise, she deleted the video of Beverly Frick dancing with the stripper. She kept scrolling back through to the photos on the courthouse lawn.

Then she saw something unexpected. There were pictures of a woman lying on her side on a bed. It wasn't Donna Vance. The woman was naked and her brown hair hung over one eye. It was unmistakably Crystal.

Jess was startled by the side door opening

and the wedding party piling into the SUV.

"Road trip!" Madison sang out excitedly. She had a mini cooler in one hand as she climbed into the seat behind Jess. "I brought water bottles for everybody."

Jess had not expected Chace's mother and her Aunt Tammy to come along. Luckily the SUV had seats for eight. Everybody squeezed in and they were off.

The Bridal Expo was being held in the Juniper ISD Multi-Purpose Arena. Jess parked and the group got in line for their tickets.

"Okay," Jess addressed the group, "we have to stay together and follow this map on the vendor floor." She passed out the maps. "I put a star on the map by each vendor we have to visit and take pictures. I will be taking the pictures today."

This announcement was met with a chorus of whining. *Aww, do we have to? I want to look around. Where are the bathrooms?* Jess felt like she was leading a field trip for preschoolers.

"I need to pick up a gift for the shower," Aunt Tammy said.

Chace clapped her hands to get everyone's attention. "Jess is right, we have to stay together and go where she says. If there's any time left over, then we can shop around."

"Thank you," Jess said.

"But seriously, can we stop at the restroom first," Chace asked. "I shouldn't have had that water bottle."

After their bathroom break, the group followed along dutifully with only a few stragglers here and there. Jess lugged along the camera bag.

Their first stop was at a booth for Fern's Floral Creations. They were doing the flowers for the wedding. The wedding party held up some sample bouquets and posed for the obligatory group photo. Jess also got a close up of Chace with a wedding bouquet.

Next the group went to Divine Destinations, the travel agency for the couple's honeymoon in Bora Bora. Jess couldn't help feeling a pang of jealousy. She had enjoyed her honeymoon road trip with Jack to New Orleans, but she had always wanted to travel overseas. The wedding party donned straw hats and sunglasses, and sipped prop cocktails in front of a large back-drop of a beach with the Divine Destinations logo.

They continued on visiting booths for china dishes, jewelry, cosmetics, and wedding invitations. Jess felt like she was getting pretty good at using the camera. The pictures were excellent and she hoped she would also get photo credit.

At the last booth of the day Chace tried on her veil. She had chosen it a couple of weeks earlier. Everyone *oohed* and *aahed* as the shopkeeper placed the veil on her head. Jess snapped the photo.

Then Jess noticed a woman in the next booth. She was admiring herself in the three-way mirror in a form-fitting, lacy, mermaid style wedding gown. It really showed off her trim figure. In the mirror, Jess could see the woman's face. It was Crystal.

"Hey!" Jess yelled as she ran toward the woman. "Crystal!"

"Where are you going?" Chace called out as she rushed past. Jess shoved the camera into Conlie's hands as she went by.

Crystal looked up, and for a moment stared like a deer in the headlights. Then she turned and ran. She stumbled on the fishtail skirt, then hiked it up and sprinted down the aisle in high heels.

"Hey, come back, you've got to pay for that," the vendor called out. He threw down his tape measure and gave chase as well. Jess was right behind him, followed by Chace in her veil, her mother, her Aunt Tammy, and all of her bridesmaids. Vendors and shoppers were squealing and shouting as the wedding party raced by.

Crystal darted to the left down another aisle and bumped into a woman carrying a basket of carnations. Flowers went flying everywhere. Crystal didn't stop.

Jess caught up with the dressmaker as he

lunged for Crystal, trying to grab the dress. He lost his balance and stumbled to the floor, grasping the skirt. Much to his horror, the fishtail skirt began tearing away at the seam. "Noooo," he cried out in anguish.

Crystal gathered up the skirt and kept running. There was a crowd of horrified onlookers standing in the aisle to the right. Jess was catching up. Crystal had come to the end of the aisle. In a panic, she went to her left heading for the exit. She turned to look at Jess and didn't see the catering trolley with a three tier wedding cake coming out of a side entrance. As she turned back, she hit the trolley, smashing into the cake. Crystal, the trolley, and the cake went down to the ground.

At that moment, Jess dove forward as if she were stealing home plate. She landed on top of Crystal who was covered in buttercream frosting. The bride and groom cake topper was wedged into the neckline of her dress.

Jess was breathing hard. She had Crystal pinned to the floor, like a wrestler. She was straddling the woman, afraid to ease up on her grasp. "What are you doing here?" she asked between breaths.

"I thought y'all came to the expo yesterday!" Crystal yelled in exasperation.

Chace and her bridesmaids caught up to the pair on the floor. "I got the whole thing on video,"

Conlie announced proudly.

"Let me go!" Crystal demanded, struggling.

"Not until we get some answers," Jess said.

The dressmaker stepped up, hands on hips and looked down at Crystal. "Well I guess you're buying that dress," he commented. "Will that be cash or credit card?"

Two security guards arrived to help the ladies up from the floor and assess the situation.

"Call the police," Jess said. "This woman is wanted for murder in Bonner County."

CHAPTER 23 – SUNDAY, FEBRUARY 11

12:30 p.m.

An hour later, Jess and the group were on the road, heading back to Grace. Police had been called to the scene and had taken Crystal into custody. Jess couldn't wait to talk to Chris about this development. She was still feeling pumped up on adrenaline as she drove. The group was buzzing.

Conlie had the camera and was replaying the video for everyone to see.

"You are a real hero," Chace said to Jess proudly. "I can't believe that girl murdered Donna Vance!" She reached over from the passenger seat and brushed some icing off Jess's arm. "Oh my gosh, you are still covered in that frosting!"

"You should have seen how you just tackled her," Taylor said excitedly. "I couldn't have done that."

"I am literally starving to death," Kennedy said. "Can't we stop for lunch?"

"We need to get back in time to get ready for the shower," Jess said.

"There's a Whataburger," Madison said, pointing ahead to the right.

"I want Whataburger," Conlie called out. "Let's just go in the drive-thru?"

Feeling a bit peckish herself, Jess relented. They went to the drive-thru and ate on the way home.

Back in Grace, Jess dropped the wedding party off at the hotel and drove back to Ms. Melody's house. She saw that the Grace PD Squad car was already there. She walked in through the kitchen door, where Ms. Melody had boarded up the broken pane of glass.

"Her real name is Morgan Field," Officer Frick said, as Jess entered the room. "We have her in custody."

Jess came in and slung the camera bag onto a chair. "Hey everybody," she said.

"It's the hero of the hour," Ms. Melody sang out when she saw Jess. "We're hearing about your daring capture of the killer."

"Alleged killer," Connor corrected.

"We were just briefing the family on the take down of Morgan Field, also known as Crystal Clearwater," Frick said. She then looked at Jess quizzically. "There's something in your hair," she said, pointing.

Jess felt her hair and gave a little laugh. "Oh, it's frosting from the wedding cake that Crystal fell into." She started trying to wipe it out.

"Wait," Frick admonished. She whipped out an evidence bag from her pocket. "Let me bag that as evidence," she said, attempting to save some of the frosting.

"That won't be necessary," Connor said, stifling a smirk.

"I need to show you something," Jess said to Chris. She took the camera out of the bag and scrolled to the pictures of Crystal on the bed.

Garrett stood up. "May I please have my camera back?"

Chris asked, "Are these pictures of the suspect?"

Garrett hurried over. "Those are private," he said, interrupting and reaching for the camera.

"Hold on just a moment," Chris said as he held the camera out of reach, "when were these photos taken?"

"That is none of your business," Garrett said indignantly.

"What's going on here?" Virginia asked.

"They won't give my camera back," Garrett pouted like a petulant child.

Officer Frick came around behind Chris and caught a glimpse of the pictures. Her mouth dropped open. "That's our suspect, nekkid as a jaybird," she exclaimed.

"Naked?" Virginia said with surprise. "You have naked pictures of Crystal?"

Garrett turned red in the face. "Those are not for anyone else to see."

"Mr. Neilson, We're going to have to take you in for more questioning," Chris said.

"There's nothing going on, I just took some photos, that's all," Garrett said. "I'm a professional photographer."

Officer Frick took Garrett by the arm. "Mr. Neilson, if you'll just come with me," she said, leading him toward the kitchen door.

Garrett started crying. "No, I didn't do anything." But he went willingly.

"I'll need to take the camera into evidence," Chris said.

"But I have all the pictures from the expo on there," Jess protested, "and all the other pictures for the magazine story."

"You'll get it back," Chris said.

"I want to see those," Virginia said, angling to get a look at the camera.

"You don't need to see the pictures," Chris said. "I'll be in touch."

"Yeah, I've heard that before," Virginia said.

Jess followed Chris outside. Officer Frick was easing Garrett into the backseat of the squad car.

"What did Crystal say?" Jess asked.

"I can't tell you that," Chris said.

"Do you think she and Garrett were having an affair? Do you think they worked together to poison Donna?"

"No comment," Chris said as he got into the car and slammed the door. As an afterthought he rolled down the window. "I'll pick you up at 3:30 for the shower."

Jess smiled, "I'll be here.

"Oh, and good job tackling the suspect. It's all over Channel 11."

Back in the house Virginia was on the phone at the kitchen table when Jess came in. "The police just took him away," she said into the phone.

Jess went past her and into the den, where she turned on the television and switched it to Channel 11. The announcer said, "Keep it here on eleven, your go to station for news. When you want news, go to eleven."

The anchor then announced that a suspect had been apprehended in connection to Donna's death and they went live to the reporter on the scene. She was standing in front of the Juniper ISD multi-purpose arena. "Leigh Ballou here, at the Bridal Expo where earlier today, a suspect in the murder of Donna Vance was apprehended." They switched to a grainy video of Jess tackling Crystal.

"We obtained this cell phone footage of the altercation," Leigh said. "I'm here with the wedding dress designer…"

Ms. Melody came in and Jess turned off the television.

"That was quite a daring capture," she said, "are you okay?"

"Just a little frosting in my hair."

"I don't know what to think. Did Crystal poison Donna? Was Garrett in on it?"

"That's just what I was wondering," Jess said.

Virginia came into the room. "That was Dean on the phone. He and I are going to the shower. We want to make sure this story is handled right, and you better get that camera back." She pointed at Jess as if she were at fault. Then she walked out of the room.

At three o'clock Jess was showered and dressed and was in the middle of fixing her hair when Ms. Melody came upstairs with a wrapped gift.

"I have to go pick up your Aunt Patsy for the shower. She wants to be early, and she said you have a date."

"Thank you, yes, I'm going with Chris Connor."

"Well that's nice," Ms. Melody said. "His partner, Beverly Frick, just brought Garrett back."

"They released him?" Jess asked incredulously.

"Beverly told me he admitted to an affair but said that was it. She doesn't think he was in on it."

"She told you all that? I can't get Chris to tell me anything," Jess said.

"Technically, she let it slip. I gave her some of my homemade snickerdoodles," Ms. Melody said.

"I never would have thought Garrett and Crystal were fooling around." Jess shook her head. "I guess she's not really Crystal."

"No, it's Morgan... something," Ms. Melody said.

"So, where is Garrett now?"

"He's outside sulking and cleaning out his SUV. I don't know what possessed me to try to run a B&B." Ms. Melody turned to leave. "Oh, and here," she thrust the wrapped gift at Jess, "This is a blender. It's a better shower gift than that silly movie poster you got from Shaun."

"I don't need you to provide me with wedding gifts," Jess said indignantly as Ms. Melody descended the outside steps and waved goodbye.

"You're welcome," Ms. Melody called out.

When Jess got downstairs, with the blender,

Garrett was in the driveway with his head in the backseat of the SUV. "Did you girls eat hamburgers in my car?" he asked angrily as he peeled lettuce off the back seat and tossed it onto the ground.

"Yeah, sorry. I guess it was a little messy," Jess said.

"I suppose you heard everything?" he said. With disgust, he swept some spilled fries off the floor and out onto the gravel.

Jess stashed the blender in the backseat of her car, right next to the wrapped, framed movie poster. "Ms. Melody just told me they brought you back. So, what happened at the police station?"

Garrett held up one hand and pursed his lips. "Okay, I admit it, I had a fling with Crystal but that doesn't make me a killer. It was a mistake and I broke it off with her. I told her I couldn't live with myself and we had to stop."

"When did you end things with Crystal?"

"That night, after the bachelorette party," he said. "She must have put poison in those smoothies out of jealousy. The girl is in love with me."

"Did you know that Crystal was really the bride from the Soggy Bottom video?"

Garrett nearly came to tears again, "No, I did not. She tricked all of us. My poor Donna!" He closed the passenger side door and moved around to the driver's side to get in.

Jess wondered if his tears were just an act. "Did Donna know about your affair?"

"Of course not. Anyway, what's with all the questions? I've already been grilled by the police." Garrett peered at Jess dubiously. "You think I was in on it with Crystal, don't you?"

"I didn't say that," Jess said defensively. "Anyway, where are you going? Aren't you coming to the couple's shower to take pictures?"

Garrett pursed his lips and gave Jess an angry look. "No I am not coming to the couple's shower! In case you haven't noticed, my wife just died. Besides, the police still have my camera so you're just going to have to handle this on your own." With that, Garrett stepped into the vehicle and slammed the door.

Jess watched as Garrett drove away. Then she went inside the house to wait for her date.

Inside Virginia was watching out the window. "I've got my eye on that bastard, and I'll tell you right now, he's getting no part of Mom's estate."

"Did she have a will?"

"She did. Her lawyer in Dallas has it. But she also had a prenup and that jackass cheated on her!" Virginia said.

"I don't know if a prenup applies in this situation. Isn't it for divorce?"

"If they got divorced, he would get nothing. Since his little piece of trash on the side murdered my mother, I don't think he's entitled to anything," Virginia was furious. "I have to talk to Dean about this."

"Do you know where Garrett is going?"

"Don't know. Don't care," Virginia answered. "Hey, I'm going to need directions to this old farmhouse. It's not coming up on my GPS."

Jess got out some paper from the kitchen drawer. "I'll draw you a map." She sketched out a map and handed it to Virginia. The doorbell rang. "That's probably my date. I'll see you at the shower," Jess said.

Jess greeted Chris at the door. "Why don't we take my car?" she suggested.

Chris opened the car door for her and then went around to the passenger side. He noticed the wrapped gifts in the back. "Oh, wait, let me grab my gift," he said. He retrieved it from his car and placed it in the back seat along with the others.

"You didn't have to bring a gift," Jess said.

"Well, I did get an invitation to the wedding," he said. "So did Officer Frick, as a matter of fact."

"I think they've invited half the town. What'd you get them?"

"It's a set of steak knives," Chris said. "I didn't have time to order from the registry and I didn't know what they needed."

"I'm sure it's a lovely gift."

They drove in silence for a while. "So, you've arrested Crystal?" Jess asked.

"Morgan Field is being held in custody. That's all I can say."

"It seems odd that she would work for Donna for three years, have an affair with Garrett, and then poison Donna for revenge," Jess speculated. "Was she really in love with Garrett?"

"She had motive, but I really can't comment about it," Chris said.

"Why did she let Donna push her around for all that time?" Jess asked.

"That's not really for me to say," he said.

"You're very tight-lipped today," she said with a pout.

Chris smiled mischievously. "No comment," was all he said.

CHAPTER 24 – SUNDAY, FEBRUARY 11

3:45 p.m.

When she pulled into the long dirt road leading to Aunt Patsy's house, Jess could already see the difference the renovations had made. The entire house had a fresh coat of paint and a new railing had been built on the front porch. The lawn had been mowed and a white arch stood in front of the porch steps.

"It's gorgeous," Jess commented. "I'll bet Aunt Patsy is over the moon."

"It's a beautiful old house," Chris said in agreement.

Jess parked and they went inside. Most of Aunt Patsy's furniture had been moved to other rooms to make more space in the front parlor and dining room. There were white folding chairs lining the parlor and flowers everywhere.

Luckily, the weather had cooperated with temperatures in the mid-sixties. The bridesmaids wore their floral print dresses and cardigans from the photo shoot. Jess had opted for a light green sweater and tan slacks. The men were in khakis and oxford shirts.

Tanya Perez was there with an older, gray-haired, Hispanic woman. *That must be Chace's abuela*, Jess thought.

The theme for the shower was high tea. Aunt Patsy's cherry wood dining table was covered in a white linen table cloth and spread with an array of finger sandwiches, scones, and French madeleine cookies arranged on beautiful three-tiered china serving towers. The sideboard housed a silver tea service and several china cups and saucers in a variety of styles and colors. Aunt Patsy was perched on her electric scooter near the sideboard.

"Jess, there you are my darling girl," she cried with her hands up for a hug. "Come over here and give me some sugar."

Jess went over and gave her great aunt a kiss on the cheek. "Aunt Patsy, the house looks great. I believe you know detective Chris Connor."

Chris bent down to shake Aunt Patsy's hand. "It's a pleasure to see you again," he said.

"You know this is my house," Aunt Patsy said, beaming. "It's been in my family for almost a hundred years. That sweet girl, Chace, wanted to have her wedding here and I said, why not."

"They've really fixed the place up," Jess said.

"Oh, a lick of paint here and there and it's good as new," Aunt Patsy said. "Did y'all bring a present?"

"Oh no, we left them in the car," Jess said.

"I'll go get them," Chris offered. He took Jess's key and went back outside.

"Let me get over to the table and grab me one of them finger sandwiches," Aunt Patsy said. "I feel just like *downtown abbey*."

Jess helped her get a plate and find a spot near a tray table in the parlor. Chace was there with her mother and grandmother.

"Oh, Ms. Patsy," Chace sang out. "I don't think you've met my Aunt Tammy yet, or my abuela. Yaya, this is Ms. Patsy. This is her house. Patsy, this is my grandmother, Lucrecia Perez. She comes from Saltillo, in Mexico."

While Chace made introductions, Chris came back and returned the key. "I put the gifts with the others." He pointed toward the front hall where the gifts were arranged on a table near the staircase.

"I've been telling everybody what a hero you are," Chace said to Jess. She turned to the others and bragged, "Jess single handedly captured that girl who murdered Donna Vance."

"Allegedly," Chris interjected.

"Well now, nobody's told me about that," Aunt Patsy said with surprise. "What did you do Jess?"

Jess began explaining, trying to downplay the incident so Aunt Patsy wouldn't worry.

"Show them the video Jess," Conlie called out

from across the room.

"Actually, I don't have it with me...."

"You'll get the camera back tomorrow," Chris said.

Jack strode into the house with Guy and the other groomsmen.

"We're here. Let's get this party started," Guy announced to the room in general.

Jack came over to the group in the corner and gave Chace a kiss on the cheek. Then he noticed Detective Connor. "Oh, hello detective. Is everything all right?" he asked.

"Everything is fine, and you can call me Chris."

"What brings you here?" Jack asked with a look of concern.

"Jack, don't be rude. He's a guest," Chace admonished.

Jess put her arm around Chris. It was a stretch to reach his shoulders as he was much taller. She ended up just patting him on the back. "Chris is my date," Jess said proudly.

"Well, well. This is new," Jack said with amusement. "How long has this been going on?"

"Actually...," Chris began.

At that moment, Virginia and Dean walked in the front door. "We had a hell of a time finding this place," Virginia announced. She glared at Jess, "That map you gave me was garbage."

Chace looked flustered. "Well, I'm so glad you did find it."

"Come on Dean. I need a drink," Virginia said, as she stalked off to the dining room.

Ms. Erika and Avery came in through the kitchen, each with two warm pies. "Good afternoon everyone," Erika announced, "Today I'm debuting a new berry pie in honor of Chace and Jack. I call it the *Miss America Pie*. It's got raspberries, strawberries, and blueberries."

Chace got up and came over to the table where Erika and Avery set out the desserts. "Oh my goodness! They're so pretty!" Chace called out. "Everybody come look."

The pie crust on top was in the shape of stars of various sizes. The blue and red berries, along with the stars, made for a very patriotic look. "And we have ice cream," Avery said. She brought out a carton of Blue Bell Homemade Vanilla and a scoop.

"I just love them," Chace cooed. She gave Ms. Erika a hug. "Somebody take a picture of these pies."

Several people took cell phone pictures and then everyone wanted a slice.

"Miss America Pie?" Virginia said, "But you're not Miss America."

"Well, I know but, it's like the song, you

know," Chace tried to explain.

Conlie began singing, "Bye Bye Miss America Pie, rode my Chevy to the levy..." Several people joined in.

"I see coffee and tea but where's the hooch?" Virginia asked loudly, putting an end to the singing.

"There's no alcohol at a high tea," Madison said.

"Whatever happened to whiskey in a teacup?" Virginia asked.

"It's fine," Dean said, handing Virginia a cup of earl grey.

"Jess, you need to be taking pictures since Garrett's not around," Virginia said pointedly.

Jess went around taking photos with her cell phone of the gifts, the decorations, the food, and some group pictures. Chris took a seat next to Aunt Patsy. Jess gave him a wave as she got a photo of the bridesmaids holding tea cups.

Taylor asked, "Are you here with that tall guy over there? He's a hottie."

"Yes, I am," Jess answered, glancing back toward Chris who was having a conversation with her Aunt Patsy. "He's a police detective."

"Oh we know. He questioned all of us the day after the bachelorette party," Kennedy said. She admired him from across the room. "He sure is a tall drink of water."

Jess chuckled nervously.

Everyone got pie and settled in. Then Jack and Chace began opening gifts. Jess took a seat between Aunt Patsy and Chris.

Chris handed her a dessert plate. "Here, I saved you a slice of pie," he said.

"Thanks," she whispered gratefully.

Each gift was opened to a chorus of oohs and aahs. Madison dutifully listed the gifts and who they were from for thank you notes.

Chris leaned over and whispered incredulously, "Is this really all we do, watch them open gifts?"

"Pretty much, and there's pie," Jess said. She took another bite of the Miss America Pie, which was delicious.

The couple opened the steak knives Chris had brought. "Oh thank you," Chace said, tilting her head a little, "you are so sweet." Jess's blender was met with a similar response.

Jack and Chace were seated near the gift table and Conlie was passing gifts to them one by one. She reached behind the table and pulled out the large framed poster. Conlie read the tag, "This one is from Jess."

"Oh no," Jess whispered.

Ms. Melody leaned across Aunt Patsy and whispered to Jess, "I told you to bring the blender."

"I did," Jess whispered back. "She already opened it."

"Did I bring out the wrong thing?" Chris asked. "There were two presents from you."

It was too late. Chace had removed the ribbon and was tearing the paper away to reveal the movie poster for *Bridesmaids* with the cast in hot pink dresses against a brick wall. "Oh," Chace said looking quizzically at the picture. "It's a movie poster." She was at a loss for words.

Jack laughed. "Interesting choice," he said looking at Jess.

"Cool movie," Conlie said.

"I don't think I ever saw that movie," Chace said.

"It's the one where they all throw up," Madison said.

"It's... I can return..." Jess began, shaking her head with embarrassment.

"Oh don't be silly. I love it," Chace said, "it's so funny." She handed the poster to Jack. "Here Honey, why don't you just set that down over there." She pointed to the spot behind the gift table.

"That did not go over well," Ms. Melody said. She stood and began to gather the torn wrapping paper.

Chris shrugged. "Sorry, I thought you wanted me to bring it in."

"No worries. You didn't know." Jess turned to her great aunt. "Aunt Patsy, do you want another cup of tea?"

"No thank you, I'm fine." Aunt Patsy changed the subject, "You know, Melody has been telling me about turning her house into a bed and breakfast. Maybe I should do something like that with this place."

"I don't know about that Aunt Patsy," Jess said. "Who would run it?"

"I can run it myself," Aunt Patsy said with indignation.

Jess noticed Avery and Ms. Erika clearing cups and plates. "I should go help with the dishes," she said. Jess brought the empty pie dishes into the kitchen. Ms. Erika was running some soapy water.

"Your Miss America Pies were a big hit," Jess said. "There's none left."

"I'm so glad everybody liked it," Ms. Erika said. "I saw some people out on the back porch a while ago. Can you see if there are any dishes out there?"

"Sure," Jess said. She went out onto the porch and picked up a tea cup that had been left on a bench. As she did she overheard a giggle. She glanced around the side of the house and saw Virginia and Dean. He stood behind her with his arms around her, nuzzling her neck.

"Stop it. Not now," Virginia said, giggling.

"What? Don't I get a kiss from my wife?" he asked.

Virginia turned and swatted his shoulder playfully, looking up at him. Jess quietly moved back around to the porch where she couldn't be seen.

"Just one kiss," Virginia said, "I'm not ready for people to find out about us just yet."

Jess went back inside, careful not to slam the door. Avery was in the kitchen packing up.

Chace and Taylor rushed in, giggling. "Jess, there you are," Chace said, "we've been looking all over."

"We want to have a girls' night in," Taylor said, "and I told Chace that movie, Bridesmaids, is a scream."

Chace continued excitedly, "So, we want to see if you want to join us, and Avery too?"

"I'm up for a movie night," Avery said.

"I hope we can get that movie at the hotel," Chace said.

"I have the Blu-ray. It's part of my Mom's movie collection," Jess said.

Chace's mouth fell open in delight, "We can hang out at Jess's apartment. She has the cutest little apartment! Oh, thank you Jess. I'll go tell everyone."

Chace and Taylor ran out of the kitchen.

Jess looked at Avery. "What just happened?" she asked.

"Looks like you're hosting a slumber party."

The Couple's Shower was winding down. After everything was cleaned up, Jess said her goodbyes to Aunt Patsy and Ms. Melody.

"I hope the weather stays nice for the wedding," Aunt Patsy said, as Jess helped her into the passenger seat of Melody's Ford Explorer. "They want to have the wedding outside on the front lawn."

"If it's like today, it will be perfect," Ms. Melody said.

"You be nice to that young man of yours," Aunt Patsy said to Jess.

Jess gave her great aunt a hug and shut the door. She looked around for Chris and saw him standing by her car.

"Shall we go?" he asked.

Jess got in and started the car.

"I've never been to a wedding shower before," Chris said.

"Well, now you can cross that off your bucket list," Jess said, smiling.

"There wasn't much in the way of food, though. How about we stop at the Grill and get some dinner?"

"Oh, I can't," Jess said. She glanced at him with disappointment, "I'm sorry, I wish I could."

"Okay," he said slowly, "I just thought..." His voice trailed off and he looked out the window. It was already dark out.

"It's just that Chace and the bridesmaids are coming over for a movie night. I wasn't planning on it, but she basically just invited everyone over to my place."

"Yeah, I get it," Chris said flatly.

There was a cold silence.

"What? I said I'm sorry," Jess said defensively. She glanced over at him. His face had hardened.

"Why did you ask me to this thing today? This wedding shower?" he asked.

Jess was at a loss for words. She sighed, "I don't know, I like you, I wanted to get to know you." It sounded more like a question than an answer.

Chris sighed. "You pretty much ignored me the whole time." He paused. "Oh, except for when Jack was around, then you were all over me."

Jess was indignant. "That's not true," she insisted.

"Admit it, Jess. You just brought me there to make your ex jealous."

"No, that's not it at all," Jess said, shaking her head. She gripped the steering wheel tighter. "You're the one who said maybe we should go out sometime. That was weeks ago and then you never asked me out."

"I've been busy. In case you hadn't noticed, we were in the middle of a murder case."

"Well, now we're in the middle of another one." Jess took a deep breath. "The reason I was 'all over you' as you say is because I wanted to show everybody that I've gotten over Jack, especially those stupid bridesmaids." As soon as she said it, Jess regretted it.

Chris was floored. "Oh, is that the reason?" he asked sarcastically. "Well, that makes it all okay then."

"No, I didn't mean it like that," Jess said. It was too late. The damage was done. She drove the rest of the way in silence. When she pulled into Ms. Melody's driveway, Chris got out of the car.

"I'll walk you to your door."

"You don't have to do that," Jess said angrily. She got out and walked up the steps to her door. Chris followed, not saying a word.

When she put her keys in and opened the

door she turned to him. "Okay, here I am, safe and sound," she said.

"Have a nice evening, Miss Hart," he said as he turned to leave.

"Yeah, you too," she said as she slammed the door behind her.

CHAPTER 25 – SUNDAY, FEBRUARY 11

7:15 p.m.

Jess fumed as she began tidying up her apartment for the impending girls' night. *Chris was taking everything the wrong way. She wasn't ignoring him the whole time and she certainly wasn't all over him, like he said. Was she?*

She found her Blu-ray of *Bridesmaids* and set it near the machine. Then she checked her refrigerator. She had nothing in the way of party food. She did have plenty of microwave popcorn and figured they could always order pizza. But there was no beer and no snacks.

She glanced at the time. The girls would be coming over in about an hour. *Guess I'm making a beer run,* Jess decided, as she grabbed her keys.

At the Brookshire Brothers grocery store Jess picked up some light beer and a variety pack of hard seltzer. She added a few bags of chips, some dips, and a couple of twelve-packs of soda. Then she decided on a gallon of decaf iced tea for Chace. *I am not helping her pretend to get drunk again,* Jess thought.

As she was coming into the produce section to get some lemons for the tea, she saw Virginia and Dean shopping together. *Secretly married,* Jess mused. *This just gets curiouser and curiouser.*

"Hi Jess," Virginia called out, "Dean and I are getting some drinks and snacks for a late night pow-wow about Mom's company. I might be late getting back to the house."

"Okay. I'll let Ms. Melody know," Jess said. She wondered why they were keeping their relationship a secret. "Where are you staying, Dean?"

"I'm at the Oasis Motel. Not a bad place." Dean smiled widely, showing off his stark white teeth. "We have a lot to go over with this new paradigm shift. I want to take Donna Vance Enterprises to the next level, but we're not sure what that looks like yet." He was gesturing with his hands as he spoke.

Jess's head was spinning from all of the corporate jargon. "When you say paradigm shift, do you mean because Donna died?"

"We don't have to go into all of this with Jess," Virginia interrupted.

Dean shifted gears. "Do you happen to have your phone with you? I need to take a look at the pictures you got at the shower?"

"Sure," Jess said. She handed her phone over. Dean began scrolling through the photos.

"Oh no, no," he said. He handed the phone back to Jess. "You got some cute shots, but the quality is not up to par."

Jess bristled at this a little.

Dean continued. "We need to loop Garrett back in on this project."

"Garrett is an ass," Virginia interjected. "His playing around got my mother killed."

Dean nodded. "I know how you feel about him, but he is a professional photographer."

Virginia rolled her eyes. "Whatever," she said.

"I'll reach out to him," Dean said. "Jess, I'll have him meet you at the Gazette tomorrow for the spa day."

"Fine," Jess said. "I need to get going."

"Oh, are you having a party?" Virginia asked looking into Jess's cart.

"No, just my regular weekly shopping," Jess said as she turned away. "See y'all tomorrow."

When she got home, Ms. Melody was just arriving after dropping off Aunt Patsy. "Oh, I thought you would still be out with Detective Connor," she said.

Jess sighed. "We had a little fight," she said.

"Oh no. How come?"

"It was stupid but, anyway, the bridesmaids are coming over in a little while for a movie night. We're going to watch *Bridesmaids*. Do you want to come?"

"Oh, no thank you. I hated that movie. All that vomiting was just gross."

"Oh, by the way, I ran into Virginia at the Brookshire Brothers' store. She's coming back late tonight, FYI." Jess considered telling Ms. Melody about Virginia and Dean's secret marriage but decided against it.

They both noticed Garrett's SUV was back. Ms. Melody sighed. "I can't believe I let you and Shaun talk me into this cockamamie B&B idea," she muttered.

At that moment, Avery pulled up in her Hyundai Santa Fe. "Am I the first one here?" she asked as she got out. "I brought some mini chocolate pies," she said, bringing out a bag from the Pie Hole. "I don't know if anybody wants sweets after the shower."

"You can never have too much pie. Thank you," Jess said. "I got some drinks and chips and I thought we could order pizza."

"You girls have fun," Ms. Melody said. She made her way to the house, sighing reluctantly about having to face Garrett.

"Here, let me help you with the groceries," Avery said. Sweet Tea followed them inside with her tail swishing from side to side.

They set out the chips and dips and put the drinks into a bucket of ice on the kitchen bar. Then the two of them sat down with a beer.

"I think the shower went well," Avery said. "Aunt Patsy's house looks amazing."

"It does, doesn't it?" Jess said. "So, I found out something weird. Dean Cartwright and Virginia Vance are secretly married."

"What? When did that happen?"

"No idea, but I heard them talking about it outside the house. I also saw them at the grocery store just now."

Jess heard footsteps coming up the side stairs and a knock on the door, followed by a burst of giggles. She let everyone in.

Kennedy held up a bottle of Rose' wine she had brought. "Rose' all day," she said as she set it on the counter.

"So, I'm going to order pizza," Jess said.

"Awesome. I am literally starving to death," Kennedy said.

"Can we order a veggie pizza?" Madison asked

Jess got everybody's preferences and put in an order for delivery. They wanted four medium pizzas; two pepperoni, one veggie, and one pineapple with Canadian bacon.

Taylor picked out a black cherry seltzer. "Hey Chace, you want one of these?" she asked.

"I also have iced tea. It's decaf," Jess interjected.

"I think I'll stick to iced tea tonight," Chace said. "We do have that spa day in the morning and I don't want a hangover." She went into the kitchen where Jess was filling a glass with ice. *Thank you,* Chace mouthed.

Everybody settled into watch the movie and Jess put a bag of popcorn in the microwave. Chace sat on the end of the sofa by Sweet Tea. "Your cat is so pretty," she said, rubbing Sweet Tea behind the ears. "Yes you are," she said in baby talk to the cat. Sweet Tea rubbed up against her shoulder and then curled up in Chace's lap.

"I can't believe you've never seen this movie," Conlie said. "It's a comedy classic."

Kennedy came up to the kitchen bar and poured herself a glass of wine. "I didn't particularly want to watch this movie tonight," she said, "but Chace always gets her way."

"Well, she is the bride," Avery said.

"Oh, I'm not trying to be ugly about it. It's fine," Kennedy said. She tossed her long red curls and selected a potato chip.

Jess sensed some resentment on Kennedy's part. "How long have you and Chace been friends?"

"We were roommates at Sam Houston State," Kennedy said. "We were both on the drill team and both in Alpha Chi Omega. Ya know, Chi-Oh 'til you die-oh." She made a symbol crossing her index fingers with her thumbs touching. "And we were both in the Miss Sam Houston Pageant."

"What is Miss Sam Houston?" Avery asked.

"That's the beauty contest Chace won before she went on to the Miss Texas beauty contest," Jess said. She had done her research.

"It's a scholarship pageant," Kennedy corrected. "Chace knew I wanted to compete so she decided to give it a go too. Our sorority chose her instead of me, so she was *Miss Alpha Chi Omega*."

"But you were also in the pageant?" Jess asked.

"Yes, I was President of the Association of Information Technology Professionals on campus, so I entered as *Miss Technology*."

"That must have been awkward for the two of you, competing against each other," Avery said.

"We were friends. We thought it was all just for fun," Kennedy said. "But then, she won and I was the first runner up. I had the title of *Miss Piney Woods*. That's what they call the runner up." Kennedy did finger quotes. She laughed a little fake laugh and tossed her hair back. "I mean, it's no big deal, but if Chace hadn't entered, I would have been Miss Texas."

"Good thing you're not still bitter about it," Conlie said. She had come up behind Kennedy quietly.

Kennedy was startled. "Oh, Conlie, I didn't see you there. I'm just getting some chips." Kennedy picked up the bowl of potato chips and carried it over to the sofa.

"I gotta keep my eye on that one," Conlie said with a wink.

"She was just telling us about Miss Sam Houston," Jess said. "You need another beer?"

"No, I'm good," Conlie said. "The thing is, Kennedy's not wrong. Chace does get what she wants. The problem is, what she wants isn't always what she needs." She opened a bag of pretzels on the counter and began munching.

"How do you mean?" Avery asked.

"Like all the attention she got when she was Miss Texas. It was fun at first, but then she felt like she was always on display," Conlie said. "It's a thin line between basking in the limelight and feeling scrutinized."

"So, she didn't really want to be Miss America, did she?" Jess asked.

Conlie considered this for a moment. "I don't think she did. You should check out her talent video. Then tell me what you think."

"What do you do, Conlie?" Avery asked.

"I'm in a band. I play guitar and sing. It's an

indie rock band in Austin," she said.

"I live in Austin. I'm at the Laurent Institute. It's a culinary school." Avery said.

"Oh yeah, I know that school," Conlie said. "You should check us out sometime. We're called *Infinite Abyss*."

"Where do you play?" Avery asked.

"Conlie, are you talking about your band?" Chace called from the sofa. "Come over here. I know I've seen this actress somewhere." She had paused the movie on a close up of Melissa McCarthy.

Conlie returned to her seat and the movie resumed.

When the pizza arrived, they paused again while everyone got a slice.

"I don't know if I can eat anything after that food poisoning scene," Chace commented as she took a bite of the Canadian bacon.

"That was so gross," Kennedy said.

Jess changed the subject, "So, what's everyone having done at the salon tomorrow?"

Madison spoke up, "We're all getting manicures and pedicures and facials."

"I'm having a hot oil treatment for my hair," Kennedy said.

"Should I get a haircut?" Taylor asked.

"What are we going to do with your hair, Conlie?" Chace asked, picking at her sisters platinum mop.

"Stop it," Conlie said, shaking her head. "You don't like my hair?"

"It's not that, it's just…" Chace didn't know what to say.

"We could put in some pink and blue streaks and you could be Harley Quinn," Kennedy said.

"No," Chace said horrified. "Don't do that!"

"Nah, I think I'll go back to my natural brown color," Conlie said, "I don't want to upstage the bride."

"Really?" Chace asked. "You'll do that for me?"

"Of course. Besides, I'm getting tired of the whole shocking blonde with dark roots thing. It's so last year," Conlie said with a smile.

"Jess, are you bringing that cute cop with you to the wedding?" Taylor asked.

"You should bring him. He was so nice when he came to talk to all of us after the bachelorette party," Madison said.

"He can question me anytime he wants," Kennedy said.

"Actually, I don't think we're going together," Jess said. "He's kind of mad at me."

This statement was met with a chorus of concerned exclamations from the group; "What?" "No?" "Why?"

"What happened?" Chace asked sympathetically.

Jess realized she couldn't tell them their entire argument. "We had a disagreement on the way home from the shower."

"Oh no," Taylor said.

"Do I need to beat him up?" Avery asked jokingly.

"No," Jess laughed. "It's just that he wanted to go out for a late dinner but I said I was having a girls' night."

"Oh my goodness! You didn't!" Madison said.

"You should have had dinner with him," Chace said. "We could have done this some other time."

"He really got mad about that?" Conlie asked.

"You have to text him," Taylor said.

"Oh, I don't know about that," Jess said.

"Tell him you want to go out on a real date," Avery said.

"How about we start the movie up again? Does anybody need another drink?" Jess asked, changing the subject.

Everybody grabbed another slice of pizza, while acknowledging that they really shouldn't, and settled in to finish the movie. Jess got her plate and an iced tea and took a seat at her desk chair. She thought about texting Chris but what would she say? She cringed remembering their conversation in the car.

She keyed in *I'm sorry* with a frowny face emoji. Then she backspaced over it. Then she texted.

Jess: *I'm sorry we argued. Can we start over?*

Chris: ...

Jess watched the dots for a minute. He didn't text back. She put the phone down and tried to concentrate on the movie. Kristen Wiig and Rose Byrne were trying to catch the attention of the policeman, played by Chris O'Dowd.

"Your cop is a lot better looking than this guy," Kennedy commented to Jess.

Everyone laughed. Jess checked her phone. Still no text back. She waited another minute. Then she texted again.

Jess: *By the way, Dean and Virginia are secretly married.*

Jess: *To each other.*

She put her phone down. *This is ridiculous*, she thought. She got up and went behind the kitchen bar. "Who wants some chocolate pie?" she asked.

"I'll take one," Conlie said.

"I don't really care for chocolate," Chace said.

Everybody got their pie, except for Chace, and sat back down to finish the movie.

During the ending credits Jess asked, "So, what did you think of the movie?"

"I hated it," Madison said. "It was stupid."

"I stand by what I said earlier. It's a comedy classic," Conlie said.

"But it was gross," Kennedy complained.

Chace looked thoughtful before delivering her verdict. "It was okay, I guess. It's not really my kind of thing." Then she smiled. "But I had so much fun tonight. You gals are the best."

Everyone said their goodbyes and filed out the door. Avery stayed behind to help tidy up.

"Interesting bunch," Avery said as she gathered up paper plates and napkins.

"Yeah, that Kennedy is a piece of work."

"I know, right? Can you believe her?"

Jess ran some water to hand wash the glasses and began putting the extra canned drinks into the fridge. "So, Chace beat out Kennedy and went on to become Miss Texas. I guess I'll leave that part out of my article."

Avery brought over the forks and set them into the hot water. "What was it Conlie said? We should watch the talent video from the Miss America pageant?"

Jess turned off the water and set some glasses in. "You know, Donna mentioned that I should watch that video too," she said. She dried her hands and they both went over to the desk.

Jess looked up the YouTube video of Chace Perez doing her talent competition at the Miss America pageant. The video showed Chace, her hair was longer and curled at the ends. She wore a long shimmery red ball gown and high heels. She looked amazing as she walked out onto the stage and stood at the microphone. The music started and Chace launched into a heartfelt rendition of the country song *Jesus Take the Wheel*. It was impressive. Chace had an incredible vocal range. Right before she reached the crescendo, Chace lifted her arms and threw her head back, singing with pure joy. She stepped back a little bit and then stumbled and fell to the floor. The crowd gasped and the host of the show ran over to help her up. Chace put her hands to her face, flustered. "I tripped on my dress," Chace said, "I'm so sorry." With that she ran off the stage.

"Oh, poor thing," Avery said. "She has such a beautiful singing voice."

Jess ran the video back a few seconds so they could re-watch the moment where Chace tripped.

"Look at her feet," she said, pointing.

They both looked closely at Chace's feet this time. Her dress swayed a bit when she moved back, but she had not stepped on her hem. Then her right knee bent and she went down.

"Wow," Jess said. "Chace actually took a fall."

Avery shook her head. "Why would she do that on purpose?"

"Unbelievable! She threw the Miss America Pageant."

CHAPTER 26 – MONDAY, FEBRUARY 12

6:30 a.m.

Jess got up early. She wanted to get to the Gazette before the spa day to show Bob what she had so far on the story. She opened her refrigerator and was greeted with an abundance of canned drinks and leftover pizza. "I'll pick up something for breakfast later," she thought.

She got her phone off the charger. Still no text from Chris.

After a quick shower, Jess gathered up her laptop bag. When she opened her front door, she saw a big bouquet of pink and red roses with lilies, along with a Valentine card and a box of candy on the picnic table of her upstairs deck. *Oh my*, she thought, *when did he leave this?*

Jess brought the gifts inside and read the card. It said:

Jess, I'm sorry for being such a grouch. We got off on the wrong foot and I would like to make it up to you. How about dinner?   ~Chris

Jess was delighted. The flowers were in a pretty pink vase. Jess set them in the middle of her kitchen table. She tucked the chocolates under one arm and left for work.

Jess drove by the front of the Gazette office. People had left more flowers, small Texas flags, pictures, and handmade posters along the front windows in honor of Donna Vance. She parked in the back and came in.

Wanda called out to her from the coffee bar in the corner, "Did you see all that mess out there?" She waved in the direction of the front windows. "I'm about to go out and take a picture of it before I bring it all inside. We can't leave that stuff out there."

Jess set her box of chocolates down on the coffee bar and poured herself a cup. "It's quite impressive. I never realized she had that many fans."

"She was considered the Queen of Texas Chic," Wanda said.

"Would you like a chocolate?" Jess asked.

"I better not. I'm trying to watch my figure," Wanda said.

"Valentine candy? Did you get a new boyfriend?" Clarence asked, giving Jess a wink.

"They're from Detective Connor," Jess said as if it were no big deal.

"Oh," Wanda said with a swish of her skirt. "I didn't know you two were an item."

"Is he that new sheriff in town?" Clarence asked.

"He's not a sheriff," Jess said, "and we're just friends." She couldn't stop the big grin on her face.

"Sure, sure," Clarence said, looking at her dubiously from over the top of his glasses. He got up to pour himself a second cup of coffee. "I saw you on the TV news yesterday."

"Oh, me too. You were so brave," Wanda said.

Jess filled them in on the happenings at the expo.

Neither Bob nor Brittney had arrived yet, so Jess set up her laptop on the freelance table and began compiling the wedding story thus far. She wished she had Garrett's camera so she could pick out which photos to use.

Wanda went out to take pictures of the tributes to Donna Vance.

Jess went back to the coffee bar and opened her box of candy. She looked them over, not sure which one to choose because she had never mastered the art of knowing which filling was inside. She hated to bite into something with a strange flavor, like orange. She picked one up and was about to venture a bite when Clarence interrupted.

"We need to help her bring in all those flowers." He pointed to the front windows where they could see Wanda struggling with an armload of detritus.

Jess set her chocolate down on a napkin and

they all went out to the sidewalk to help carry in the flowers and other items left by Donna's fans.

"Did you get some good pictures?" Clarence asked.

"I sure did," Wanda answered.

Once inside Wanda began arranging the flowers around the office in various containers. Jess went back to work on her story and Clarence went back to his desk.

A moment later, Bob and Brittney came in the back door with a new carpet all rolled up for Brittney's office.

"Clarence," Bob called out. "Get over to the county lockup. I want to know if they're making an arrest for Donna's murder."

"I'm on it," Clarence said, as he gathered up his notebook and coat.

"Should I go too?" Jess asked hopefully.

"No, you're busy with the wedding story," Brittney said.

"Hey, Jess. Good job catching the suspect yesterday. I saw it on the news," Bob said before he and Brittney went into her office to lay out her new rug.

Jess wrote her story through the couple's shower and outlined the rest of the article. There was still the spa day today, then the rehearsal dinner on Tuesday, and the wedding on Wednesday. *I'll be glad when this is all over,* she thought.

She looked out the front windows. There were still several TV news vans parked around the square. She wished that she could be out there with the other journalists, covering the crime story.

She decided to call Chris. Maybe he would tell her what was going on with Crystal. *Not Crystal, Morgan Field,* Jess reminded herself. Her call went to voicemail. "Hi Chris. I wanted to say thank you for the nice valentines you left on my deck this morning. That was so sweet. And yes, I would like to go to dinner. How about Saturday, just the two of us? Give me a call later. I'm curious about what's going on with Crystal's ...." The voicemail beeped and an automated voice told her that she had run out of time.

It was after 9:00 a.m. now. Time to get ready for the spa day. Jess wondered if she should spring for a manicure herself. She texted Chace.

Jess: Meet me here at the Gazette office. Garrett is coming to take pictures.

Chace: Garrett is weird. Why don't you take the pics?

Jess: Dean says it has to be Garrett.

Speaking of Garrett, Jess thought, *where is he? Do I have to give him a wake-up call?* At that moment, Garrett walked in through the front door.

"Bad news," he announced as he worriedly

smoothed his mustache. "They're releasing Crystal."

Jess couldn't believe her ears. Before she could say anything her cell phone buzzed. It was Ms. Melody.

"Hey, Ms. Melody. Did you hear the news?"

"They are releasing Crystal. I can't believe it."

"What happened?" Jess asked.

"There wasn't enough evidence," Ms. Melody said. "Crystal, I mean Morgan Field, called me and she's on the way to the house now to pick up her things." Ms. Melody's voice rose with worry. "I'm stuck here at the store."

"Can't you leave? Where's Shaun?"

"It's his day off and I can't get him on the phone," Ms. Melody said. "Can you please go meet her at the house? She said she doesn't want to stay there anymore and frankly, I don't want her there either."

"I can't, I'm working on the magazine story."

"I don't want her in my house without somebody being there!" Ms. Melody almost shrieked. "She's a cold-hearted killer and Virginia is there now. It's just a nightmare!"

"Okay, I'll go now. I'll work it out." Jess clicked off. *Now what?* she thought.

Brittney was at the coffee bar. "Are these chocolates for everybody?" she asked.

"Oh, are there chocolates?" Garrett looked over with interest.

"Yes, help yourself," Jess said. She walked over to the coffee bar thinking, *maybe Brittney would help.* "So, Brittney," Jess said as she approached, "how would you like to go to the spa day with Chace and the bridesmaids this morning? You could take some notes. Garrett's getting the pictures, right Garrett?"

"Yes. I got my camera back from that Officer Frick lady this morning. She's the one who told me they were releasing that vile woman."

"Jess, are you asking for my help?" Brittney said pointedly.

"Yes, I'm sorry. Ms. Melody needs me to take care of something at home. It's kind of an emergency."

Brittney rolled her eyes. Begrudgingly she agreed. "Okay, I'll do you a favor, this time."

"Thank you so much. It's at 9:30 a.m. at the Serenity Salon. The bridal group will meet you here any minute." Jess grabbed her purse and headed out the back door.

At the house, Crystal, also known as Morgan, was waiting in the patrol car with Officer Frick. They got out of the car and met Jess at the door. Morgan pulled out her key to the house.

"I'll need to get that back from you," Jess said.

"Fine," Morgan said angrily, as she thrust the key into Jess's hand. "It's not like I would be using it anyway."

"Where will you be staying Ms. Field?" Frick asked. "You do know that you can't leave town."

Jess opened the door and they all went inside.

Morgan was aggravated. "I don't know where I'm staying. I just know that I can't stay here with Garrett and Virginia. I guess I'll get a motel room or something."

"Damn right you can't stay here," Virginia said as she emerged from the den where she had been watching the news. "This is outrageous! You should be in jail."

"Ma'am, please remain calm," Frick said, "The suspect is here to retrieve her belongings."

Jess went upstairs with Morgan and watched somberly while she packed her suitcase.

"I didn't kill Donna, in case anyone cares," she said crossly. "There was no poison in those smoothies."

"Is that why they released you?" Jess asked.

"They don't have any evidence that I did anything," Morgan said as she zipped up her suitcase.

"Is that all your stuff?" Jess asked.

"I have some things in the bathroom."

Jess followed her down the hall and watched as she retrieved her shampoo and toothbrush.

"What's the matter? Do you think I'm going to steal something?" Morgan snapped.

Jess shook her head. "Let's just go."

As they came downstairs, they could hear Virginia arguing with Officer Frick.

"... and why don't I get police protection? I'm the one whose mother got killed!"

"Under the circumstances..." Frick began.

Virginia pointed at Jess. "You're supposed to be covering the spa day at the salon right now with Garrett."

"It's okay. Brittney is filling in for me," Jess explained.

"Who the hell is Brittney?" Virginia demanded.

"Brittney Barnes, from the Gazette. You met her," Jess said.

"Do you have all your things Ms. Field?" Frick asked.

"Yes, I'm ready to go," Morgan said.

"Good, get out of here," Virginia said.

They shuffled toward the front door.

"Jess, we need to have a story meeting this afternoon. I'll set it up with Dean," Virginia called out before she slammed the front door.

This isn't even her house, Jess thought. She regretted ever suggesting that Ms. Melody turn her home into a bed and breakfast.

Morgan walked to the patrol car with her luggage. "So, where's the nearest hotel?" she asked.

"Oh, I'm not taking you to a hotel," Frick said. "I'm needed back at the station."

Morgan's face fell in surprise. "What am I supposed to do? I can't walk all over town carrying my suitcase. I'll be attacked by all those reporters."

"You are released on your own recognizance," Frick said as she opened her door.

"What about police protection?"

"You are a person of interest. You are not afforded police protection," Frick said. With that she got into her car and started the engine.

"Thanks for nothing." Morgan yelled as Frick drove away. She dropped her suitcase on the gravel drive. She had tears in her eyes.

CHAPTER 27 – MONDAY, FEBRUARY 12

10:15 a.m.

Jess sighed. "Come on. I'll take you to the Oasis Motel."

On the drive over Jess cleared her throat, "So, you're the girl in the Soggy Bottom video?"

"Yes," she admitted. "That's the only thing they have on me."

"Okay, what's the deal? If you don't mind my asking. Why did you work for Donna after what she did to you?"

Morgan shook her head. "By now you know that my name isn't Crystal Clearwater. I'm Morgan Field."

"Right," Jess said, "but I still don't understand why you changed your name, your appearance, all of it."

She looked at Jess, distrust in her eyes. "Are you trying to get an exclusive interview for the paper? There's no way I'm talking to you."

Jess looked ahead at the road. "I understand. I mean, I would love to get an interview and tell your side of the story. But, more than that, I'm just curious."

Morgan was silent.

Jess continued, "I saw the way Donna treated you. Why would you put up with that for so long? Three years, is that right?"

"Yes, just over three years actually. If I wanted to kill her, I wouldn't have waited this long."

They arrived at the motel parking lot and got out. "We're here," Jess said cheerily. *And just when you were opening up to me, too*, Jess thought with disappointment.

The light in the window said *No Vacancy*.

"Shoot, they don't have any rooms," Morgan said.

"It won't hurt to ask," Jess said.

They went inside. The desk clerk said they were expecting some of the news crews to be checking out later that morning.

"Can we put a name down, in case you get a vacancy?" Jess asked.

Jess gave the young man her name and cell number. She and Morgan got back in the car.

"Do you want to get coffee while we wait?" Jess suggested.

"I'm afraid those reporters will see me," she said sadly.

"I know what to do." Jess drove to the Pie Hole and parked in the alley behind the shops. "How do you take your coffee?" she asked.

"Cream and two packs of Equal," Morgan said.

"Oh, the Pie Hole is famous for having no equal," Jess joked.

Morgan laughed.

"I couldn't resist. Be right back." Jess ran in the back door and emerged five minutes later with two to-go cups of steaming hot coffee.

"Thank you," Morgan said, clutching the cup for warmth. "You really are a lot nicer than most reporters I've met, even though you did tackle me yesterday."

Jess chose to ignore that comment. "We'll just stay in the car until you can get a room," Jess said. She pulled out of the alley and drove a few blocks to the park, which was deserted.

"All right now, why the secret identity?" Jess asked.

"The thing is, that Soggy Bottom video humiliated me," Morgan said. "It ruined my life." She took a sip of her coffee.

"How did it ruin your life?"

"Well, everyone knew it was me in the video, all my friends did anyway," she said. "This is off the record, okay?"

"Of course," Jess said.

"Okay, well, my so-called friends all started

calling me Soggy Bottom. My husband, he took it personally. He got ribbed about it at work and our marriage went downhill from there."

"All because of that video?" Jess asked.

"Yes, all because of that video!" Morgan said vehemently. "We were only married for four months before Greg filed for divorce. Can you believe that? Four months?"

"Wow," Jess said sympathetically.

"I hated Donna Vance! She ruined my life. So yeah, I wanted revenge." Her hair flopped down into her face. "But not like this."

"So what did you do?" Jess prodded.

"After the divorce, I decided that I wanted to get Donna Vance, but good. She ruined my marriage, so I was going to ruin hers. You've seen that book of hers, *The Second Time Around*? What a joke!"

"So, you changed your identity?"

"I lost weight and colored my hair dark brown. Then I faked some credentials to make myself the perfect personal assistant. It wasn't hard at all."

"Wow," Jess said. She took a big gulp of her coffee. "And the whole time she never recognized you?"

"She didn't have a clue. So, then I started an affair with Garrett." She shuddered like the mere thought of him made her sick. "That idiot has no idea how repulsive he is."

"Garrett said it was a fling," Jess said.

"A fling? He was in love with me." She sipped some more coffee. "That was my plan all along. He was going to leave her for me, and I was going to be right there when he told her. I wanted to see the look on her face when her perfect marriage fell apart. But then she died and she never knew any of it." Morgan looked profoundly disappointed.

"Oh, okay," Jess said as if this was perfectly normal. She thought for a moment. "So, why did you run off to Juniper?"

"I knew it was only a matter of time before somebody blamed me," she said. "I just wanted to disappear again. But first, I wanted to see myself in a wedding dress, without the big derriere."

Jess made a pouty face. "You did look beautiful. Sorry I tackled you."

"Thanks. I guess it was stupid of me to try and run. But y'all were supposed to go to the expo on Saturday, not Sunday."

"Where were you all day Saturday?" Jess asked.

"I rented a car and basically just stayed away. I didn't want to be around Garrett. I was going to get a hotel room in Juniper, but Officer Frick ran into me at the grocery store and brought me in for questions."

"You rented a car?"

Morgan took a breath and sipped some more coffee. "I parked it a block away from the house. Then I slipped out in the night and drove to Juniper."

"Why make it look like you were kidnapped?"

"I didn't want the police to think I had skipped town," Morgan said. "Like I said, it was stupid of me."

Jess's phone rang with a call from the motel. "Hello, this is Jess," she said.

It was the clerk at the Oasis Motel. "There's a room available now. Do you still want it?"

"Yes, we're on the way."

"They have a room for me?"

"They sure do," Jess said as she backed out of the space.

"Thanks for letting me unload on you. It feels good to get that off my chest."

"Hey, anytime. And if you ever want to do an interview for the Gazette, give me a call," Jess said.

"I don't know, maybe," Morgan said.

Jess pulled into the parking lot of the Oasis Motel. "Let me give you my number," Jess said. She pulled out a Grace Gazette business card and wrote her name and cell number on the back. "Here. I'll help you with your bag."

"Thank you, Jess. You're a lifesaver."

"I do have a question," Jess said. "Who do you think killed Donna?"

Morgan shrugged. "Maybe a crazy fan?"

"You don't believe that, do you?"

"No, to be honest I don't. I think it was Virginia."

"Her own daughter?" Jess asked incredulously.

"She's not upset that her mother has died. And, she has the most to gain - all that money and maybe taking over Donna's company."

"You have a point," Jess said. "But what about Garrett?"

Morgan rolled her eyes. "He doesn't have it in him. Believe me, he was afraid of Donna."

Jess's phone rang again. This time it was Chace calling. "I have to take this."

"Okay, thanks for everything," Morgan said as she dragged her suitcase into the front office.

Jess spoke into the phone. "Chace, what's up?"

"Jess, you've got to get over here! Everyone's getting sick," Chace said frantically.

"Where are you?" Jess asked as she slid into the driver's seat of her blue Ford Fusion.

"We're at the salon. I don't understand what's going on. They're all throwing up!" Chace's voice was becoming shrill.

"Who is throwing up?"

"All my bridesmaids. It's just like that terrible movie last night!" Chace squealed. "I think they all got food poisoning. You've got to do something!"

"On my way," Jess pulled out in the direction of the town square. *What does she think I can do?* she asked herself.

Jess sped over to the Serenity Salon and Day Spa. She parked right in front and ran inside.

Chace met her at the door. "It's just a nightmare!" she said.

Brittney was doubled over, clutching her stomach. Conlie had her hair in foils and was vomiting into a shampoo sink.

Michelle, the owner of the salon, was standing near Conlie with a towel in her hand. She was cringing and looking very distressed. "The others are in the bathroom," she said, "If they are sick, they have to leave."

"Are you okay?" Jess asked Chace.

"I feel fine," she answered.

"What did everybody eat?" Jess asked.

"We had the breakfast buffet at the hotel," Chace said.

"Call Jack and see if everyone else is okay," Jess said.

"I think it was the mimosas they gave us," Conlie said, holding a wet towel to her face. "Oh my stomach."

"There is nothing wrong with the mimosas," Michelle said defensively. "It's fresh squeezed orange juice and champagne. Champagne does not go bad." She held up a mostly empty pitcher of mimosas.

Jess went over and sniffed the pitcher. It smelled normal. *What am I even sniffing this for?* she wondered. She took a deep breath. *Keep it together, Jess. Act like you know what you're doing,* she told herself.

"Where's Garrett? Is he sick?" Jess asked.

"I don't know," Brittney moaned. "He took some photos at the beginning, then he left." Her eyes got watery. "I can't hold it." Brittney ran for the bathroom but didn't make it.

"Noooo," wailed Michelle.

Jess tried to call Garrett but got no answer.

Chace held her phone to the side. "Jack said everybody's fine at the hotel."

"All right, tell him to come pick you up," Jess said, "I'll deal with the others."

A timer dinged. "It's time to take the foils out," the salon assistant said.

"Conlie, you've got to get that hair color rinsed out," Jess said.

"Okay," Conlie said, "I feel a little better since I barfed." She moved to a different shampoo sink and laid back in the chair.

Michelle was mopping up the floor where Brittney had thrown up.

"Did you serve any other food or drinks?" Jess asked.

"No, it was nothing I gave them," the woman said indignantly.

Brittney stood nearby looking miserable. "I'm going home," she said.

"Okay Brit, I'll catch up with you later," Jess said. Then she tentatively knocked on the restroom door.

"Come in," Madison said in a deep voice.

The restroom reeked so badly, Jess started to feel queasy herself. It was a one-person restroom. Madison was leaning over the toilet, Taylor was still throwing up in the trash can, and Kennedy was trying to rinse vomit out of the sink.

"Worst spa day ever!" Kennedy said.

CHAPTER 28 – MONDAY, FEBRUARY 12

11:30 a.m.

Jack arrived and the bridal party piled into his car, Conlie with her hair still wet. Chace promised to text Jess an update on how everyone was doing.

Jess walked across the square to the Gazette. Garrett was there at the freelance table, chatting with Wanda.

"I just tried to call you. Why weren't you at the salon?" Jess asked angrily.

Garrett held up his phone. "Battery's dead. Besides, I got all the pictures I need right at the beginning."

"Didn't you think you might need before-and-after pictures?"

"Oh, yeah. Are they done now? I'll go back over." He started to pick up his camera bag.

"Don't bother. They all got sick," Jess said.

"What happened?" Wanda asked.

"Are they okay?" Garrett asked.

"They were all throwing up. It was awful," Jess said.

"Oh no," Wanda said. "Everybody got sick? Even Brittney?"

"Yes, Brittney went home. But Chace is okay, thank goodness."

"Did they go to the emergency room?" Garrett asked.

"No, they all went back to the hotel. I think they felt a little better after they threw up," Jess said.

"Do you think it was a stomach bug? How are you feeling?" Garrett asked.

"It sounds like food poisoning," Wanda said.

"Maybe it was something they had at the hotel this morning," Jess said.

"Well, I'm glad everyone is okay," Garrett said. He began scrolling through the photos on his camera.

The phone rang and Wanda answered it.

Jess went over to the coffee bar, although the last thing she needed was more coffee. She noticed her box of candy was empty now. "Hey, what happened to my box of chocolates?" she asked.

"Oh, your Valentine's candy? Sorry, those girls made short work of that when they stopped in to meet Brittney," Wanda said.

Jess reluctantly tossed the box into the trash. "I never even got to have any."

"For the record, I didn't have any either. I'm watching my figure," Wanda said with a little shake of her hips.

"Oh, that's right, you got candy and flowers from that police detective," Garrett said. "I saw him this morning going up to your apartment."

"You saw him?" Jess asked. She couldn't help smiling.

"Yeah, he came by really early," Garrett said. "I didn't know you two were dating."

"We're not really dating. Not yet anyway."

"How come you weren't at the salon this morning?" Garrett asked.

"Oh, I had to go back to Ms. Melody's and sort of supervise while Crystal ... I mean, Morgan Field, got her things. Ms. Melody couldn't make it. She's stuck at the antique store. In fact, I should call her just to let her know it's done."

Wanda got off the phone. "Clarence was hoping to get an interview with Morgan Field. He's down at the police station now, trying to talk to someone about her release."

"She won't be giving any interviews," Jess said.

"I can't believe they let her go. She killed my angel." Garrett was near to tears again.

"Do you really think she did it?" Wanda

asked.

"Yes, I do. It's obvious. She was the Soggy Bottom girl," he said. "Jess, don't you think she's guilty?"

Jess sighed. "I honestly have no idea." She looked at Garrett dubiously, wondering how sincere his grief was in light of his affair. She really wanted to hear his side of the story but wasn't sure how to go about it. "Garrett," she said treading lightly, "what if we go get some lunch? I know a really good burger place just a few blocks away from here. Maybe the media circus hasn't found it yet. Do you like burgers?"

Garrett looked up and straightened his mustache. "I do like burgers."

"I love burgers," Wanda said. "Are y'all going to the Burger Barn?"

"Yeah, let's go," Jess said. She stood up and hung her bag across her shoulder. "I'll drive."

"Okay, I am hungry," Garrett said. "Should I bring the camera?"

"Yeah, bring it," Jess said, "We can take some burger pics, just for fun."

"Bring me back a bacon cheeseburger with avocado and mayo," Wanda said, "It's called the California Dream."

"What happened to watching your weight?" Jess asked.

"Ah, screw it," Wanda said, waving her hand like she was swatting a fly. "I'm famished. Bring me back some sweet potato fries too."

The Burger Barn was one of Jess's favorite hang outs. Their claim to fame was that they would put anything on a burger, including a tostada or a slice of pizza. Likewise, you could use anything for a bun; an oversized glazed donut or even two complete grilled cheese sandwiches with a burger patty in between. Jess had never been crazy enough to try those options.

The restaurant was in an old house, painted red and decorated like a barn inside and out. There was a painted tin rooster by the front door.

After they had placed their order, a turkey burger with lettuce and tomato for Jess and a mushroom Swiss burger for Garrett, they filled up their drinks and began looking for an empty table.

Jess had been wrong. The media circus had discovered the place and almost every table was occupied. Jess had her eye on one booth and rushed over as soon as it was vacated. She began clearing away the cups and napkins herself. The booth had wagon wheels forming the seat backs. It wasn't the most comfortable thing but it fit the barn motif.

"So, what did Crystal say?" Garrett asked as they slid into the booth.

"About Donna? She said she didn't do it," Jess answered.

Garrett huffed. "That's a lie." He sipped his soda. "How could they release her?"

"All they had was circumstantial evidence," Jess said. "There was no poison in the smoothies they took from the house."

"Circumstantial? She was the girl in the blooper video! She tried to escape and make it look like she got kidnapped!" Garrett was insistent. "Doesn't that tell you she's guilty?"

The man at the counter called out, "number eleven, your order is ready."

Garrett started to get up to get their order. "I'll go," Jess said. "You stay here and hold this table." There were already people eyeballing their booth.

Jess brought the trays back to the table and the two of them dug in. Jess was hoping to ask him about his affair, but figured she had better lead up to it.

Through a mouthful of fries Garrett asked, "Are you telling me you think Crystal is innocent?"

Jess shrugged. "I really don't have any idea."

"You don't think I poisoned my own wife do you?"

"No, no. Of course not," she reassured him. She remembered what Morgan had said about Garrett being afraid of Donna. They munched in silence for a moment.

"This really is a good burger," Garrett said, taking another big bite. Jess noticed a drop of ketchup dribbling down his chin and looked away.

"So, tell me about you and Donna."

"We really were the perfect couple," he said. "Donna always said we were a team."

"You've been together, how long?" Jess asked, knowing it was ten years.

"We were coming up on our ten year anniversary in June. We were going to tour Europe," he said sadly. He dipped another French fry into the ketchup. "We met when I was assigned to take pictures for her *Party Cakes* cookbook. It was love at first sight."

"Aww, how sweet," Jess said, trying her best to sound sincere. She took a bite of her burger and waited, unsure of how to approach the subject of his affair.

Someone from another table was pointing and glancing in their direction. Both Jess and Garrett noticed. "Is that the assistant?" they heard in a loud whisper.

Someone else whispered, "No, she's the one that caught the assistant and wrestled her to the ground."

Garrett glared at the onlookers. "That's what bothers me so much. The news media got word of my indiscretion and now I'm persona non grata," he said.

"So, what happened with you and Morgan Field?" Jess said.

"Morgan Field? Oh, you mean Crystal. She tricked me," he said. "She tricked all of us."

"How long were you two involved?"

"Not long really. It was only a few times, but it meant nothing to me."

"So, you weren't in love with her or planning to leave Donna for her?" Jess picked up a fry.

"Is that what she said?" Garrett asked.

"There's no way he would leave my mom," Virginia said, coming around to their booth from the drinks station. "I told you already, they had a prenup. If he left her, he would get nothing."

Garrett was taken by surprise. "Have you been listening to our entire conversation?" he asked indignantly.

"I heard enough you slimy piece of trash," Virginia spat.

Jess noticed someone across the room taking a cell phone video.

Garrett stood up. "Leave me alone Virginia. I don't have to take any crap from you!"

Virginia's face screwed up in anger. "You can go straight to hell!" she shouted. With that she threw her soda into his face.

"No, don't," Dean called out as he came around from the drink station.

"Aaaahh," Garrett cried out. He stood up, ice and soda dripping down his face and shirt.

Virginia stormed off, followed by Dean.

"You ugly little troll!" Garrett yelled after her as she walked out the door.

CHAPTER 29 – MONDAY, FEBRUARY 12

1:05 p.m.

After a quick trip back to Ms. Melody's for a change of clothes, Jess and Garrett returned to the Gazette. Jess was relieved to find that Virginia was not at the office. She could see Dean seated behind Brittney's desk. Clarence was bent over his computer and Wanda was on the phone. She set Wanda's bag of food down on the counter and made her way to the freelance table. She tapped Clarence on the shoulder. "What's he doing in Brittney's office?" she asked, pointing toward Dean.

"Bob and Brittney are out of pocket right now. I'm not in charge," Clarence said, barely looking up.

Wanda called out to Jess, "Phone call for you, Jess. It's Bob." Wanda patched the call through to the phone on the freelance table and Jess picked up.

"Hi Bob," she said.

"Jess, I'm on my way to the office now. I understand from Wanda that Dean Cartwright is there."

"Yes, he is," she confirmed.

"Do not talk to him about the wedding story.

He has no say in it."

"Okay," Jess said a little shakily.

"See you in a few," Bob said before he clicked off.

Just then, Dean opened Brittney's office door. "Garrett, Jess, a word please."

Dutifully, they shuffled over. Dean held the door for them and ushered them into the two chairs opposite the desk before he took Brittney's seat.

"Isn't this rug fantastic?" he asked, indicating Brittney's new yellow and blue patterned rug. "It's a Donna Vance design from the *Donna Vance At Home* line."

"Yeah, it's awesome," Jess said nervously.

Garrett was still fuming from the incident at the Burger Barn. "You got back from the burger place pretty quick."

"First of all," Dean said, "I'd like to apologize on behalf of Virginia. She lost her temper and I know she feels just terrible about it." He flashed a big smile full of blindingly white teeth.

Sure she does, Jess thought.

"You tell that girl she better steer clear of me," Garrett said, pointing at Dean angrily. "I will not be treated that way."

"Like I said, I do apologize," Dean continued. "I would like to shift gears now and interface with you two about the magazine story, maybe workshop some ideas on the direction we're taking with that. This will be Donna's last article so it has to be cutting edge."

Jess squirmed in her seat. *Who made you the boss?* She wondered.

"So, Jess, let's unpack what you have so far," Dean said.

Jess wasn't sure exactly how she should put it. "I don't really think you have editorial control on this piece," she said.

Dean leaned forward and placed his hands on the desk. "Now Jess," he said, "I am the CEO of Donna Vance Enterprises."

"I understand that," Jess said calmly, "but this article is an assignment for *Texas Bride Magazine*, part of Lone Star Publications. I answer to them."

Dean put his fingers to his forehead in aggravation. "Listen here, missy. If you're not going to cooperate...."

As he was speaking, the door opened and Bob came into the office. "Mr. Cartwright, What are you doing in here?" he asked.

Dean smiled. "Bob, what can I do you for?" he asked as if they were old friends.

"Mr. Cartwright, you need to leave this office," Bob said.

Dean was taken aback. "Is there some misunderstanding? Virginia told me this room was to be our workspace while we're in town."

"No, this was the temporary workspace for Donna Vance. This is the office of our Associate Editor," Bob said, not smiling. "Once again, I am asking you to leave."

Dean raised his hands as if in surrender. "Okay, okay, no need to get hostile." He picked up his briefcase and left the room, followed by Jess and Garrett.

Dean looked around at the few empty desks in the bullpen. "So, can I just take one of these?" he asked, pointing.

Bob cleared his throat. "Actually, no. I'm asking you to kindly leave the premises. You don't work for Lone Star Publications and we are not in the business of providing free office space."

"Unbelievable," Dean said, shaking his head. "So much for small town hospitality."

Wanda held the pass-through up for him. Nobody said a word as he walked out the front door.

Everyone breathed a sigh of relief and went back to work. Garrett sat at the freelance table, deep in thought. "I have to move out of the B&B," he announced. "I can't stay there with Virginia. She'll kill me." He turned to Jess, "How about that hotel where you took Crystal? What's it called?"

"The Oasis Motel, but they might not have a vacancy. I think she got the last available room."

Garrett got out his phone. "I'll call them," he said, tapping the name into his smartphone. He stood and walked to the back of the room while he made the call.

Bob opened his office door. "Jess, have you got a minute?"

Jess gathered up her notes and went into Bob's office. She took a seat across from his desk. "Thank you for kicking Dean out of here," she said.

"I can't believe he had the gall to come in here and try to boss everyone around like he owns the place," Bob replied.

"How is Brittney doing?" Jess asked with genuine concern.

"I think she's going to be all right. It must have been something they ate or drank at the salon."

"I hope she feels better soon."

"I'll tell her you said so. Anyway, where are you on this wedding story?"

Jess got out her itinerary. "Well, I have been writing a piece about each of the pre-wedding events as they happen. I haven't written anything about the spa-day yet and, in light of everyone getting sick, I don't know how to salvage that. Garrett got pictures at the beginning."

"Do you think we can reschedule the beauty shop for tomorrow?" Bob asked.

"Maybe so. I'll call the salon," Jess said.

"Luckily this whole thing is picture heavy. For the writing, keep it light."

"Absolutely. I just want to make the sponsors look good."

"But, you also want to put in some fun human interest stuff," Bob said. "How are you handling the expo coverage? Anything about your capture of Morgan Field?" Bob asked.

"I didn't think that should go into it. I don't want to take focus away from the wedding or get into the murder investigation," Jess said.

Bob nodded, "Good call. So what do we have next?"

Jess checked her itinerary, although now she knew it by heart. "There's the rehearsal dinner tomorrow and then the wedding itself. It's an early wedding, so I can have the article done by that afternoon."

"I'd also like you to submit a short piece for the paper, covering the wedding. More of a straight news announcement with a few photos."

"Sure. No problem."

"Great. It sounds like you are on top of it." Bob said. He sat back and shook out a tic tac from the pack on his desk. "Now, I got an email from the editor of the magazine. She wants you to do a separate piece on Donna Vance."

Jess gave him a quizzical look.

"It's actually just a small part of a bigger piece they're doing, as a sort of tribute to Donna."

"Why me?" Jess asked.

"They want a first-hand account of what it was like to work with her," Bob assured her. "Nothing about the murder or anything morbid like that."

"She was only here for one day," Jess said. "I didn't really work with her that much."

Bob shrugged, "They want three hundred words. I'm sure you can come up with something. They're getting submissions from different people who knew her."

"Okay, sure," Jess nodded her head. "I can write about what I learned from her."

"There you go. That's a good angle," Bob said. "Now, you better go see about rescheduling that salon appointment."

"You got it," Jess said. She gathered her things and went back out into the bullpen.

She looked around. "Where's Garrett?" she asked.

"He left to go get a motel room," Wanda said.

Do I need to go babysit him moving out too? Jess

wondered. She checked the time. No, Ms. Melody should be home by now. She would be glad to have one less guest to worry about. That would leave only Virginia.

Jess decided to walk over to the salon and talk to Michelle about rescheduling the spa day.

"That's a hard pass," Michelle said, shaking her head, "I will not have that group back in my salon. No way. No how. I had to cancel our next three appointments while we cleaned up that disgusting mess."

"But we wanted to get the pictures of the salon treatments. You did pay for a sponsorship," Jess pleaded.

"You can get your pictures the day of the wedding. My assistant Mimi and I will be out at the farmhouse to do everybody's hair and nails before the wedding."

"Okay, fine," Jess said dejectedly. As she was walking back to the Gazette her phone rang. It was Jack.

"Hey, Jack. How's everyone feeling?"

"Better, they've all been taking it easy in Chace's suite."

"Good," Jess said. "I hope it wasn't the pizza from last night."

"Jess, I wanted to talk to you about tomorrow," Jack said.

"Sure, we have the rehearsal dinner tomorrow, right?" Jess said. "Garrett and I will meet everyone at the hotel at 6:30 for a group photo ...."

"No, that's the thing," Jack said.

"You want us there earlier?" Jess asked.

"We don't want you there at all," Jack said.

"What do you mean?"

Jack sighed. "That didn't come out right. The thing is, we want the rehearsal dinner to be just family."

By now Jess had arrived at the front of the Gazette office. She stood outside the door. "But, I thought ...."

"Chace wanted me to call you. She's sorry, but it will be just family and the wedding party at the rehearsal dinner."

"Of course," Jess said. She felt deflated. "I'll tell Garrett. See you at the wedding."

"I'm sorry Jess."

CHAPTER 30 – MONDAY, FEBRUARY 12

6:15 p.m.

When she got home Jess saw that both Ms. Melody and Virginia were out. Jess padded up the stairs to her apartment. Sweet Tea darted up after her and beat her to the door.

What do I care about the stupid rehearsal dinner? She let herself and Sweet Tea in. *I never even wanted to be part of this wedding in the first place*, she said to herself.

She took a look into the refrigerator. Leftover veggie pizza, half a can of cat food, and plenty of beer. That was it. She closed it again.

"I still need groceries," she told Sweet Tea.

The cat jumped onto the counter and began walking back and forth with her tail in the air.

"Are you hungry girl?"

"Meow," Sweet Tea replied affirmatively. Jess gave her the cat food she had been saving. Sweet Tea did not mind that it was cold.

Jess texted Avery.

Jess: Do you want to get some dinner?

Avery: Busy with prep for the wedding

buffet.

Jess: Boo (frowny face emoji)

Avery: Lunch tomorrow?

Jess: Yes!

"Guess I'm going shopping, again," Jess said as she wriggled back into her jacket.

At the Brookshire Brothers' Jess picked a cart and was bypassing the produce section on her way to the frozen food in the back when she spotted Chris Connor perusing a bin of squash. She strolled up behind him.

"Howdy stranger," she said.

"What?" he looked up. "Oh, Jess, it's you."

"So, what's a guy like you doing in a place like this?" she asked playfully.

He laughed. "I have no food in the house," he admitted.

"Me neither," she said. "I was on my way to pick up a frozen dinner. How sad is that?"

"Yeah, I couldn't figure out what to make." Chris paused for a moment. "What if we skip the shopping," he said, indicating their empty carts, "and go get some dinner, on me?"

"I like it," Jess said nodding. "Sounds like a plan."

"How about the Grill?" Chris asked. "They've

got a good chicken fried steak."

Jess thought about Brooke at the Grill. Surely she wouldn't be working the evening shift. "Okay, sounds good. Guess we don't need these," she said, indicating their carts.

They each took their own car. At the Grace Grill, Jess looked around but didn't see Brooke. *Thank goodness for that*, she thought.

They took a seat in a booth by the windows. Jess felt a little awkward with Chris. Was this a date? She hadn't dressed nicely or retouched her makeup.

The menus were tucked behind the napkin holder. Chris handed her one. "Do you know what you want?" he asked.

"Good question," she said, looking at him as if sizing him up. "Oh, you mean from the menu."

He smiled. There was something in that smile that Jess couldn't put her finger on. Maybe it was the way his green eyes seemed to sparkle. He looked like he knew something, but he wasn't saying.

"I know what I want," he said, meeting her gaze. He leaned back in the seat. "You take your time."

Jess looked down at the menu. She didn't really have to. She knew it well and was just trying to decide when her thoughts were interrupted.

"Well good evening to you Detective Connor," Brooke said as she sidled over with her notepad. She nodded in Jess's direction, "Jess, how are you? What can I get you two to drink?"

Jess was taken aback. "Brooke, I didn't know you were here this evening."

"I'm always here," Brooke complained. "They've got me working a double with all these reporters hanging around. No offense."

"None taken," Jess said.

"I'm off duty so I think I'll have a beer. I'll take a Buffalo Bayou More Cowbell." Chris said.

"Corona Light for me," Jess said.

"B-R-B," Brooke said as she sashayed off.

"B-R-B?" Chris asked.

"Be right back," Jess answered.

Jess perused the menu and decided on the grilled chicken with mashed potatoes and a side salad. Brooke returned with their drinks and took their orders. She showed no signs of her previously spiteful demeanor.

Once Brooke had left, Chris took a swig of his beer. He sighed with satisfaction.

"Busy day?" Jess asked.

"It's been crazy. We've been getting tons of phone calls about the release of Morgan Field, as I'm sure you're aware."

Jess noticed a layer of foam across his lip from the beer. She wondered what it would feel like to kiss those lips. "You've got some foam," she said pointing to her own lips.

"Thanks," he said, wiping his mouth.

"So, any leads on who killed Donna?"

"Off the record?" he asked.

"Off the record," she answered.

"No comment," he said with a sly grin.

Jess laughed. "Oh come on, don't be that way."

"We're looking into a few leads, doing some interviews," he said, "nothing conclusive yet."

"Have you talked to Virginia?"

"We have talked to everyone close to the case," Chris said. He took another sip from his beer. "Excuse me for a minute. I need to visit the little boy's room. B-R-B."

Jess laughed. Then she noticed Brooke wiping the table next to them. "Brooke," she said quietly. "Could I talk to you for a sec?"

Brooke turned toward her. "Sure thing. What's on your mind?"

Jess took a breath. "The other day, when you mentioned Jack and '*some woman*' at his motel room …" she squirmed uncomfortably but felt she needed to clear the air. "You're not going to say anything…."

Brooke interrupted. "It was you, wasn't it?"

Jess closed her eyes, mortified. "Please don't say anything. I would hate for it to get back to Chace."

Brooke pursed her lips and shook her head. "It's not any of my business. I don't go around spreading gossip. So, don't worry about it."

"Thank you," Jess said meekly.

"Besides, I would never do anything to hurt that poor, sweet, little Miss Texas gal," Brooke continued.

"Okay, good," Jess said, nodding.

"Now my cousin Cecil is a whole 'nother story. He works over at the Oasis and he has a mouth on him, I'll tell you what."

"What are you two talking about?" Chris said as he returned to his seat.

"Nothing at all. I gotta get back to work," Brooke said with a wink toward Jess.

Chris eyed Jess suspiciously. "Are you trying to get information out of the town gossip?"

"What? No. We were just talking about ... girl stuff," Jess said dismissively. She took a sip of her beer and batted her eyelashes.

"Okay," Chris chuckled. "I won't ask."

It wasn't long before their food arrived. "Chicken for the lady," Brooke said, setting down

Jess's plate. "And our signature chicken fried steak with no gravy for you, Detective Connor."

"Thank you. And please, call me Chris," he said.

"Sure thing Chris," she said with a wink as she walked away.

Jess wasn't sure what to make of Brooke.

"They really do have the best chicken fried steak," Chris said as he cut into it.

"So, who is the most likely suspect?" Jess asked. She cut a bite of her chicken.

"Well, the question to ask is, who had access to anything that Donna ate or drank that night," Chris said. He tried a bite of his steak and chewed appreciatively.

"She never ate anything. All she had were those smoothies and water," Jess said.

"And apparently an entire box of chocolates."

"Did Beverly find anything in her dumpster diving?"

"Apart from banana peels and toner cartridges, not a thing," Chris said.

"I wonder what happened to that box." They pondered this while they ate. "Oh wait, she was drinking iced water at the bachelorette party," Jess said.

"So, that makes everybody at the party a suspect," Chris said.

"Which brings me back to Virginia," Jess said. "They had a terrible argument that night."

"So, what do you think happened?"

Jess thought this over while she chewed. "Maybe Virginia was waiting for her mother outside and went back with her to the Gazette, and poisoned her there by force feeding her the chocolates."

Chris chuckled. "Maybe so," he said.

Jess cut off another piece of her chicken. "I notice you're being very elusive. You're not really telling me anything."

"I can't discuss the case with you, on or off the record."

Jess made a pouty face.

Chris took another sip of his beer. "Let me ask you this. How did you find out about Dean and Virginia being married?"

"I overheard them out behind the house at the shower," Jess said. "Virginia has everything to gain from her mother's death. She inherits everything, including the company. She found out her mother had her podcast cancelled and she was furious about that. She always said that she had a terrible childhood." Jess was counting on her fingers, "and she's not at all upset over her mother's murder."

"So, you've eliminated Morgan Field as a suspect?" Chris asked.

Jess felt a little like he was humoring her. "I talked to her this morning. She says that Garrett was in love with her and was going to leave Donna. Actually, that was her plan for revenge all along, not to kill Donna, but to see her face when Garrett said he was leaving her."

"Do you believe that?" Chris asked.

"It sounds crazy, but I think she meant it," Jess said.

"What does Garrett say?"

Jess looked affronted. "How do you know I talked to Garrett?"

"Because you're nosy," he said with his knowing smile.

Jess took a sip of her beer. "Garrett says it was just a fling and he had no intention of leaving Donna. Apparently, there was a prenup, so he wouldn't get any money anyway if they divorced."

"So, there was a prenup if they divorced. Does he inherit anything now, or does it all go to Virginia?"

"Actually, I don't know," Jess said deep in thought.

Chris glanced around the room. "Where is that waitress? I could use some more steak sauce."

Jess looked up and saw Brooke helping a man at the counter. It was Dean Cartwright.

"Speak of the Devil," Jess said, pointing discreetly toward the counter.

Chris turned to look. "Well, if it isn't Dean himself," he said under his breath.

Brooke handed Dean a to-go bag and his credit card. Jess overheard her say, "Here you go Sugar, now you take care." When Brooke looked up, Jess waved her over.

"How's everything over here?" Brooke asked when she got to their table. "Y'all ready for a second round?" She indicated their half empty beer glasses.

"No thanks," Chris said, "Did you want another one Jess?"

Jess shook her head no.

"I would like to get some more of that steak sauce," he said.

"So, that guy at the counter..." Jess began.

"Oh him, he's been coming here almost every night since Friday. I think he's one of them reporters." She waved her hand dismissively. "But he always orders a lot of food. I don't know where he puts it, trim guy like him."

"He's actually Donna Vance's manager," Jess said. Then she wished she hadn't.

Brooke's eyes got wide, "Her manager? Wow!"

"You know, you shouldn't gossip about people," Chris said.

Brooke rolled her eyes. "It's not gossip if it's true. Anyway, I'll be right back with that sauce." She patted Chris's arm before rushing away.

"I think Brooke has a thing for you," Jess said, as she finished off her potatoes.

"Does that bother you?" Chris's steady gaze and knowing smile were maddeningly appealing.

"I don't think it's fair that you get special treatment just because of your good looks," Jess said. As soon as she said it, she regretted it. She could feel the color rushing to her cheeks.

"Oh, my good looks huh," Chris said smiling widely.

Jess took a big sip of her beer to hide her embarrassment. "Just forget I said that."

"Oh, I'll never forget that," he said, still smiling. "I'll never let you forget it either."

They both laughed. Jess finished the last of her Corona. She thought for a moment. "Wait a minute. Did Brooke say Dean had been coming here since Friday night?"

"I think so," Chris said. "That would be the night of the ...."

They both said, "murder," in unison.

"Are we talking about murder?" Brooke whispered conspiratorially as she set a small ramekin of sauce on the table.

"Brooke, did you say that customer, Dean Cartwright, came in here on Friday night?" Jess asked.

"Yes, he did," she replied nodding. "He's been in here almost every day."

"Are you sure it was Friday night?"

"Absolutely. I remember because he came in at the same time as all those bachelor party guys. They were real sweet too. Gave me a big ol' tip."

"So, what time would that be?" Chris asked.

"I guess he came in a little bit after eight. That's the one time he dined in and he asked me where to get a hotel room too. I told him, there's only two hotels in Grace, the Bluebonnet and the Oasis Motel." Brooke laughed. "Come to think of it, that was before Donna Vance got herself killed."

Someone called out from across the restaurant. "Can I get a refill over here," The man had raised his glass in the air and was shaking it, rattling the ice cubes.

"How rude," Brooke said to Jess and Chris before she turned her smile to the thirsty customer.

"Dean said he got into town early on Saturday morning," Jess said.

"So, it seems that he was lying," Chris said.

"Does that make him a suspect too? Maybe he and Virginia conspired together to kill Donna."

"You're as bad as Brooke," Chris said.

Jess ignored that remark. "What are you thinking? Should we go and question him?"

"*We* are not questioning anybody," he said with a smile. "May I remind you that you are not on the police force?"

Jess smiled, "I could be a consultant. I have a keen eye for details."

"That you do," Chris agreed. "I guess that's why you're an investigative reporter."

"Aw shucks," Jess said, basking in what she considered praise.

They finished their meals and Brooke came to offer them dessert, which they declined.

"I'll just pay the check," Chris said, handing her his credit card.

"Thanks for dinner," Jess said. "So, does this count as a real date?" She made air quotes around *real date*.

Chris gave her a sly smile, "I don't know. It depends what happens next."

Jess felt a jolt of excitement. *What was he saying?* She realized she could get lost in his smile and his sparkling green eyes. *Why hadn't she noticed this when they first met? Oh yeah, he was dragging her in to the police station as a murder suspect, that's why.*

Just then Jess's phone buzzed with a text. Instinctively, she checked the message.

Morgan: I know who killed Donna. We need to talk.

CHAPTER 31 – MONDAY, FEBRUARY 12

8:05 p.m.

Jess stared at the message on her phone, then she texted back.

Jess: Who?

Morgan: ...

Chris finished up the remainder of his beer. "What is it?"

Jess showed him the text message. "What should I do?"

"Try calling her," he said.

Jess called the number. It went straight to voicemail. She texted again.

Jess: Call me.

Morgan: ...

"No answer and she's not texting me back," Jess said.

"Give it some time," Chris said. They both waited.

They could see a crowd at the counter where Brooke was standing at the cash register.

"What is taking so long with the receipt?"

Chris wondered aloud.

They overheard Brooke saying to her customer, "It's this old credit card machine. It's just taking longer than usual. Sorry about that, Sugar."

Jess stared at her phone. "Why isn't she texting me back?"

Brooke finally finished with the group at the counter and came back with the credit card and receipt. "Sorry it took so long. Our system is overloaded with these out-of-towners. Still, it's good for business," she said. Chris signed the receipt and they got up to leave. "Good night you two," Brooke cooed. "Stay out of trouble."

In the parking lot, Jess checked her phone again. "No reply," she said. "I'm going to try calling again."

Chris waited as the phone rang and again went to voicemail. "Let's go over there. I'll drive," he said.

Jess climbed into Chris's red Ford F-150. "She's at the Oasis Motel. I'm not sure which room she's in."

As Chris started backing out of the parking space, a news van from Channel 11 in Juniper pulled up behind them. Chis hit the brakes abruptly. Jess jolted forward and dropped her phone under the seat. They both reached for the phone and bumped heads, hard.

"Ouch," Jess cried out, putting her hand to her head.

"Oh, sorry," Chris said. He cringed. "Are you okay? That was quite a bump."

"I'm okay, are you?"

"Yeah, I'm fine." He picked up her phone and handed it to her. Still no text.

The news van was still blocking their exit. "What the hell is the matter with these people?" Chris said in frustration. He opened the door and stood up to see what was going on.

"You need to move your vehicle," he shouted to the driver, who was getting out of the van.

"We're just picking up some sandwiches to go for the news crew," the man said. "It'll only take a minute. There's just no parking around here."

Chris flashed his badge. "You need to move your van," he repeated.

"Okay, okay," the man said, holding up his hands in surrender. "I'll move the van." He got back in and waited as another vehicle slowly maneuvered around him.

"What is wrong with that guy?" Jess asked with annoyance.

Chris got back into his truck. "Dang news media," Chris muttered. "No offense."

At the motel, Chris talked to the desk clerk

and was told that Morgan Field was in room 2B.

As they drove around to the second row of rooms, Jess noticed Virginia's car in the parking lot. She craned her neck to see if she could also spot Garrett's SUV, but it wasn't there. *Why didn't they all just stay here in the first place?* she wondered.

Chris parked in front of room 2B and they knocked on the door. No answer. Jess knocked again and called out, "Morgan, it's me, Jess. I got your text message."

They were met with silence.

Chris banged on the door. "Police, open up," he barked in a commanding voice.

Again, silence.

"I guess you have to kick the door in," Jess said.

Chris shook his head. "I'm going back to the office to get the key. Do you want to wait in the truck?"

"No," Jess answered.

"I don't want you waiting out here alone," Chris said.

"I don't mind," Jess said.

"Come with me then."

"Do you think it's not safe out here?" Jess asked.

"Something like that," Chris answered. "Come on."

They walked to the front office and the clerk gave him the master key to open the room.

Jess was worried about Morgan. She checked her phone again. There were no new texts. "Maybe she's just in the shower or something," Jess said hopefully.

When they got back to the room Chris knocked one more time. Then he used the key and opened the door.

"Police," he called out. "Is anyone here?"

Chris walked into the room with Jess right behind him. It was dark inside so he turned on the lights. The room was deserted. There were clothes on the bed and an open suitcase on the dresser.

Once again Chris called out, "Police, is anybody here?"

They could hear water running and saw a light on in the bathroom. Cautiously, Chis made his way to the bathroom. Jess was following right behind him. The sink and bathroom counter were open to the room. As they approached, Jess could see that the bathroom door was open.

"Ms. Field, this is the police," Chris called out again.

They rounded the corner to the bathroom. The tub was overflowing. Water was splashed everywhere. Morgan was fully clothed and had slipped under the water, which was pink with blood. Her wrists were slashed and she wasn't moving.

CHAPTER 32 – MONDAY, FEBRUARY 12

8:50 p.m.

Jess gasped. "NO!" she cried out. She rushed forward. Chris held her back. She cried into his shoulder.

"Wait outside," he said. "Here, go to the truck." He handed her the keys. Using a washcloth, he turned off the water.

"Maybe we can save her," Jess said going toward the bathroom.

"No, it's too late," he said.

Jess noticed a toilet paper wrapper on the carpet near the bathroom. There was some writing on it. "What's this," Jess asked? She reached down and picked it up. Scrawled in uneven handwriting the note read: *I killed Donna and I can't live with myself. I'm sorry. Goodbye cruel world. Crystal.*

Chris read the note over Jess's shoulder. "Jess, please, don't touch anything. You need to get out of here. This is a crime scene now."

She laid the paper on the bathroom counter and turned to go. Chris walked her out and helped her into the passenger seat. He stood outside the truck while he called in the incident.

Jess stared ahead in shock. *Why had she killed herself?* She had just texted about half an hour ago.

Chris got off the phone and opened his car door. "Officer Frick is on her way over. I've asked her to drive you home."

"Do you think she killed herself? Should we analyze the handwriting?" Jess asked.

"Jess, leave the police work to us. You need to go home and calm down."

Jess nodded, "Got it. But I don't see why she would have texted me that she knew who the killer was...."

"We'll talk later," he said.

Jess heard sirens in the distance.

Later, when Officer Beverly Frick arrived in the squad car, Jess was feeling a bit calmer. She wondered if Morgan had really killed herself or if the suicide had been staged.

It had started to rain. As she pulled out of the parking lot, Officer Frick said, "That's two bodies you've found in just three days. You're like one of those cadaver dogs."

"Cadaver dogs?" Jess said with surprise. "Are you joking?"

"Yeah, I'm just joshing you," Frick said, trying to back pedal. "Sorry. Was she your friend?"

"Crystal? I mean Morgan. No, not really a

friend. I just met her on Friday. But I did feel sorry for her."

"Oh, I remember, you tackled her at the bride convention. I saw the video. That was awesome the way you just chased her down and then ... pow!" Frick pounded her fist into her hand for emphasis. Then she had to grab the wheel to prevent the car from swerving.

Jess glared at Frick, who was red in the face.

"Sorry," Frick said again. "Listen it's not your fault. Suicide is a sign of mental illness." She began scratching her arm.

"I don't think it was suicide," Jess interjected. "I don't believe she killed herself."

Frick drove past the town square. She scratched at her neck as she made a left turn toward Jess's neighborhood.

"Oh, wait, can you take me to the Grace Grill instead of my house? My car is parked there," Jess said.

"Yeah, sure. No problem." Frick circled back. "So, you're saying she was poisoned with arsenic too?" Frick asked. She scratched her neck again.

"No, it's just that she texted me that she knew who the killer was."

"Maybe she knew because she's the one what done it," Frick said.

"It just doesn't make sense. Something seemed off in that motel room."

"Wait a minute. You're not putting any of this in the newspaper are you?" Frick asked.

Jess reassured her. "No, it's all just my speculation." She noticed Frick's eyes were watery and her nose was red. Frick was out of uniform, wearing a bright blue pullover sweater. "Are you getting sick or something?" Jess asked.

"Nah, it's just allergies."

"Nice sweater," Jess commented. "Is it from the Alpaca Sweater shop?"

Frick smiled. "Thanks. Yeah, I got a bunch of those alpaca sweaters at the grand opening sale."

"Do you think maybe you're allergic to alpaca wool?"

"No. I have a lot of allergies, but that's not one of them." Frick pulled into a space at the end of the parking lot. "I think I'll go in and get some fries," she said. "Do you want any?"

"No thanks." Jess said. "Thank you for the ride. Tell Chris he can call me tonight, if he wants."

Frick got a sly look on her face. "Ooooh, you and Detective Connor." She winked and shot a finger gun at Jess.

"Stop it," Jess said, failing to suppress a smile. She got out and ran through the rain to her car. *Why does everybody act like a twelve-year-old when they find out we're dating?* Jess wondered.

When she got back to her own car, Jess noticed Garrett's red Escalade parked nearby.

Back at home, Jess was too wired to sleep. Instead, she thought it was a good time to write her memories of Donna for the magazine.

MY DAY WITH DONNA - BY JESSICA HART

I was privileged to work with Donna Vance on the cover story for this issue, the wedding of former Miss Texas Chace Perez to local attorney Jack Ketchum. I had a dual role as liaison to the town of Grace and cowriter for the wedding piece. It was a great honor. Even in the short time we worked together, I learned a lot from Donna Vance, both professionally and personally.

One of the first things Donna said to me was that in order to be a good writer, you cannot worry about what other people think. That's good advice for writers, but it applies in other walks of life as well. It's about having courage and not being afraid to speak your mind. Donna was not afraid. When she wanted something, she went for it.

I also learned that Donna likes to cover a story from all the angles. She told me, "Nothing I write is ever a puff piece." I think we should all take this to heart and do our best in everything we do, even if it seems trivial.

Lastly, I learned the value of family relationships. Donna was known as the Queen of Texas Chic. From home decor, to weddings, to good food, the bottom line in everything Donna did was family. We don't always remember to cherish our family members, but nothing is more important.

CHAPTER 33 – TUESDAY, FEBRUARY 13

7:00 a.m.

When Jess woke up, she checked her phone. Chris hadn't called or texted. *Should I text him?* She wondered. She was itching to know what he had found out about Morgan Field's death.

She showered and shuffled into the kitchen for some coffee. She opened her little drawer to find she was out of K Cups. *I never did the grocery shopping*, she remembered. Jess sighed. There were other places to get coffee, downstairs for instance.

She knocked lightly on the back door of Ms. Melody's house before sticking her head in. Ms. Melody was in the kitchen putting frozen waffles into the toaster.

"Good morning," Jess sang out with a big friendly smile.

"Oh, thank God you're here," Ms. Melody said.

"Were you expecting me?" she asked as she came inside. Jess helped herself to a cup from the pot of coffee.

"No, but I am glad to have somebody else here." She was speaking in a loud whisper. She cocked her head in the direction of the kitchen table where Virginia sat scowling into her cell phone.

Jess nodded and made her way to the table. Obviously, Ms. Melody needed a buffer.

Virginia looked up from her phone. "Oh, it's you," she said with disdain, "Dean told me how you kicked him out of the Gazette office yesterday. That's not cool."

"Bob asked him to leave," Jess clarified. She decided to be direct with Virginia. "I'm surprised you're still sleeping here and not at the motel with Dean."

"What is that supposed to mean?" Virginia said.

Ms. Melody came over to the table. With a clunk, she set down a plate of waffles and a plastic bottle of syrup in front of Virginia. She walked away without a word.

"I have to say, the quality of the breakfast around here sure has gone downhill," Virginia yelled after her. "Don't I even get a fork?"

Ms. Melody returned with a fork and knife wrapped in a paper towel. She slapped it down on the table. "Will that be all, Madam?" she asked sarcastically.

"More coffee?" Virginia asked, shaking her empty cup.

Silently, Ms. Melody took the cup and refilled

it. She set it down with another clunk.

Jess didn't like to see Ms. Melody in such a rotten mood. "I saw your car at the Oasis Motel last night," she said to Virginia.

"I wasn't there. I don't know what happened," Virginia spat out. She began dousing her waffles in syrup.

"How do you know something happened?" Jess asked.

"I don't. What are you even talking about?" Virginia answered.

"Last night, police sirens, at the motel. Doesn't that ring any bells?"

"Like I said, I wasn't there when whatever it is happened." Virginia stuffed a big bite of waffles into her mouth.

"Well, Morgan Field died last night in her motel room, not that you care," Jess said. She felt a strong dislike for this woman.

"Died?" Ms. Melody called out from the kitchen where she was tidying up. "What happened?"

Virginia spoke through a mouthful of waffles. "Oh, Crystal? She probably killed herself, knowing that mousy little piece of trash."

Jess's mouth dropped open. She stared at Virginia. *How could she be so heartless?*

Virginia looked up from her plate, "What,

was I right?"

"What happened, Jess?" Ms. Melody asked. She took a seat between the two at the round table.

"Detective Connor and I found her dead in her room. I don't think I should say anything more."

"Whatever," Virginia said. "She killed my mother so she got what she deserved." She devoured her last bite of waffle. "Can I get some more?" she asked.

"The kitchen's closed," Ms. Melody said with finality. With that she got up and tramped upstairs.

"I'm giving you a bad yelp review," Virginia called out after her.

Jess pressed on. "Speaking of your mother, how are you holding up?"

"Fine. I am just fine. Now, if the police would just release her body, we could all go back to Dallas and get out of this hell hole."

Jess looked at her dubiously.

"What?" Virginia spat out angrily.

Jess shrugged. "You just don't seem upset, that's all."

"What has gotten into you? Is this *Attack Virginia Day*, because I didn't see it on the calendar?"

"I'm not trying to attack you," Jess said. She got up from the table and went into the kitchen for more coffee. "I'm just sayin'."

"You want me to cry? Crying is not my shtick."

"Okay, okay. I guess I just don't get your relationship with your mom."

"Am I sad about my mother? Yes, of course I am. Don't get me wrong. I'm just not a showy, emotional person, not that it's any of your business."

"No, it's not," Jess agreed.

"Besides, you heard what she said. My mother's last words to me were 'nobody loves you.' Maybe I should get that stitched onto a pillow." Virginia picked up her coffee cup and stared into it.

"So you're still angry at her?"

Virginia banged the cup down on the table. "The woman sabotaged my career. She got my podcast cancelled." She let out a breath. "She was always hard on me, even as a kid. If I didn't do something perfectly, I had to start over. You try growing up with that for a mother." She took a deep breath and downed the rest of her coffee.

Jess had enjoyed a close relationship with her own mother before she passed away. She almost felt sorry for Virginia. "I shouldn't have said anything," she said.

Virginia went into the kitchen for a third cup of coffee but found the pot empty. "I want to circle back to what you said earlier." She looked pointedly at Jess. "You said something about me and Dean."

Jess looked her directly in the eye. "I know you two are married. I heard you outside the house at the couple's shower."

"Fan-frickin-tastic!" Virginia said. "You're like a bloodhound or something."

"I just wondered, why keep up this pretense?"

Virginia stared daggers at Jess. "So, I guess you've already sold the story to all the news outlets."

"I haven't told anybody," Jess said. "I'm not like that."

"You work in the news media. Of course you're like that," Virginia shouted. She banged her empty cup down on the counter. "I wish I had never told Mom to let you co-write, you nosy little two-faced jerk!"

Ms. Melody was just coming back down the stairs with a laundry basket, followed by Sweet Tea. She had heard the last part of Virginia's tirade. "That's it. Pack your bags. I want you out of here."

"What?" Virginia said incredulously. "You can't do that."

The cat hissed at Virginia and ran off.

"The bed and breakfast is closing up permanently." Ms. Melody proclaimed, hands on hips. Jess didn't know if she'd ever seen her angrier.

Jess and Ms. Melody waited in the living room as Virginia packed her suitcase, while keeping up a steady stream of protestations. They both breathed a sigh of relief as they heard Virginia's car peeling out of the gravel driveway.

"And then there were none," Jess observed.

"Never again," Ms. Melody said.

"I'm sorry we got you into this."

"I blame Shaun," Ms. Melody said as she got up from the sofa. "I better get to the store. He's been opening by himself so I could make breakfast for that sorry lot."

"Do you want me to come by after lunch and help out?" Jess asked. "I don't have much going on today. I got uninvited to the rehearsal dinner."

"You did? Well, bless your heart. I would love some help at the store."

"Great, I'll be by after lunch."

Jess came in the back door of the Gazette. Bob was talking to Brittney in her office. They waved Jess over.

"Brittney, how are you feeling?" Jess asked as she came through the door.

Brittney sighed, "Better, a lot better. It must have been those mimosas."

"I understand Morgan Field committed suicide last night," Bob said. "Can you give me two hundred words on that?"

"Okay. You know I was there," Jess said.

"We know," Brittney said. "We've already talked to Officer Frick this morning."

"So, what's the official word on it?" Jess asked.

"She said suicide," Brittney answered.

"I think that's wrong. I think she was murdered."

"Don't speculate. Just say it was an apparent suicide," Bob said. "I'd like to have your copy on my desk in about an hour."

"Sure thing. Oh, and I've got my piece on Donna for the magazine," Jess said.

"What piece on Donna?" Brittney asked.

"Texas Bride just wanted a blurb about what it was like working with the Queen of Texas Chic," Bob explained.

Brittney looked disappointed but said nothing.

"All right, later." Jess went over to the table in the middle.

"I heard you had quite a night," Clarence said.

"What did you hear?" Jess asked dubiously.

"You found Morgan Field dead in her motel

room."

"Yes. I was there with Detective Connor. Have you been talking to Beverly Frick too?"

"Actually, I heard it from Brooke when I got my breakfast platter at the Grill this morning."

"That woman needs to keep her trap shut," Jess said. "Besides, how did she know?"

Clarence shrugged. Then Jess remembered. Frick had gone in for fries.

Jess called the police station and got Officer Frick.

"Beverly, hi. It's Jess at the Gazette."

"Hey Jess, how's it going?" Frick asked.

"Good, good. So, what was the cause of death for Morgan Field last night?"

Frick sounded like she was reading. "I am not at liberty to say."

"Bev remember, I was there. I saw her in the bathtub in the motel room."

Frick was silent for a moment. Then she whispered, "Are you calling me as Jess or as a reporter?" she asked in hushed tones.

"Both," Jess said hopefully.

"I am not at liberty to say," Frick said.

"Have there been any new developments?"

"I am not at liberty to say."

"Come on, Bev. Did she die from drowning or did she bleed out from the cuts on her wrists?"

Silence.

"Bob said you called him this morning. I just want clarification."

"I told him that Morgan Field was found dead of an apparent suicide." she said, "That's all I can say."

"Do you think it was suicide?"

"The thing is, Jess, I can't tell you anything else about her drowning. Detective Connor gave me strict instructions."

So it was drowning, Jess thought. "Where is Chris? Can I talk to him?"

"I am not at liberty to say."

"Thanks so much. You've been very helpful." Jess hung up the phone.

She got out her laptop and began work on the article.

GRACE GAZETTE - FEBRUARY 13
Suspect in Donna Vance Murder Found Dead
– by Jessica Hart

The body of Morgan Field, age 32, was found yesterday at the Oasis Motel after an apparent suicide. Authorities were called to the scene late Monday after Detective Chris Connor discovered the body in a bathtub in one of the motel rooms.

Morgan Field was a suspect in the recent poisoning death of lifestyle maven and Queen of Texas Chic, Donna Vance. Field had been working as Vance's assistant for the past three years under the assumed name Crystal Clearwater. Field was featured on the Donna Vance website in the *Epic Wedding Fails* blooper reel and had come to be known as Soggy Bottom. The blooper reel features embarrassing moments and mishaps from wedding videos.

Field's death is being treated as an apparent suicide. The poisoning death of Donna Vance is still under investigation by local law enforcement.

CHAPTER 34 – TUESDAY, FEBRUARY 13

11:30 a.m.

Jess clicked submit and gathered up her bag. She looked around for Bob to let him know she was done for the day, but he wasn't in his office. She saw Brittney at her desk and knocked on the glass. Brittney waved her over so Jess stuck her head in. "I turned in my story. I'm heading out and I'll see you tomorrow at the wedding."

"You're not coming back after lunch?"

"I'm all caught up on the wedding feature so I told Ms. Melody I would close the antique store today. She needs a break."

"Fine," Brittney said with a sigh. She pulled angrily on her bottom desk drawer. "Dang it," she muttered in aggravation.

"What's wrong?" Jess asked.

"I can't get this stupid drawer open," Brittney said. She yanked on it harder. "It's just not working."

"Here, let me try." Jess went over to the desk and tried to help. "It seems like something is stuck." Jess saw a letter opener on the desk and used it to un-wedge the obstacle while Brittney tugged. After much jiggling and pulling the drawer finally opened.

The object that had jammed the drawer was a now mangled, empty, heart-shaped candy box.

Jess stared at it in disbelief. "Oh my," she said.

"What?" Brittney asked.

"This is the box that Donna got on Friday. Probably those chocolates were poisoned."

"Oh my God," Brittney exclaimed. She dropped the mangled box and backed away, holding her hands up as if it were hot to the touch.

Jess called Chris on his cell phone. The call went to voicemail so she clicked off.

"This came from Candy's Candies," she said. "I'm going over there. Do you have a plastic bag?"

"What? No."

Jess took a tissue from Brittney's desk and gingerly picked up the box from the floor where Brittney had dropped it. "I need to talk to Candy about this."

"You can't take that. It's evidence." But Jess was already out the door.

She took off down the street and marched into the candy store with the mangled box. The small shop was all awash in pink heart-shaped boxes and the smell of chocolate was heavenly.

Candy, a small dark-haired woman, was behind the counter. "Hello. How can I help you?" she asked. Then she noticed the torn up box and Jess's stern demeanor. "Oh no. What happened?"

Jess took a deep breath. "I want to know who ordered these chocolates."

"I don't really know about that," Candy began.

Jess started again. "Last Friday somebody delivered this box of chocolates to the Gazette for Donna Vance. Can you tell me who ordered the candy?"

"I don't remember delivering anything to the Gazette," she said. "Let me check my records." She began flipping through a binder on the counter behind them. "No, we didn't deliver to the Gazette on Friday."

Just then the door opened and in walked Officer Frick followed closely by Brittney.

"Miss Hart, I understand you have removed a piece of evidence from the crime scene," Frick said. "I'm going to have to ask you to turn that candy box over to me."

"I told you not to take it," Brittney said, shaking her head.

Jess sighed and held the box out to Beverly. "Here." She noticed that Officer Frick's eyes were red and puffy and she was scratching her arm again. "You really need to see somebody about those allergies."

After receiving a stern warning from Officer Frick, Jess walked to the Pie Hole for her lunch with Avery.

When she arrived, there were several members of the news media enjoying pie and coffee and occupying all the tables. Todd was at the counter and motioned for Jess to come back to the kitchen.

In the kitchen, she was met with the aroma of Avery's beef tenderloin coming out of the oven. "That smells amazing," Jess exclaimed.

"Thanks. I thought I'd give you a preview of the wedding luncheon," Avery said. She checked the temperature on her meat thermometer. "Perfect," she said. She began cutting off the string that tied the cut of meat.

"What can I do to help?" Jess asked.

"Go ahead and grab the potatoes out of the other oven," Avery said, tossing an oven mitt to Jess. The dijon roasted potatoes looked amazing and the aroma made Jess's stomach growl.

Avery had carved about half of the beef. "I'll leave some for Mom and Dad," she said.

"Thank you," Ms. Erika said as she emerged from the walk-in freezer. "Now you two get your food and scoot. I've got to start another batch of custard pies for all these out-of-towners."

Avery fixed two plates and set them on a tray.

"All the tables are taken," Jess said.

"That's okay. Follow me to the employee break room," Avery said with a smile.

"You don't have an employee break room," Jess said. With curiosity, she followed Avery out the back door.

Outside, Avery turned left and went into the shop next door. "Ta-da," she said. "Welcome to the Pie Hole employee break room, for now."

The space was empty except for a small bistro table and two chairs. The table was already set with silverware, cloth napkins, two iced teas, and a rose in a bud vase in the middle.

Jess smiled widely. "Oh my goodness, this is great. Your dad told me he leased the space next door."

"This is going to be Ms. Erika's Tea Room, but it's going to have an opening to the Pie Hole on that wall." Avery beamed, pointing.

Jess looked around imagining the space filled with elegant tables. "This will be fantastic."

"Have a seat," Avery said. "I want to know what you think of the food for the reception."

"Wow, thank you. I thought we were going out for lunch, but this is way better than anything at the Grill." Jess sat and put her napkin in her lap.

Jess tried the beef tenderloin. "Oh, it just

melts in your mouth."

Avery smiled and took a bite herself. "It's good," she said. "It might need a little more garlic."

Jess protested, "no, it's perfect, just the way it is."

As they ate, Avery filled Jess in on her plans for the wedding reception. "I'm making all the food for the wedding here and then taking it out to the farmhouse kitchen to keep it warm. I hired three high school kids to help out."

"That sounds awesome," Jess said, "I'll ask Garrett to take some pictures tomorrow and add this to my article."

"Thank you," Avery said.

The two ate in blissful silence for a while before Avery spoke again. "So, what happened with that Soggy Bottom girl? That must have been awful finding her dead like that."

"Yes it was," Jess agreed. "It could have been suicide but I'm not convinced. Unfortunately Chris kicked me out of his crime scene and I can't get him on the phone today."

"Do you think she was murdered?" Avery asked. She took a sip of her tea.

"That's my theory," Jess said. "I just can't get a handle on who would want her dead. And why make it look like a suicide?"

"Why do the police think it was suicide?"

"Because her wrists were cut and there was a suicide note," Jess said.

"Ewww," Avery gave a little shiver. "I bet there was blood everywhere."

"There was blood in the water but the cause of death was drowning," Jess said.

"What did the note say?"

Jess pictured the note. "It was written on the toilet paper wrapper. It said something like: I killed Donna. I'm sorry. Goodbye cruel world. Crystal."

"She signed it Crystal?"

Jess's eyes got wide. "That's weird. Why would she sign Crystal instead of her real name?"

"Do you think she killed Donna Vance?" Avery asked.

"No, I don't," Jess said. "She was a bit off the deep end, but I don't believe she poisoned Donna." Jess related the story of Crystal's plan for revenge against the Queen of Texas Chic by seducing Garrett and ruining their marriage.

"That girl was one crazy, twisted, hot-mess," Avery said, finishing up her lunch.

"Yep," Jess agreed. "But, that doesn't make her a killer."

Avery began clearing the lunch dishes. "Do you have time for dessert?"

"I've got to get. I'm closing at the Emporium today," Jess said.

"Later Gator," Avery said.

As Jess walked across the street to the Antique Emporium she again wondered about the signature on the so-called suicide note. *Why didn't I notice that before? And who really wrote that note?*

CHAPTER 35 – TUESDAY, FEBRUARY 13

1:00 p.m.

When she came into the Emporium, Shaun was at the counter and Ms. Melody was putting together a new window display. She had a doll and a large teddy bear seated at a child's play table with a floral print tea set. Around it, she had set out big pots of silk flowers in an array of pinks and yellows. Jess stopped to observe. "Nice little tea party," Jess commented.

"It's not too early to get ready for springtime, is it?" Ms. Melody asked.

"Not at all," Jess said.

Shaun came over. "It's a lovely garden party," he said.

"Thanks. I'm feeling creative now that I've gotten rid of all the negativity in my home," Ms. Melody said deliberately. She got up from her kneeling position and dusted off her hands. "Now that you're here to hold down the fort, I am going home where I will be blissfully alone."

"Shall I stop by with a bottle of wine?" Shaun joked with a raised eyebrow. "We could see where the evening takes us."

Ms. Melody giggled. "Shaun, you are so bad." She swatted at him. "You're a married man." They all chuckled at how bad Shaun was.

Jess rolled her eyes. "Aren't you going to stay and close with me?" she asked.

"Fear not, fair maiden," Shaun said as he picked up Jess's right hand and gave it a kiss. "I shall stay and protect you from all vagabonds and highwaymen." Still grasping her hand he held it to his chest.

Jess pulled her hand away and wiped it on her jeans. "Thanks." She would never get used to Shaun's flirtatious ways.

"Thanks for closing tonight, Jess." Ms. Melody said before making her exit.

Jess took her spot at the register and Shaun stayed out on the sales floor to provide customer service and to tidy up his booth. Jess texted Chris again:

Jess: I'm closing at the antique store until about 6:30. Call me. (smiley face)

As soon as she sent it, she wondered if it sounded desperate. She texted again.

Jess: Something is not right about that suicide note.

She wondered, *Should I have suggested dinner again or would that sound even more desperate?* The truth is, she was dying to talk to him about Morgan's so-called suicide.

As she pondered, a lady came up to the counter with a basket full of mismatched tea cups and saucers. Jess recognized her as Leigh Ballou, the Channel 11 news reporter from Juniper.

"You're Leigh Ballou," Jess said, "I've seen you on TV."

"Thank you," Leigh said, although Jess hadn't really complimented her. She tossed her big blonde hair and began setting her purchases out on the counter. "I saw those cute tea cups in the window. I wanted to get some kind of souvenir before leaving town."

Jess began wrapping the cups in craft paper. "Oh, you're leaving Grace already?"

"That girl killed herself. I filmed my report in front of the motel this morning so we are done here. My news crew left already. I just hung around to do a little shopping," Leigh said, getting out her wallet. "How much do I owe you?"

Jess rang up her purchases. *Should I tell her it might not be suicide?* She wondered. "That will be $60.62."

Leigh got out a credit card and handed it to Jess. She looked at her quizzically for a moment. "You're that girl from the expo video," she said excitedly. "You tackled the killer in a wedding dress!"

Jess shrugged, "Yes. That was me."

"I can't believe my crew has left. I would love to interview you," Leigh said.

"I don't think I should do any interviews," Jess said.

Shaun came out from the center aisle with a floral print ceramic teapot in his hands. "Miss, I think this will go nicely with your flowery tea cups." He approached the counter and offered the tea pot with a slight bow.

"Oh, thank you," Leigh said, taking the teapot from him. It had hand-painted bluebonnets across both sides. "This is lovely."

"The color matches your eyes, if you don't mind my saying so," Shaun said with a big grin.

Leigh smiled coyly, "Of course not." She passed the teapot on to Jess. "I'll take this too."

Jess rang up the tea pot and hoped Shaun would distract Leigh from her request for an interview.

Shaun held out his hand for a shake, "Shaun Johnson at your service."

"I'm Leigh Ballou."

Shaun held his hand to his heart. "You are a lady who needs no introduction. I'm a big fan."

"Thank you," she said with a smile. "I was just trying to convince your friend here to give me an exclusive interview for Channel 11. She's a hero you know."

"She is quite the little heroine," he said.

"Actually, I'm not doing any interviews. I work for the Grace Gazette and I think it would be a conflict of interest," Jess said. "Your new total comes to $82.26." Jess held up the credit card, half expecting Leigh to balk at the total.

"That's fine," Leigh said, "let it rip." She turned to Shaun and offered him a business card. "Call me if your friend changes her mind."

Jess wrapped the tea pot and double bagged everything. "Be careful with it," she said, handing Leigh the bag.

Leigh gently took her mismatched tea set. "And here's a business card for you. My offer still stands if you want to do an interview. You could come down to the studio in Juniper. We'd do your hair and makeup." She said this like it was an incentive.

Jess took the card and smiled. "Thanks."

Leigh left with a wave to Shaun. He blew her a kiss.

Shaun pocketed the business card and strutted closer to the counter. "Well, well, well. I've still got what it takes."

"What is that exactly?"

"Sex appeal," he answered, adjusting his collar.

Jess groaned. Now Shaun would be unbearable.

"And I get my profit on that tea pot."

"Was that from your booth?" Jess asked. "I thought you only dealt in memorabilia."

Shaun pointed across the store. "I got me a new second booth space just for the chicks, man." Jess glanced over and saw an end cap with a hutch full of floral dishes, handmade soaps, and candles.

"Nice. I'm impressed," Jess said.

"Say, how did the happy couple like that movie poster you got?"

Jess cringed a little. "It wasn't really their jam, if you know what I mean?"

"Oh well. All sales are final. Listen, I'm going to take a little break and go next door for a sandwich. You want anything?"

"Can you bring me back a diet cola?" Jess asked.

"Sure thing little lady," Shaun said, shrugging into his jacket. "I'm going to go see if Brooke is working. She's a real firecracker."

I don't even want to know what that means, Jess thought.

She checked her phone again. Still no word from Chris. *Dang it!* She started a new text, then deleted it and put her phone down. She pulled out some receipt paper from the register printer and began making a grocery list. Coffee, Milk, Cereal, Cat Food, Bread .... The landline rang.

"Antique Emporium," she said into the phone.

"Jess, this is your father."

"Hi Dad, why are you calling on the store phone?"

"I just took a chance that you would be working. I saw you on the TV news the other day."

"Oh that," Jess said. "It's no big deal."

"It looked like you knocked over that bride at the convention. Is she the one that's marrying your husband?"

"No, Dad. She's the one who was accused of killing Donna Vance. Then she went missing. Anyway, Jack is not my husband anymore."

"That's a shame. I thought you two might still have a chance."

"He's getting married tomorrow, Dad."

"So, this girl you caught in the wedding dress, you say she killed someone?"

"Allegedly, but I don't think so."

The bells on the door jingled and someone came in and began browsing.

"Are you getting involved in another murder investigation?" her father asked.

"No, not at all," Jess lied.

"Who did she kill? Donna Vance you say?"

"Well, people think she may have killed Donna Vance," Jess said. She didn't want to worry her father.

She heard him talking to Eleanor, her stepmother. "Is Donna Vance that lady on TV who does all the cooking and crafts and gardening?" He came back on the phone. "Eleanor really likes Donna Vance. She's so sad to hear that she died right there in your town."

"Yeah, it was pretty awful," Jess said. She didn't want to tell him that she had found Donna's body. She glanced across but didn't see the man who had come into the store. *He must have gone to the back*, she thought. "Anyway, Dad, I have a customer so I had better get off the phone."

"Oh, well, the reason I called is - this weekend is Jeremy's birthday party," her father said.

Jess heard Eleanor in the background correcting him. Her father came back on the line, "Sorry, no it's Chad's birthday. He'll be thirteen. I wanted to see if you could come out on Saturday for his party."

Jess felt dubious about her stepbrother's birthday party. "Does he want me there?"

"Of course he wants his big sister there. I'm inviting Tom too. It's a family party."

Jess sighed, "Yes, I'll come. I just thought a teenage boy would rather have a party with friends and play laser tag or something."

"No, he's excited about having the whole family over."

"Okay, I'll be there Saturday," Jess said. *So much for having a real date with Chris this weekend.*

"All right, we'll see you this Saturday. I'll email you the details and where he's registered. Bye Sweetheart."

"Bye Dad," Jess said before hanging up the phone. *Since when did kids register for their birthday gifts?* Jess wondered.

Before she looked up she heard a man's voice. "What are you doing here?" She looked up to see Dean Cartwright with a pistol in his hand.

CHAPTER 36 – TUESDAY, FEBRUARY 13

2:30 p.m.

"Dean," Jess said with surprise. "What are you doing with that gun?"

"There's no price tag on it, so I wanted to ask how much it is. Are you working here?" he asked.

"Yes, I work here part time," she said. "Those antique pistols are supposed to be in a locked case." She came around the counter and gently took the pistol from him.

"Are you going to kick me out of this place too?"

"No, no," Jess said trying to smooth things over. "We can check with the vendor on this pistol. He's actually working tonight ...."

Dean interrupted. "Don't play nice with me. I tried to work with you," he said pointing a finger in her face. "I'll have you know, I put in a call to *Texas Bride Magazine* to have them take Donna's name off this wedding story."

"You did?" she said. *What would that mean?* Jess wondered. *Would they kill the story or would she get full writing credit?* "Listen Dean, I think we got off on the wrong foot."

"Don't try to sweet talk me now," he said. "Virginia told me what a sneaky, two-faced little back-stabber you are."

"What? Where does she get that from?"

"She said you were eavesdropping on us at the wedding shower. So much for keeping our marriage a secret. And she said you kicked her out of the B&B."

"First of all, I just happened to overhear you two outside the house," Jess began.

"I don't want to hear it." Dean turned to leave.

Jess called out to him, "I know you were in town the night Donna died."

Dean stopped in his tracks. He turned around slowly. His lip curled up in a menacing snarl. "No I wasn't. I got in on Saturday morning, early."

"There was a witness that saw you on Friday night at the Grace Grill next door," Jess said nervously. "The police know about it too."

"I have already spoken to the police," Dean said, "and this is none of your business."

"Did you kill Donna Vance?" Jess asked boldly.

Dean chuckled. "Don't be absurd."

"You're the one that sent her those chocolates. Did you poison them?"

"I never sent any chocolates. Flowers yes, but no chocolates."

Jess was not convinced. She stood with her arms crossed.

"Why would I kill off my biggest revenue stream?" Dean asked.

"I don't know, maybe to boost sales of her books? Maybe to put Virginia in Donna's place?"

The bells on the door jingled as Shaun came back into the store with a cold soda for Jess. "Diet soda for the lady," he said as he set the drink down in front of her. He could sense the hostility in the air. "Is everything okay?" he asked.

Dean cleared his throat. "Everything is just fine and dandy. Nancy Drew here just has the wrong end of the stick."

Just then Dean's cell phone rang. He turned and answered the call. Shaun and Jess looked on. Suddenly, all of the anger was gone and his faced turned ashen. They heard him say, "Oh no. We're on our way." He ended the call and rushed out of the store without another word.

Shaun turned to Jess. "I can't leave you alone for five minutes," he said.

After closing the Antique Emporium, Jess was determined to get herself some groceries. She drove straight to Brookshire Brothers and began filling up her cart. She picked out apples, bananas, and was contemplating the potatoes when her phone

CHACE SCENE

rang. *Finally Chris is calling me back*, Jess thought as she fumbled in her purse for the phone. Her caller ID indicated that the call was from Chace.

"Hello," she said tentatively.

"You need to get over here to the hotel," Conlie said. "We're in the middle of the rehearsal dinner and Chace is having a meltdown."

She could hear Chace's sobs echoing in the background. "What's going on?" Jess asked. *And why am I always the one who has to put out the fires?* She wondered.

"We are in the ladies room," Conlie explained. "Everybody was making speeches at the dinner and telling funny stories, then Taylor made some joke about Jack having a girl in his hotel room before Chace came to town. Well, then Chace burst into tears and ran into the ladies room so here we are."

Jess went cold. Brooke must have said something. "Why are you calling me?" she asked meekly.

"Chace said to call you."

She heard more sobs in the background. Then Chace took the phone and wailed, "I can't believe he's cheating on me! Jess, I want you to come here and tell me the truth!"

CHAPTER 37 – TUESDAY, FEBRUARY 13

7:35 p.m.

Jess's heart was racing. *Did she know?* Jess abandoned her cart and hurried to the car.

Outside the hotel, Jack was slumped on a bench, waiting for her. He had two dark red splotches on his crisp white shirt.

"What happened to you," Jess said, indicating the stains. "Did she shoot you?"

"Oh, Chace threw a couple of shrimp at me from her shrimp cocktail."

"She's not supposed to be eating shrimp."

Jack ran his hand through his hair. He took a deep breath. "You just can't tell her what happened, you just can't." He reached out to Jess's shoulder and she noticed that his hand was shaking. "If she knows we slept together..." Jack shook his head in desperation, "she'll leave me." He looked into Jess's eyes, pleadingly.

Jess hated to lie but she had promised to keep their night together a secret. "The last thing I want to do is hurt her," Jess said. "I already told you I wasn't going to say anything." Jess shook his hand off angrily and marched into the hotel. This was all his fault. Jess had no idea he was engaged when he came to town and they had reconnected. If anyone was going to tell Chace about it, it should be Jack.

The bridesmaids were waiting in the lobby. "There you are. She's right in here," Madison said leading the way to the ladies restroom. Jess glanced into the banquet hall and saw all the family members milling around worriedly.

Inside the ladies room, she could hear Chace crying from the large handicapped stall at the end. Conlie was sitting on the counter by the sink. She looked good with her chestnut colored hair pulled into a bun. "Jess is here," Conlie called out to her sister.

Chace sniffed loudly, "Jess? Is that you?"

"It's me," Jess answered.

"Okay Conlie, you can go," Chace said.

"Fine," Conlie said, clearly indicating that it was not fine. Conlie gave Jess a menacing look and her heart sank.

Once she had left, Jess spoke tentatively, "Do you want to open the door?"

"No, I don't want you to see me like this."

"So what happened?" Jess asked.

Chace took a deep breath. "Okay, so, Taylor got up to say something at the rehearsal dinner. She made some stupid joke about how she heard a rumor that Jack had been catting around with another woman when he first got to town. She said he had some blonde in his hotel room."

Jess observed herself in the mirror. She guessed her light brown hair could be considered blonde. "Did she say who it was?"

"No, just some blonde girl who stayed all night long," Chace wailed again. "That can't be what's true."

"Where did she hear this rumor?" Jess asked. *And why would she bring this up the night before the wedding?*

"I don't know," Chace sobbed. "Jess, you have to tell me the truth."

Jess gulped. She wasn't sure what to say. "Why do you think I would know anything about it?"

Chace sighed heavily. "You know him better than anybody. It had to have been that first night, and I know you were sitting in the jail cell all night long but... I thought maybe you saw somebody or heard something. I mean, how was he acting when you talked to him? Did he act suspicious?"

Jess breathed a sigh of relief. Chace believed she had spent the night in jail. "No. He didn't seem suspicious at all. Have you talked to Jack about it?"

Chace blew her nose. "No, I just threw my shrimp cocktails at him and ran off."

Jess saw a box of tissue on the counter and passed it under the stall door. "Here, this is better than toilet paper."

"Thanks."

"The thing is, Chace, this is a small town and people spread rumors all the time. It's probably just a big lie that somebody made up. And anyway, there's blondes coming in and out of that motel all the time. How do they know it was Jack's room, or even what night it was?"

Chace sniffed loudly but didn't say a word.

Jess thought of something. "You know what? I bet it was that blonde with the big ponytail."

Chace gasped. "What? You saw him with somebody?"

"I sure did. They were at Casa Maria the other night. She had her ponytail through a baseball cap and she had on some little tiny pink glasses. I thought it was tacky myself."

Chace laughed. "Jess, that was me and you know it."

"He only has eyes for you, Chace. You've got nothing to worry about."

"I guess you're right. I shouldn't have made a big scene." Chace's voice got quieter, "Do you think I'm crazy for marrying Jack? I mean, we've only known each other for six months."

Jess didn't know what to say. "I don't know, Chace. I'm really not the best person to give advice on relationships."

Chace laughed. "I probably shouldn't be asking his ex-wife about it, especially on the night before my wedding. It's weird, right? But I really do think of you as a friend."

Jess felt a pang of guilt. "I do too. Why don't you come out of there?"

The door swung open and Madison and Conlie rushed in. "Chace, you need to straighten up and come back to the table. Mom is going crazy and Jack is nearly in tears," Conlie said.

Chace came out of the stall. Her mascara had run down her cheeks and she caught a glimpse of herself in the mirror. "I look terrible," she cried out.

"Here. I've got a makeup wipe," Madison said, handing her a wrapped towelette.

Chace went to work on her makeup while Conlie and Madison fussed around her. Jess backed away. *I guess my work here is done*, she thought.

Chace looked up. "Thank you for coming, Jess. I don't know what I would do without you."

"Do you want to stay and have some dinner?" Madison offered. "There's lots of food left."

"No thanks, I'll just pick up a Lean Cuisine," Jess said as she headed for the door. She practically bolted out into the parking lot and rushed to her car. Then she let herself cry. That sweet girl deserved so much better than Jack. When she first met Chace she had hated her, but now she was consumed by guilt. Now, she wouldn't hurt Chace for the world. *How did I get into all this drama?* Jess wondered.

As she drove away Jess glanced at the clock. The Brookshire's would be closed now. She kind of missed the 24-hour supermarkets in Houston. She drove by the Gazette office and decided to stop at the Side Bar.

She parked and went in. As she descended the steps just inside the door, she saw Clarence was seated at the bar, nursing a beer. Good old Clarence.

"Hey, fancy meeting you here," she said jokingly.

"Jess, come on over and take a load off," he said, dusting off the bar stool next to him.

Norman was behind the bar. "Corona Light for the lady?" he asked.

Jess climbed onto the bar stool. "Sure, thanks."

"How's tricks?" Clarence asked.

"Oh, I don't know," Jess sighed. "Okay, I guess."

"Sounds like you've got man trouble," Clarence observed.

Jess smirked at him. "Well aren't you nosy."

"Hey, as a journalist, I take that as a compliment. Now, what's troubling you?"

"Oh, I don't know. I've been thinking about Donna and Crystal. I mean Morgan. I'm trying to figure out what happened." Norman set down a cold bottle of Corona with a lime wedge. Jess squeezed the lime into her beer.

"And here I thought you were feeling sad about your ex getting married tomorrow."

"Well, yeah, there's that," Jess said with a shrug. She took a big sip of her beer. "I just had to go to the rehearsal dinner and put out a fire, so to speak."

"Is that so?"

"Let's just say the bride was having second thoughts."

"And you want her to go through with the wedding?"

Jess pondered this. "Yes, I do. I really want this whole wedding thing to go off without a hitch."

"Is that because you want your ex to be happy or because you want this magazine cover story?"

Jess's mouth dropped open in mock offense. "What kind of a question is that?"

"I'm just calling it like I see it," Clarence said.

Jess laughed and took a swig of her beer. "What have you found out about Morgan's apparent suicide?" She did finger quotes around suicide. "I was thinking about that suicide note. It was signed Crystal, not Morgan. Don't you think that's suspicious?"

"Well, just between you, me and the lamppost," Clarence began, "Morgan Field was murdered."

"I knew it," Jess exclaimed. "How did it happen?"

"According to my source at the police department, somebody held her under the water until she wasn't breathing. Then they cut her wrists. Of course we can't print anything yet."

"Who did it? Dean? Garrett? Virginia?"

"Person or persons unknown," Clarence drawled. He finished his beer and pulled out a $20 bill. "I better get home to my own ball and chain." He called out to Norman and waved the twenty before laying it on the bar, "this covers her drink too."

"Thanks Clarence, you're a true gentleman."

He tipped his imaginary hat and made his way to the stairs.

Jess sighed. One beer would have to be enough on an empty stomach. She was about to ask Norman if he had any snacks when her phone rang. It was Chris. *Finally!*

Before he could even say hello, Jess said, "Chris I have been trying to get ahold of you all day."

"Sorry, I should have called. It's been very busy today."

Jess cleared her throat. "Did you find out anything new ... about the case?"

"We're looking into a few things. Are you at home?" Chris asked.

"No, I'm at the Side Bar."

"That super-secret speakeasy?"

"Yeah. Do you want to come join me for a beer?"

"Listen, I want you to go home now and lock your door, just in case."

"Why? What's going on?"

"Dean and Virginia have skipped town. We've got an APB out for them. They're both wanted in connection with the death of Morgan Field."

CHAPTER 38 – WEDNESDAY, FEBRUARY 14

9:30 a.m.

Ms. Melody drove her Ford Explorer under the awning at the Heritage House Assisted Living Facility to pick up Aunt Patsy for the wedding. Jess hopped out of the passenger seat to help Aunt Patsy get in. She was sitting on her electric scooter, ready to go.

"It sure is a pretty day. They couldn't have asked for nicer weather." Aunt Patsy observed. The sun was peeking out through the trees. It was sixty degrees and there wasn't a cloud in the sky. "I have to say, I was a little bit worried about that."

Jess got her great aunt situated in the back seat and Aunt Patsy fastened her seat belt. "It is risky to have an outdoor wedding in February," Patsy said.

Ms. Melody chimed in. "You know what they say about Texas. If you don't like the weather, just wait a minute." They all chuckled and Ms. Melody pulled out onto the road.

"You know they say that about the weather in every state," Jess observed.

"Jessica, darling. Everybody at the home has been watching you on the *you tubes*, how you ran after that girl in the wedding dress. That was a hoot. I'm so proud of you."

"Thanks Aunt Patsy," Jess said. She started to say that the girl in the wedding dress had been murdered the very next day, but she thought better of it.

At the farmhouse, Jess helped get Aunt Patsy out of the car and onto her scooter. They made their way toward the house. They were very early. Jess did not see Garrett's Escalade yet.

The front of the house was all set up for the wedding. The new archway was festooned with pink and red roses. Rows of white wooden chairs were set up with a center aisle and big floral arrangements on both sides of the arch. There was a small white tent in the back to the left of the seating. Jess was glad they had decided against the bales of hay.

Aunt Patsy's eyes glistened. "It's just beautiful. Why haven't we ever had a wedding here before?"

Jess had to admit, it did look lovely. "What's this little tent for?" Jess asked.

Aunt Patsy piped up. "The bride and her wedding party will be in there before they walk down the aisle. Chace and her mother told me all the plans when they were fixing up the house."

"Oh, I see. Listen, I'm going to have to cover the wedding for the magazine, so I won't get to stay with you the whole time," Jess explained.

"Is that why you wore slacks today?" Aunt Patsy asked. "I wasn't going to say anything, but you should have put on a nice dress."

Jess rolled her eyes. "It is not necessary for you to judge my attire every single time we go somewhere," she said with irritation.

Ms. Melody cut in, "now you two stop that bickering. This is Chace's special day."

They carefully lifted the scooter up the front steps and into the house. The front parlor and dining room had been set up for the reception with several round tables, topped with pink tablecloths and centerpieces made from Mason jars and roses. Small heart-shaped boxes of candy in pink and red adorned each place setting. It looked kitschy, but very cute. More tables were set up beyond the butler's pantry in the large sunroom.

Avery came in from the kitchen. "Good morning, everyone. What do you think?" She spread her arms to indicate the décor.

"Avery, did you do all this?" Aunt Patsy asked.

"No, Chace and her mother put together all the centerpieces. They provided everything. Mom and I just helped set it all up."

"It's gorgeous," Ms. Melody said.

"Would you like some coffee?" Avery asked.

"I would love some," Jess answered.

They all crowded into the kitchen and got coffee.

Avery had the kitchen all set up for the reception food prep. "Mom's my sous-chef today," she said. "My other helpers will be here soon."

Ms. Erika came in the backdoor with a box. "That's right. I am second in command." She turned to Avery, "I've got the champagne chilling out in the van."

Jess smiled. "I'm impressed. Look at you, running your own show. I'll get Garrett to come in and take some photos during the prep and then later when the food is ready," Jess said.

Aunt Patsy looked around. "I've got a lot of memories in this kitchen. Where's the cake?"

"In the fridge," Avery said. "I have all three tiers ready. I just need to assemble it and put on the decorations and piping."

"It sounds like you've got a lot to do. We better let you get to it," Ms. Melody said.

"Thank you for the coffee, Avery," Aunt Patsy said. They finished up their cups and went back out into the dining room.

"Isn't it beautiful?" Chace called out from the landing on the staircase. The railing was adorned with a garland of silk roses in pink and red. Chace was beaming in a pink bathrobe with her hair in a towel. "Jess, come on upstairs, we're all getting ready."

"Okay, are the ladies from the salon here yet?" Jess asked.

"They sure are. We're all getting our nails *did* and I'm about to have my hair put into a chignon."

"Garrett needs to get pictures of that," Jess said with irritation. "Where is he?"

"I'm right here," Garrett said defensively as he came out of the downstairs powder room in the hallway. "I just had to take a leak."

"Excellent, I'm glad you're here," Jess said. She turned to Aunt Patsy and Ms. Melody. "So, will you two be all right down here?"

"Don't you worry about us, you've got work to do," Ms. Melody said.

"I'm just happy to be back in my old house again," Aunt Patsy said.

As she went up the stairs, Jess heard Aunt Patsy say, "I'm so glad those two are getting along. I was worried Jessica might still have feelings for Jack." Jess cringed and hoped Chace hadn't heard.

She needn't have worried. Chace was chattering away to Garrett, "You have got to get a picture of my sister Conlie's hair now. It is so different from when you first met her. And all of our manicures are going to be pale pink. My colors are blush and bashful."

They stopped at the doorway to the master bedroom. "Just let me make sure everyone is dressed." Chace stuck her head in the door. "Everybody get your robes on. I've got the photographer here."

There were a few squeals and Jess heard someone say, "Wait a minute. Where's my robe?"

Chace giggled. "Y'all decent?" She asked.

"Okay, come on in," Madison said.

Jess went in behind Garrett. All of the bridesmaids were in matching pink robes with Jack and Chace Forever stitched above the right pocket, courtesy of Corporation T-Shirt. The mothers of the bride and groom were seated together on an antique chaise lounge. There were three ladies from the Serenity salon, working on hair and nails. Kennedy and Madison were standing near the closet with their hair in curlers.

Garrett began snapping candid photos.

"Don't take my picture with rollers in my air," Kennedy squealed with her hands up to block the photograph.

Jack's mother, Kathy, noticed Jess as she came into the room. "Jessica? Is that you?"

"Hey, Mrs. Ketchum. Nice to see you," Jess said with a smile. Kathy's hair was redder than Jess remembered, and in a shorter style.

"What are you doing here?" she inquired.

CHACE SCENE

"Chace honey, don't tell me you made her a bridesmaid too?"

Jess bristled at this. She started to answer. "I'm here for..."

Chace laughed and put her arm around Jess. "Oh no, Jess is just my good friend."

Jess leaned down and shook hands with Kathy. "I'm doing a feature story about the wedding for *Texas Bride Magazine*," she said with a huge grin. She turned to summon Garrett over. "Let's get a shot of the mothers." She shook hands with Tanya as well. Garrett snapped a few photos of the mothers and got a few close-ups of the beauty treatments in progress.

"We'd also like to get some portraits later on the staircase," Tanya said to him.

"I'm a photojournalist, not the wedding photographer," Garrett said tersely.

"Don't worry, Mama. The other photographer will be here a little bit later." Chace assured her mother.

"Well, we better let you finish getting dressed." Jess said.

There was a knock at the door, which was still part way open. "Mind if I come in?" It was Chace's father Manuel, a good looking Hispanic man in his fifties. "How's my baby girl?" He gave Chace a quick kiss on the cheek.

"Daddy," Chace sang out, grinning from ear to ear. She gave her father a big hug.

Jess stepped over to shake his hand. "Mr. Perez, it's nice to meet you. I'm Jessica Hart." She motioned toward Garrett who was putting a lens cap onto his camera. "We're here for *Texas Bride Magazine*."

"So, you are part of the media circus," he said jokingly. "Delighted to meet you."

"We're just going down to the kitchen to get some photos of the catering," Jess said. She and Garrett headed out the door.

As she was closing the bedroom door she overheard Kathy say, "Poor Chace, it's such a shame having Jack's ex hanging around all the time. Can't even enjoy her own wedding." Jess clenched her fists and took a deep breath. *She's not my problem anymore*, she thought.

Once they got downstairs, Garrett turned to Jess. "We didn't get a chance to talk earlier. Did you know they caught Dean and Virginia?"

"No, I didn't," Jess said incredulously. "Where were they?"

"They got all the way to Corsicana. They were trying to get back to Dallas. What a couple of idiots. Did you know they were married?"

"Um, yeah ... so, where are they now?" Jess asked. She looked around and noticed Ms. Melody and Aunt Patsy sitting in the corner of the parlor. They were both listening intently.

"Officer Frick said they're in police custody. They brought them back to Grace late last night. The police found a bag with the poison in Dean's motel room." Garrett seemed pleased. "Finally, justice for my Donna. I just can't believe her own daughter poisoned her."

"Wow," Jess couldn't believe it either. "So they were in on it together?"

"Looks like it." Garrett said. "So, you wanted to get photos in the kitchen?"

Jess's mind was still reeling from the news. "Yes, pictures," she said getting back to business. She led the way to the kitchen and Garrett got a few shots of the food prep while Jess waited in the hallway. It was a small kitchen and she didn't want to get in the way.

Jack came down the hall. When he saw Jess he stopped. "Thank you for talking to Chace last night," he said. "We really dodged a bullet there."

Jess narrowed her eyes at him. "You better watch yourself, Jack. Grace is a small town and gossip travels fast."

"What do you mean?" he asked, confusion across his face.

Jess poked his chest with her index finger. "I mean, if I ever hear about you running around behind her back again, you will be sorry."

CHAPTER 39 – WEDNESDAY, FEBRUARY 14

10:45 a.m.

Jack started to say something but the kitchen door opened and Garrett came out. "I got the pictures. Now let's get a few shots of the table settings and the flowers."

Jess kept pointing at Jack as she followed Garrett into the parlor. "I'm watching you."

Garrett took all the pre-wedding pictures they could think of. Then they sat near the back of the arranged chairs. The ushers arrived along with the rest of the groomsmen and began milling around. The photographer Chace had hired was getting pictures on the porch for their wedding album.

Then all of the men went inside while Chace and the bridesmaids emerged from the back door. They came around the side of the house to wait in the white tent. Jess marveled at how well orchestrated it was.

"People will start arriving soon," Jess said, checking her watch.

"I'll circulate around and get some shots during the wedding, then afterward I'll want a few close ups of the couple and the bride for the cover." Garrett said. He got out a cloth and began cleaning his lens.

Jess heard someone coming up behind them and turned to look. It was Chris. "Howdy stranger," he said with a smile.

Jess jumped up, "Chris, I wasn't sure you would make it." She ran over to him and stopped awkwardly. *Should I hug him?* She wondered.

"Hey, how's it going?" he said. He clapped her on the shoulder and shook her hand. He nodded at Garrett, "Good to see you."

Garrett stood up. "Officer, have you charged Virginia and Dean with Donna's murder? I was told they were just brought in for questioning."

Chris smiled. "I'm happy to say that we did make an arrest. Their preliminary hearing will be tomorrow morning."

"Why were they running away to Dallas?" Jess asked.

"Dean's father went into the hospital. He had chest pains but he's okay," Chris said.

"That's a likely story," Garrett said. "I'm just so glad we finally have justice for poor Donna and poor Crystal."

"Morgan Field was her real name," Jess corrected him. "Speaking of Morgan, did they confess that they staged her suicide?"

"No more talk about the case, we're here for a

wedding," Chris said. "May I sit with you?"

"Certainly," Jess said. She looked up and saw Ms. Melody maneuvering the scooter out of the front door. "Oh, wait, I had better get Aunt Patsy."

"Allow me," Chris said. He rushed up the porch steps and helped Aunt Patsy down. He motioned for Jess to join them near the front.

"I want to be where I can see everything," Aunt Patsy said.

"Are we sitting on the groom's side or the bride's?" Chris asked.

"The bride's," Jess answered without hesitation.

They took their seats in the second row. Little by little, the guests filed in and the wedding commenced. Garrett and the official photographer jockeyed for position around the outskirts. The front porch was the backdrop.

The groomsmen waited near the front, looking dapper in their pale gray tuxes with pink boutonnières. The flower girl was a little cousin of Chace's with long dark curls. Then the bridesmaids did the slow walk down the aisle, one by one.

Garrett was getting pictures of everything. *He certainly is a trooper,* Jess thought. *His wife died just a few days ago but he was still working like a pro.*

The keyboardist began playing the wedding march and everyone stood. Chace emerged from the tent and walked down the aisle. She was a vision of loveliness. The alterations had been completed so the dress fit perfectly. The ruffles and full skirt swayed as Chace stepped slowly down the aisle.

"I can't see," Aunt Patsy complained. When Chace came into her view, she whispered to Jess, "Well isn't she a stunner?"

The wedding ceremony went off without a hitch and everyone came into the house for the reception buffet. Jack and Chace were at the foot of the stairs, smiling and shaking hands, as everyone filed in. Jess maneuvered Aunt Patsy around to the sun room so they could all enjoy the beautiful weather. Also, she didn't want to intrude too much on the family celebration.

Jess went to the buffet table and fixed a plate for Aunt Patsy. Ms. Melody and Officer Frick joined them at their table. Bob and Brittney were seated nearby and Jess made sure Garrett got photos of the buffet and the beautiful three-tiered cake.

The harpist was set up near the entrance to the sun room playing softly for everyone to hear.

As the guests were finishing up their beef tenderloin, the couple got up to cut the cake. Both photographers were in tow.

Jess was enjoying herself. It was a beautiful day and the wedding was lovely. Aunt Patsy was happier than Jess had seen her in a long time. Jess had been watching the goings on with the eye of a journalist but she didn't feel like she was really part of it. *I'm an outsider,* she thought. *Garrett has this covered. I don't really need to be here right now.*

She leaned over to Aunt Patsy and said, "I'm going to take a little walk down to the creek. It's such a nice day and they don't really need me here anymore," she said.

Chris was watching the couple, as was everyone else.

Before Aunt Patsy could say anything, Jess had slipped away through the crowd and around to the front of the house. She walked through the field to the tree-lined creek. She wasn't sure why, she just felt the need to get away from it all, if only for a moment. She knew she would have to talk to people and smile and get with Garrett later to choose the pictures for the magazine story. She would have to write the final chapter of this wedding article.

She wasn't sad exactly. She wasn't in love with Jack anymore. She felt melancholy somehow. It had been a stressful week with all the wedding activities and the murder of Donna and then Morgan.

She got to the creek, which was a little high due to the recent rain. Even so, it was calm and quiet. Jess closed her eyes and listened to the water and breathed it all in.

She heard a rustling through the path and opened her eyes. It was Chris.

"Jess. What are you doing?" he asked.

She smiled. "Just taking a moment for myself," she said.

"Do you want me to leave you alone?"

"No," she reached out and motioned him over. "Come over here and just listen to the quiet. I love this spot."

He came over and took her hand in his. He took a deep breath and listened to the water flowing, the birds chirping, and the slight breeze through the branches. "This is nice," he said.

She turned to look at him.

"Are you feeling sad about Jack getting married again?" he asked tentatively.

"No, that's not it," she said. "I just want to give them some space. I used to come here as a child and go wading. My brother Tom would catch frogs to try and scare me." She laughed. "How are you doing? I know it's been a tough week for you."

"It sure has. I haven't had much sleep."

"I guess when you came to tiny little Grace, Texas; you didn't expect all this excitement."

"I did not," Chris said. "I also didn't expect to meet someone like you."

Jess felt him pulling her closer. She looked up. *He certainly is tall,* she thought.

He brushed the side of her face with his hand

and tilted up her chin. Then he lowered his mouth to hers.

Jess should have expected the kiss, but she didn't. Her heart fluttered. She grasped his shoulders and stepped on tiptoe to reach him, not wanting the kiss to end. His lips felt soft and wonderful and all she wanted was more.

Their first kiss quickly led to their second and third. After the fourth time, Jess lost count. They broke apart. Jess was all smiles.

"I've wanted to do that for a long time," he said.

"Really?" Jess moved in and kissed him again. "Me too."

They held each other for a moment.

"I'm glad you followed me out here," Jess said.

"I had a little prodding from your Aunt Patsy," Chris admitted.

"That little sneak," Jess said with a laugh. "I guess I had better be getting back. Things are probably winding down."

Chris helped Jess up the pathway back to the open field.

As they walked back toward the house Jess said, "Oh, once again I want to thank you for the beautiful flowers and the Valentine candy."

"Candy? I didn't get you any candy," Chris

said. "That must be from some other guy."

"Come on, it was there with the flowers, a big heart-shaped box of chocolates."

"Nope, it wasn't me," Chris said. They both stopped.

"But Garrett told me he saw you leaving flowers and chocolates," Jess said. "If it wasn't from you, then who?" Jess thought back. "I never did get to try any of the chocolates. They disappeared from the coffee bar at work. I think Brittney had some."

"Was this the day she got sick at the salon?" Chris asked.

"Yes, it was. Everybody got sick," Jess said, "Do you think Dean poisoned my chocolates? He's the one who sent those chocolates to Donna."

"He swears he never sent chocolates, just a card and some ...."

"Flowers," Jess finished.

"Did Garrett say he saw me put a box of candy on your deck?"

"Yes he did." Jess's mind was racing. "Did he try to poison me? Did he poison all those bridesmaids? And Brittney?" Jess was getting angry. "I took him out for a hamburger!"

"Garrett must have tampered with Donna's chocolates and told everyone they were from Dean," Chris said.

CHACE SCENE

Jess began running back to the house.

"Wait," Chris called, running after her.

They got to the house together. There was a crowd of people outside, lining the walkway between the house and Jack's BMW. *Just Married* was written across the back windshield and balloons were tied to the bumper. Jess scanned the crowd for Garrett.

"I'll go around back, you check the sunroom," Chris said.

Jess ran around the edge of the crowd to the sunroom. As she did, Jack and Chace emerged from the front door and made their way to the car, amid shouts of well wishes and people throwing birdseed.

Jess went through the sun room and found Garrett standing near the buffet table eating another slice of cake.

With his mouth full Garrett said, "This cake is really good."

"You," Jess said pointing accusingly, "you gave me poisoned chocolates!"

Garrett dropped his plate and ran toward Jess, knocking her down. She slid into a table as Garrett kept running. Chris came in through the kitchen.

He bent to help Jess up and they both chased after Garrett. He was running around the crowd with Jess and Chris in hot pursuit.

Chace was getting into the passenger side of the car and Jack was standing near the driver's side with the door open. He was waving and making his parting remarks.

Before he could slide into his seat, Garrett ran up and pushed Jack away, sending him careening into the crowd. Garrett got into the BMW and sped away before anyone even knew what was happening.

The crowd gasped.

"He's got Chace!" Tanya screamed.

Officer Frick emerged from the crowd. "We've got to follow them," she shouted and ran for the squad car. Chris followed.

Conlie ran to her Harley and hitched up the skirt of her bridesmaid's dress. She fastened her helmet.

Jess ran over to the parking area before realizing she hadn't brought her car. "Here, hop on," Conlie shouted, tossing Jess a helmet.

Without a second thought, Jess put on the helmet and mounted the motorcycle. She held on tight to Conlie and they were off.

Chris and Frick were right behind with sirens blaring. Following them was a procession of vehicles from the wedding.

Jess and Conlie spotted the wedding car heading back into town. Garrett was driving erratically, swerving nearly off the road. Conlie came up closer behind them. The balloons on the back of the car were bobbing crazily in the wind.

Jess peered around to try to see inside the back windshield through the JUST MARRIED sign. It looked like Chace was hitting Garrett and he was trying to push her off of him.

There was a curve in the road and Jess hung on for dear life. The wind was whipping up Conlie's dress. The bow on the back flapped in the wind and then blew off. Jess was glad she had worn slacks.

"You bastard," Conlie spat through clenched teeth as she gunned the motor.

"You're gaining on him," Jess said, though she was sure Conlie could not hear over the sounds of the Harley and the sirens. *What*, Jess wondered, *would Conlie do when she caught up to them?*

Conlie pulled up closer and Jess looked around her through the back windows again. Chace had her veil and was trying to wrap it around Garrett's neck. *She's going to get herself killed*, Jess thought.

They were coming into town now, but Garrett did not slow down. They blew past the Oasis Motel. Garrett looked like he was clutching at his neck. Chace grabbed the steering wheel and the car veered into the other lane, narrowly missing a pick-up truck going in the opposite direction.

They barreled into the town square with Conlie only a few yards behind them. The car sped through the intersection and past the Pie Hole. It swerved around the corner past the Gazette and made another corner before it took a sharp left turn. It jumped the curb onto the courthouse lawn and veered around the courthouse. Conlie slowed to a stop. She and Jess got off and began running. The car was still in motion heading directly for the World's Second Largest Hanging Flower Basket. The squad car stopped in the street in front of the Antique Emporium. Frick and Connor got out.

"Chace!" Conlie screamed as she ran toward the car.

The BMW finally came to an abrupt halt when it plowed into the flower basket. The pergola buckled and the basket came loose from its chain. It broke apart on the hood of the car.

The driver's side door opened and Garrett tumbled out with the bridal veil wrapped tightly around his neck. He lay on the ground clutching at the veil.

Chace unfastened her seat belt and ran around the back of the car to the driver's side where Garrett lay. She fell on him and began pummeling him with her fists. "You rotten bastard," she screamed. "You have ruined my wedding."

GRACE GAZETTE – FEBRUARY 15
Killer Confesses in Donna Vance Murder-
– by Clarence Irvin

Garrett Neilson, former husband of lifestyle maven Donna Vance, was arrested yesterday for the murders of Vance and Morgan Field. Neilson was apprehended after abducting former Miss Texas Chace Perez following her wedding to local attorney Jack Ketchum. Neilson is charged with two counts of first degree murder, conspiracy to commit murder, kidnapping, and grand theft auto. Neilson later confessed to the murders and is being held without bond.

Vance died late February 9 at the office of the Grace Gazette, where she was working on a story for *Texas Bride Magazine*. She died from poisoning after ingesting several pieces of chocolate that had been injected with arsenic.

Field was found dead from drowning on the evening of February 12 at the Oasis Motel in Grace. The scene in the motel room had been staged to look like a suicide. The Bonner County coroner determined that Field's wrists were cut post mortem.

Neilson also confessed to the accidental poisoning of several members of the bridal party and Grace Gazette Associate Editor, Brittney Barnes. They consumed a second box of chocolates laced with arsenic on February 12.

All of those involved survived the incident after suffering from stomach distress. Their survival is attributed to the smaller amount of arsenic consumed and the inhibiting effect of alcohol on the poison. In his statement, Neilson confessed that this second box of poisoned chocolates was intended for local news reporter, Jessica Hart.

Charges against Dean Cartwright and Virginia Vance have been dropped in light of Neilson's confession. Neilson admitted to planting a bag containing arsenic inside a room at the Oasis Motel which had been recently vacated by Dean Cartwright and Virginia Vance.

Donna Vance is survived by her daughter, Virginia Vance, whose podcast *Yeah, Right* was recently cancelled. Virginia Vance announced yesterday that she was married last year, to her mother's former business manager, Dean Cartwright, in a private ceremony. A memorial service will be held next week in Dallas to honor the life of Donna Vance, who was known as the Queen of Texas Chic.

GRACE GAZETTE – FEBRUARY 16
Alpaca Sweater Shop Shut Down Amid Allegations
– by Jessica Hart

The Alpaca Sweater Shop on the town square has been shut down amid allegations that the wool used in the sweaters was made from dog hair spun into yarn. Store owners, Sonny and Skye Bleu, claim that their merchandise was made exclusively from alpaca wool.

Allegations were initially made by Beverly Frick of the Grace Police Department. In a statement released today Frick said, "I bought three sweaters from the Alpaca Sweater store and I noticed soon after I began wearing them that I was having an allergic reaction. I was itchy and had sinus trouble. I have always been allergic to dogs, so that raised a red flag."

In answer to these allegations, Sonny Bleu said, "I stand by our product. Our sweaters are made from 100% alpaca wool. We haven't had any other complaints."

Despite his claims, Bleu has closed the store permanently. No charges have been filed at this time. Mr. and Mrs. Bleu plan to relocate to Austin.

JESS SAYIN' BLOG POST – FEBRUARY 16

State of Grace Address

It's been an exciting week in Grace, to say the least. I hope everyone enjoyed Valentine's Day. Mine had its ups and downs. I won't be taking anymore motorcycle rides for a while, that's for sure. However, I did enjoy my walk down to the creek on Aunt Patsy's farm. That was especially nice.

By now you've all read about the daring rescue of Chace Perez and Garrett Neilson's confession to two murders. I still can't get over the fact that he tried to poison me! ME?? I hope they bury him under the jail.

Coming soon, check out the March issue of *Texas Bride Magazine*. Chace Perez (now Chace Ketchum) former Miss Texas, is on the cover. The feature story on her fabulous wedding was co-written by yours truly and the late Donna Vance. Be on the lookout for that.

My hope is that now, things can get back to normal. This brings me to the ...

Save the Flower Basket Fundraiser - All this weekend the Grace Garden Club will be on the courthouse lawn selling potted petunias, begonias, and geraniums. The flower sale will raise money for rebuilding the hanging flower basket on the courthouse lawn.

Garden Club President Katy Hockley said,

"Having the world's second largest hanging flower basket is a matter of pride for our community. We hope everyone comes out to support our town and buys lots of flowers."

This weekend I will be visiting my father and Eleanor for Chad's 13th Birthday. Happy Birthday, Chad! It should be a lot of fun. Next week I will be back at work. Stop by Nesbitt's Antique Emporium and say *Howdy.*

PIE HOLE BASIC PIE CRUST

Ingredients:
- 2 ½ Cups all-purpose flour
- ½ Cup butter
- ½ Cup shortening
- Pinch of salt
- Ice Cold Water (about 6 – 9 tbsp)

Combine dry ingredients. Make sure butter is cold and cut into small cubes. Cut shortening into slivers. Rub dry ingredients into the fat. Add tablespoons of ice cold water one at a time as needed until the dough is cohesive and no longer crumbly. When the dough is ready, break it into two balls and chill in the refrigerator for 30 minutes. Roll out on wax paper, adding flour so it won't stick. Place into 9 inch pie pan. Crimp edges.

To blind bake pie crust – Pierce the bottom and sides of crust with a fork. Place parchment paper into crust and fill with dried beans or pie weights. Place baking sheet on a lower over rack and heat to 425 degrees. Place pie pan on baking sheet and reduce heat to 400 degrees. Bake for 10 to 12 minutes until edges turn golden. Remove from oven. Discard beans and parchment paper. Bake for 6 to 8 additional minutes until the bottom begins to color. For cream pies or refrigerated pies, bake an additional 7 minutes or until the entire crust is golden brown.

CHOCOLATE PIE

Filling Ingredients:

- 8 oz semi-sweet chocolate chips
- 1½ tsp. vanilla extract
- 1/3 cup sugar
- 2 ½ cups whole milk
- 6 tbsp. salted butter, cubed
- 6 large egg yolks
- 2 tbsp. cornstarch

Whisk egg yolks and cornstarch together in a bowl.

In a medium sauce pan combine sugar and milk. Whisk together over medium heat. Bring to a simmer, whisking frequently. Gradually add a few spoonfuls of the hot liquid into the egg yolk mixture and whisk. Add a few more spoonfuls and whisk again. Then slowly add the egg yolk mixture into the saucepan, whisking constantly. The mixture will thicken. When it comes to a boil, remove from heat and gradually whisk in the butter, one cube at a time. Whisk in the vanilla and chocolate chips. Stir until smooth.

Pour filling into a cooled pie crust and smooth it out. Place a sheet of plastic wrap on top, touching the filling, and refrigerate for 4 or more hours. Remove plastic after the filling has cooled.

Topping Ingredients:

- 1 cup heavy whipping cream
- 1½ tsp. vanilla extract
- 2 tbsp. powdered sugar
- Chocolate sprinkles or shavings

In a mixing bowl, mix the whipping cream on high speed for 1 to 2 minutes. Add sugar and vanilla. Continue mixing for 2 to 3 more minutes, until soft peaks form. Spread topping over the cooled filling and top with chocolate sprinkles or shavings.

MISS AMERICA PIE

Crust Ingredients:
- Pie Hole Basic Pie Crust – not blind baked
- 1 beaten egg
- 1 tbsp. sugar

Start with unbaked pie crust. Place into 9 inch pie pan and crimp edges. Take additional pie crust dough (about 8 oz) and roll on a lightly floured cutting board to a thickness of 1/8 inch. Using star shaped cookie cutters, cut out several varying sizes of stars. Place pie pan and stars on a baking sheet. Brush edges of pie crust and stars with beaten egg and sprinkle with 1 tbsp sugar. Chill for 30 minutes.

Filling Ingredients:

- 1½ cup blueberries
- 1½ cup chopped strawberries
- 1¼ cup raspberries
- ¼ cup sugar
- 1 ½ tbsp. cornstarch
- Pinch of salt

In a large bowl, stir together all filling ingredients. Let sit, tossing occasionally, for 8 to 10 minutes. Spoon filling into pie crust and place stars on top in whatever arrangement you like. Bake at 375 degrees for 35 minutes or until fruit is bubbling and crust is golden brown. Serve warm with vanilla ice cream.

CHICKEN FRIED STEAK FROM THE GRACE GRILL

This is a favorite of Detective Chris Connor.

Ingredients:

- 8 cubed steaks (6 oz.)
- 3 eggs
- ½ cup buttermilk
- Flour for dredging and breading (about 2 cups)
- 1/3 cup vegetable oil

Beat eggs with buttermilk in a wide, shallow dish. A pie plate works well for this.
Salt and pepper steaks to taste.
Spoon out about a cup of flour onto a plate. Dredge each steak through the flour until coated. Dip coated steaks in the egg mixture.
Get a second plate of flour. Coat each steak with flour again and set them on wax paper.
Heat oil in a frying pan over medium heat. Pan fry each steak at medium until golden brown.

Serve with gravy, steak sauce, or Worcestershire sauce.

DONNA VANCE'S VEGAN PROTEIN SMOOTHIE

Ingredients:

- 1 cup soy milk
- ½ scoop protein powder
- 1 frozen banana
- ½ cup chopped frozen mango (optional)
- 2 tbsp. dried spinach
- 2 tbsp. kale
- 2 tbsp. wheatgrass
- 2 tbsp. hemp hearts
- ¼ cup pumpkin seeds
- ¼ cup mineral water

Layer vegetables, mango, and banana into a large blender. Add in all other dry ingredients. Then pour in soy milk and water. Blend for two minutes or until smooth.

ACKNOWLEDGEMENTS

Many thanks to all of my helpers. Thank you to Natalie, Dan, and Dani for listening to my crazy ideas. Thank you Sue Lieberman, Candella Musselman, and Shela Burdge for all your feedback. Thanks also to everyone at Write Here for all the advice. Especially Brent who warned me against having a wedding at a farmhouse.

ABOUT THE AUTHOR

Cherry Northcutt

Cherry Northcutt is a native Houstonian. She worked for a number of years as a freelance features writer before branching out into fiction.

Cherry lives near Houston with her husband, their two children and a very opinionated cat.

For more information visit www.cherrynorthcutt.com. To see other books by Cherry Northcutt visit amazon.com/author/cherry.northcutt

Thank you for reading Chace Scene – A Grace Texas Mystery. If you enjoyed this book, please leave a review on Amazon or Goodreads.

Be on the lookout for Babbling Brooke - A Grace Texas Murder Mystery, coming soon.

Made in the USA
Columbia, SC
14 February 2024